ALL NEON LIKE LOVE

Dan Gennoe is a London based writer and novelist. A former music journalist, he's written cover features, interviews and reviews for *Esquire*, *GQ*, *Arena*, *FHM*, *Q*, *Mojo*, *Red*, *Time Out*, *The Independent* and *The Mail on Sunday*. He's mixed with rappers and rockstars, ghosted celebrity memoirs, and worked as a music editor for *Google*. *All Neon Like Love* is his first novel.

www.dangennoe.net

All Neon Like Love

DAN GENNOE

JOE BONES

Published by Joe Bones 2015

ISBN: 978-0-9931788-1-8

First published in Great Britain in 2015 by Joe Bones.

Cover design by Nathan Burton www.nathanburtondesign.com

For Kyrstie, who knows everything.

'The miracle of love, which in order to exist, must be kindled not only in our own hearts but in those of others as well.'

Alberto Moravia, *Contempt*

'Everybody's looking for something.'

Eurythmics, *Sweet Dreams (Are Made Of This)*

Chapter One

The room's dark but there.

He can make out shapes.

Edges.

Vague details.

The neon K of K West glows blue outside. Its light flooding the room. Filling the spaces with a blue haze. Making sides and corners. Picking out things. The chair. The writing desk. The luggage stand. The edge of the bed he's sitting on. The clothes on the floor next to it.

His clothes. Dropped as one at the foot of the bed.

Hers. Trailing from the door. Coat. Shoes. Dress. Underwear.

All black in the pale light.

All tangled in each other.

Knots and dark patches.

Straps and heels and collars and clasps and sleeves and legs and hems and zips and buttons. Piled at the foot of the bed. Scattered across the floor.

Black against blue.

Everything in the room is lit blue.

The white carpet under his feet.

The tall curtains.

The bathrobes on the back of the door.

The flowers, the neatly arranged hotel stationery, the bed sheets. All white turned blue. All there but distant. All dim neon highlights in the darkness.

He lights a cigarette. Breathes more blue into the room.

He feels the bed move under him.

He feels the sheets tug and pull and the warmth of her as she slides up behind him.

As she touches him. Presses herself into him.

He feels the sadness melt away as she pulls her arms tight around him. Spreading her warmth across his back. Down his sides. Onto his stomach.

He feels the weight of her head against his.

Of her chin on his shoulder.

Of her cheek against his ear.

Of her nose.

Her mouth.

Her breath.

Her breath.

Hot on the side of his face. Damp on the side of his neck.

Slow. Deliberate.

Breathing herself into him. Breathing him back into her. Long, deep lungfuls of him.

Holding him in.

One. Two. Three.

Letting him go with a shudder.

His shoulders tense. But he doesn't move. Doesn't react. Doesn't encourage or reciprocate.

He stays still.

Passive.

As still and passive as he can.

Enjoying the attention. Wanting more of it.

He closes his eyes.

2

He feels the bed shift under him and her slide in closer.
Closer.
Pressing against him.
Breathing him in.
Closer.
Breathing him out.
Reaching around.
Placing her hand on his.
Pulling it up.
Back.
Up to where her mouth should be.
He opens his eyes. Strains to see her put the cigarette to her lips.
She watches him watching her drag hard and long and exhale.
He exhales with her.
Slowly. Deliberately.

She smiles.
Pleased to get a reaction.
Pleased to have his attention.
Watching him watching her while she decides what to do with it.
She puts her lips back against his ear.
Breathes.
Slowly. Deliberately.
She closes her eyes and goes to speak.
He feels her lips move.
He feels their shape change from suspended vowels to a smile and back again.
He can hear the wetness of her mouth as she holds the words back: turning them over on her tongue, letting the wait become unbearable.
He can feel the sighs and syllables as she thinks about releasing them: filling his head until it's light and heavy and stupid with all the things she might be about to say.

He can smell the perfume in her hair, the cigarette on her breath, the excitement on her lips as she slowly, deliberately breathes into his ear: 'Put that out and come back to bed. I don't think I've had enough of you yet.'

He wakes up and he's alone.

He knows he's alone before he even opens his eyes. He always is. Every morning it's the same. He knows that when he opens his eyes he'll be in his bed, in his room, in Peter's flat. He knows that the blue-white glow of the suite at the *K West* will be gone, replaced by the empty grey of morning and the monochrome of Peter's taste in bachelor decor. He knows that she won't be there next to him, no matter how long he keeps his eyes closed. He knows it as soon as he wakes. His first thought of the day is that she isn't there.

Still, he feels the space next to him to be sure. Because he has to be sure before he opens his eyes, so he can give up the hope that he'll see her there when he does. Because knowing that she won't be there, even seeing that she isn't, won't be enough to break the feeling that a moment ago he was with her, that she was touching him, that he could feel the warmth of her skin and the weight of her breath as she breathed her words into his ear. He has to feel that she isn't there to accept it.

The space next to him is cold.

The sheets and the pillow untouched by her.

As he knew they would be.

As they have been for weeks.

But still, every day he wakes up hoping to reach out and find a different answer: if not that they're really still together, then at least that he's still asleep. That he's waking up not in the morning but in his dream; that his hand is about to feel the warm of her next to him and when he opens his eyes he'll be back in the *K West*'s big white bed with her, curled up and contented, lost together in the crisp white sheets and the room's blue neon glow. He imagines the relief of finding out that the morning isn't real. He imagines how happy he'll be realising that he's still got a few more minutes with

4

her. He imagines that he isn't holding his eyes tight shut. That this isn't the conscious thought that he knows it is.

And he knows it's months now, not weeks. He knows before he's awake enough to pretend otherwise, but still he tries to pretend that he doesn't. He tries to pretend that he's not keeping count, that he's not sure how long it's been, that waking up without her again won't push their last day together one day further into the past, that it won't make her more of a memory and less a part of his life.

He feels his way down the sheets and across the bed.

To be sure.

He feels the sadness grow the further he reaches.

He opens his eyes.

He lies in the dark, looking up at the ceiling, trying not to think. Leaving his mind blank. Hoping the darkness will wash in and send him back to sleep, knowing that it won't. He's wide awake, but he doesn't feel rested. He feels tired. Like he hasn't slept in days. Weeks. The only reason he knows he has is because he saw her. If he saw her he must have been asleep, at least for a little while.

He can barely see the ceiling that he's trying not to focus on. The empty grey of this morning darker than yesterday's; the days getting shorter, the nights getting longer, yet his time with her stays the same almost to the second. The darkness of the room, like the chill in the air which makes him want to pull the covers tight round him, tells him that it's still early, but he knew that already. He knows what time it is without looking at the clock on the bedside table because it's the same time every morning. He knows that the clock will tell him that it's 06:30, but he looks anyway. To be sure.

The clock says 06:29.

He watches it.

Waits.

One. Two. Three. Four. Five. Six. Seven.

The clock flips to 06:30. He hears the heating click on and the boiler fire up. Give it ten minutes and the room will be warmer. He hopes that the warm will send him back to sleep, although he knows from morning after morning of hoping that it never does.

5

The clock says it's Nov 01. Tuesday. Seventeen weeks and five days. Four months and one day. As he lies awake in the darkness, eyes wide open, staring up at the ceiling, trying not to focus, trying not to think, trying not to add another day to the other one hundred and twenty-three days since he last woke up to find her there, as he lies there waiting for the warmth to come, hoping that it will take him back to sleep, back to his dream, back to her, he tries not to think about getting up and starting his day. He tries not to think about what he might do with it. He tries not to think about how he will spend the hours between now and being back here, in the dark, waiting to see her again. He tries not to think about finding something else to do to fill the minutes, something else to think about, something other than her. He doesn't want to think about her, because thinking about her is thinking about being without her. He wants to see her. He wants to touch her. He wants to smell again the perfume which he doesn't want to admit he's forgotten.

The clock says 06:31.

It's no good. He has to think about it. He has to think about finding something else to do today, otherwise he knows that he'll do the same thing that he did yesterday, the same thing that he's done every day for a week, the thing that he does because doing it is better than doing Nothing. He can't do Nothing. Nothing means waiting; letting another day go by; sitting around Peter's flat, surrounded by Peter's things; sitting out on Peter's terrace, smoking cigarettes, watching people he doesn't know moving along the walkways, walking up and down the staircases, going in and out of flats; watching his nameless neighbours sitting alone by the ornamental lake, keeping their own company by the fountains, keeping themselves to themselves in the residents-only gardens below. Or when he can't take sitting in Peter's flat any more and it's too cold to sit out on Peter's terrace watching unfamiliar outsiders come and go through the glass doors of the Barbican Centre on the other side of the ornamental lake, Nothing means joining them in the warmth and light of the Centre's coffee shop or bar, watching them stir their lattes or sip their glasses of wine; it means sitting in the foyer with them, watching them read books, make notes, stare at laptops, stare

6

into space, stare at each other; watching them meet friends, become couples, laugh and joke together; watching them head into the restaurants, the cinemas, the galleries, together. He had weeks of doing Nothing. He can't go back to it. But if he can't go back to Nothing and if he doesn't think of something else, something definite, something concrete, something important to do with today, then he knows he'll be back in the coffee shop across from her office, watching her workmates come and go, watching clients arrive and sign in at reception, watching to try to see her; wondering why he never does. Exactly as he did yesterday and Friday and Thursday and Wednesday and last Tuesday and Monday. And that would do him no good at all.

He thinks that maybe he could try to do some work. He could make some calls, send some emails, do some writing. He's got work outstanding, things he should have done for deadlines that he's long since missed. The magazine probably aren't expecting the work anyway. They've probably given up on seeing anything from him. He's sure that Audrey only keeps giving him work so she's got a reason to stay in touch; chasing copy is her way of checking in, keeping an eye on him, making sure he's not doing anything stupid while trying to get him to do something sensible like think about something else. She's trying to keep him occupied, not employed. She knows that he doesn't need the work for the money now, but she probably thinks he needs it for something to do. She's probably right. She usually is. Even when she isn't. Even when all her well meaning and good intentions cause more problems than they solve, when all the things she does to help him come back to bite her, when all her efforts to rescue him are the last thing that he wants or feels he needs, her assessment of the situation, her assessment of his needs, is rarely wrong. Audrey always knows best, but he'll be the last to admit it. He should thank her really; show her that, whatever her reason, the gesture of work and her patience with his lack of delivery are appreciated. He should show her that he is grateful for the fact that she's always there for him, always going out on a limb for him, always willing to make life harder for herself, for him. He should be a better friend to her, as she is always trying to be to him.

7

He knows all of this, but still, a part of him can't help but blame her for most of it in the first place. It's not her fault, not entirely. She didn't break everything. But she helped. Just as she helped start it, she helped end it. Audrey always helps. Somehow she's always there, ready and willing, when it would be best for everyone if she left well alone. Sometimes she's too helpful. Sometimes he's not sure who she's really helping, him or herself. He thinks that for once he would have been better off if she hadn't come to his rescue, if she hadn't been there for him. But then again, lying in the dark, looking up at the ceiling, trying not to think, he tries not to think that Audrey's probably right, as she usually is.

He tries to think that work might be good, that he might enjoy having something to think about other than her. He tries to think that he might relish actually achieving something, getting something done, making use of his day rather than having it as just another protracted prelude to closing his eyes and dreaming of her again. He tries to believe that if he puts his mind to it, if he makes a concerted effort, if he has it as his intention from the moment he gets out of bed to be an active participant in his day, to do something constructive, to use the next eighteen hours for some positive purpose, if he can focus on that thought, hold on to it while he's in the shower, having his breakfast, as he sits down at the table in Peter's black-and-white living room, as he turns on his laptop, as he focuses on the blank screen in front of him, if he can do that, then he might stand a chance of doing some of the work that Audrey's probably given up on ever seeing. He knows that work is the answer. He knows that if he could get started, if he could stay with it long enough to become absorbed, then the rest would come and he would end the day feeling better, less empty, less guilty for always letting Audrey down. He knows work is the way to break the spell he's been struggling under. He knows that all he really has to do is try. He knows all of this. And he knows that no matter what his intentions are, or how hard he tries, or how much he wills himself to focus, his day of work will drift into a day of Nothing, and a day of Nothing will only make it harder.

He rolls over.

He looks at the empty space next to him.

He tries not to, but he thinks of all the times she stayed over. He thinks about being woken by her 06:30 alarm. He hears himself trying to convince her to stay in bed, not to go. He hears her laughing, already wide awake, telling him that she has to, that she has to get to the office, that she has work to do, telling him to go back to sleep.

He thinks about her saying it. He can hear her voice, or rather the voice that he gives to her now that he's only got odd moments of her sound left to base it on. He hears the sweetness, the softness, the excitement and the happiness in it. Whatever else, he's sure about the excitement and the happiness. She was always so happy. Always. The thought of work only made her happier. In the odd moments of her that he can still sense and hear, she's never happier than when she's leaving him to go to work. She had to get to the office, to her papers, to her clients. Not because she loved defending the interests of large companies, but because every day she spent in the practice of corporate law on their side of the argument was an opportunity to learn things that would one day make her better at attacking them from the other side of it, or so she used to tell him.

He closes his eyes. He sees her getting ready. Dressing. Straightening her grey skirt. Tucking in her white shirt. Brushing her hair. Putting on her lipstick. Putting on her heeled shoes. Putting on her grey jacket. Gathering up her things. Her coat. Her briefcase. He feels her kissing him on the lips. Kissing him goodbye with the passion of an idealist and the confidence and determination of someone altogether more capable.

He closes his eyes tighter, desperate to obey her instruction to go back to sleep. He imagines that she's there in the room now, about to lean over and kiss him. He imagines the softness and the warmth and the perfume of her lipstick which will stay with him once she's left. He imagines her firm kiss sending him back to the contented sleep that her alarm, or more recently his anticipation of it, pulled him awake from.

He closes his eyes as tight as he can, but it's no use. He

won't sleep again. Not now. He's too awake, he's done too much thinking already.

He opens his eyes, rolls back the other way and for a moment he thinks of Peter.

Work was everything to Peter too. The flat, with all its toys and gadgets and designer minimalism and its lack of a wife or children to soften the granite surfaces and chromed edges, is the lasting proof of that fact. How jealous he'd been of his older brother. Growing up in Peter's wake, watching him build up his business, devote every part of himself to it, become defined by it; how he'd wondered what it must feel like to find something, anything, so absorbing. And then he met her.

He rolls onto his back and tries to focus on the ceiling.

And then he met her.

He tries to focus on the empty grey above him.

And then he met her. Then he knew what it felt like. How it was to have something that could hold every part of his attention. Something that could consume his thoughts to the point where he had none left for anyone or anything else. Then he knew what it was to be absorbed. What she and Peter found in their work, he found in her.

Lying there in the dark he knows that work will never do it for him. Not today, not ever. He knows work is never going to fill any of the emptiness he feels, no matter how hard he tries to make himself believe otherwise. Now he knows for certain that, for him, work will always lead to nothing.

And now he knows for certain that he's awake and that there's no hope that he will go back to sleep. To see her again he'll have to wait until tonight. He's not yet out of bed and already today is turning into the protracted prelude that he was hoping to avoid.

He thinks about her pulling on her coat. He thinks about her leaving at 07:15 every morning. Leaving for her glass-fronted office building in the City, on Gresham Street, a ten-minute walk from Peter's Barbican flat. She liked to be at her desk before everyone else started arriving at 08:00. She told him that she liked the peace and quiet of the office then. No phones ringing. No insistent emails. No knocks at her office door. Just her and her papers, getting on. She told him that her office had glass walls; that people always knew when she was in; that to some that was as good as an invitation to come and share with her whatever was on their mind. She told him that she hated the feeling of being on display; that people could see her; that she was being watched.

He thinks about getting up.

He thinks about catching his breath as his feet touch the cold laminate floor of the bedroom. He thinks about the unwelcoming grey slate of Peter's bathroom tiles and the stinging heat of the shower that he still hasn't learned to adjust to anything other than scalding. He thinks about going down the dark and narrow hallway to Peter's equally narrow kitchen, boiling Peter's beautiful stainless-steel kettle, negotiating his way around all the other equally beautiful and stainless machines and utensils to make his breakfast, and sitting down to eat it, alone, at the table in Peter's black-and-white living-dining room.

He thinks that he'd prefer to stay where he is, warm, just a little while longer; there's no hurry, it's not like he's got anywhere to be or anyone to be there for.

He thinks about how he envied her, having somewhere that she was that desperate to get to every day; somewhere that she felt so strongly she needed to be. He thinks about how he used to lie in bed and listen for the sound of her opening the front door and closing it behind her. He thinks about how he used to hold his breath: one, two, three; waiting for the sound of the front door opening again, of her coming back in, of her having forgotten something. He thinks of how he used to listen and hope that she would come back, and how she never did. He thinks about the smell of her lipstick and her perfume, how he used to breathe them in and close his eyes and wait, and how even now the memory of them makes the sadness melt away for a moment.

He closes his eyes one last time and tries to breathe in the memory.

He thinks that if he tries really hard, if he can focus on that thought, if he can hold onto it, then he might just be able to smell her again, and if he can do that, then he'll be able to feel her presence, remember her touch, have her back again.

He thinks that if he gets going he can be in his position in the coffee shop opposite her office before she gets there.

He thinks that if he gets there early enough he can be there before she arrives for work, and that today, finally, he might see her. He thinks that that's all he needs: to see her.

The bedside clock says it's 06:33.

Chapter Two

He met her at the magazine's Christmas party. Audrey introduced them. Audrey liked introducing him to people.

He hadn't wanted to go. He'd said so every time the subject had come up and had repeatedly tried to get out of it, but Audrey had insisted the way Audrey always did when she thought something would do him good, and as usual when Audrey insisted, it was easier to accept her good intentions than argue with them.

Parties were Peter's thing, not his. He wanted to like them but could never find a comfortable way to strike up conversation with people he only vaguely knew, never mind complete strangers. Parties were an art that he was incapable of learning no matter how much he wanted to or how often he'd watched Peter at them. Peter was good at parties. Peter had that effortless way that people who are good at parties have of moving from group to group, never looking lost or out of place, saying hello to everyone and never getting too caught up with any particular group or conversation. He didn't have that. He spent parties in corners, hoping Audrey hadn't forgotten about him; wishing he'd gone with her to mingle, as she'd suggested; wishing he'd let her introduce him to all the editors and other contributors she was always so eager to introduce him to; wondering if it was too late to go and find her and get her to introduce him now. The rest of the time he usually spent wondering how long he should wait before leaving, on his own, as he always did.

He had briefly thought, hoped even, that he might not be invited to the Christmas party, given that he hadn't written anything for the magazine since July, but then he knew that there was no way Audrey would allow him not to be, so convinced was she that it would do him good. This inevitability only added to his already significant sense of dread: that she might have told people about Peter; that the editors and other contributors she was always so eager to introduce him to might not know what to say, or worse, might approach him with sympathy and kindness, which would make them all feel awkward.

He'd tried to appeal to her, but she'd told him that it was what he needed, to get out, to see people, to start mixing again, to have some fun, to stop moping. To the last point he had snapped back that the date of the party would be four months to the day since Peter's funeral; all things considered, he was hardly moping. He'd then added, with uncharacteristic but deliberate cruelty, that he was sorry if the fact that it was taking him a while to get over burying his brother was boring for her. After an uncomfortable moment which lasted long enough for him to regret every word of what he'd just said, Audrey picked up her point and carried on, undeterred, as only Audrey could, telling him that it would do him good to show his face, remind people that he was still around, still available for work, adding with characteristic wisdom that while she realised that, with what Peter had left him, he didn't need the money any more, he still needed to work. If anything, he needed to work more than ever, if only to get out of the flat and put him in contact with people again. She'd said that showing his face and wishing a few of the right people a merry Christmas at the party was the best way of doing it.

After another uncomfortable moment, which lasted long enough for him to wonder what made Audrey so determined to care, and to be grateful that she did, he'd finally agreed that she was, as always, right: partly to show that he hadn't meant what he'd said; partly because he wanted her to be.

The party was at a bar in Shepherd's Bush: a cavernous room of brushed metal and exposed brickwork, dimly lit yet uncomfortably exposing for anyone who wasn't good at parties.

From the relative safety of the far end of the bar he watched the more socially aware and gifted, which accounted for almost everyone else there, as they smiled exaggeratedly, nodded emphatically, dropped jaws in mock horror and laughed to excess in order to communicate their interest and opinions above the drone of obscure hip hop and the pounding of pneumatic electro beats. He watched as individuals found each other in the understated glow of hidden purple strip lighting; as they introduced strangers to friends, friends to colleagues and colleagues to anyone who happened to be standing around them, or so it seemed to him.

The venue was different every year, but the scene was the same: the conspicuously style-conscious people of the moment, in the conspicuously-style conscious bar of the moment, entertained by the editors and management who liked to think that they had been responsible, in full or in part, for making their guests the people of the moment that they were, but in truth were just grateful that they had turned up and spent most of the evening fawning over them to prove it. He wasn't sure which part of it was meant to be fun. It all looked like so much hard work. All that smiling, all that nodding, all that trying to hold onto the attention of someone who's so clearly not interested, who's already looking over your shoulder and around the room for more interesting people to talk to. His conspicuous lack of company aside – Audrey had been spirited away by another commissioning editor almost as soon as they got there – he was grateful not to have to make the effort to be part of it. If he had to be there, he was grateful to be able to watch.

Across the other side of the room a group of older men in suits, whom he didn't recognise but who at a guess he would have said were from accounts or corporate, were smiling and nodding, albeit with much less conviction. The company they were entertaining was clearly less demanding, with less ego to stroke or less potential for escape. From where he was he couldn't see who they were talking to, his view partly obstructed by a purple-glowing tropical plant, but something about the ease with which they talked, and their unaffected interest in what the person hidden from view said back to them, made him suddenly envious. After an hour or more of watching people trying to convince each other of the good time they were having, the group of older men in suits and, he presumed, the unseen focus of their attention, were the first guests he'd spotted having what appeared to be actual fun.

He watched the older men in suits take it in turns to speak and then nod or laugh their approval to each other and then collectively pause to listen to the person he couldn't see. Attentive as they were to each other, when the other person spoke their attention visibly heightened. He watched as the older men in suits leaned in to hear over the scratchy beats. He watched as their smiles slowly widened, as they nodded in unison and laughed, not excessively but with genuine appreciation of the humour of what had been said.

He moved a few places along the bar to try to get a better view. Still unable to see who they were talking to, he moved further along again; further away from the relative safety of the far end of the bar; further into the exposing edge of the party. As he did so one of the older men in suits stepped to the side, giving him clear sight of the hidden speaker. That's when he saw her for the first time. Tall, blond, centred, about his age: early to mid thirties; she was listening to one of the older men in suits – who, on getting a clearer view, he thought might be something to do with legal affairs – as he expounded his point and gesticulated with his wine glass. She listened with her eyes. She fixed her gaze on his face, keeping it there, not letting it slip from him, showing him that she was listening, that she was interested; narrowing her eyes as he got into detail, smiling them wide again as she understood his meaning.

She had a softness about her, a kindness in her face that even from a distance didn't go with the businesslike demeanour the rest of her projected. The encouragement in her eyes; the smile of her mouth; the way she tipped her head to the side with all her hair over one shoulder, exposing her neck and the delicate line of her jaw; all seemed intended to play down strength and confidence. As if she was aware she could intimidate and was doing her best not to. As if she wanted to be liked.

He couldn't take his eyes off her.

It wasn't that she was attractive, or not *just* that she was attractive physically – he didn't come to realise how beautiful she really was until much later, when at unexpected moments he'd find himself watching her face, amazed that eyes and a nose and a mouth and eyebrows and cheeks and a chin and the freckles that only came out in the sunshine could be so perfect together, combining as they did to give her the prettiness of a girl with the strength and allure of a woman. It wasn't the way her sleeveless black dress discreetly clung to her slim yet definite figure or the way she shifted her weight from one foot to another, easing out her corresponding hip to form a curve that anyone watching would be drawn to run their eyes along. It wasn't even the way she smiled with the whole of her face or that she laughed from her shoulders up. It was that she made you want to tell her everything.

He knew instantly, the moment he saw her, even from halfway across a crowded room, that he wanted to tell her everything. As he watched her listening to the man from legal affairs, her elegance and femininity reminding him of a French actress whose name he couldn't remember, he found himself wishing she was listening to him instead. He wanted her eyes to be fixed on his. He wanted them to narrow and widen as she listened to and understood him. He wanted them to encourage him to tell her more and more and more until she knew all there was to know about him; until she knew all that he thought and felt; until she knew him better than he did. He didn't know *exactly* what the everything that he wanted to tell her was, but looking across at her listening so carefully, so deeply to the man from legal affairs, he wanted to find out. For the first time in a long time, he felt the sadness start to subside.

The man from legal affairs was flattered by her attention, although he wasn't aware of it: he talked freely because she made him feel interesting, but not self-consciously so. Watching her listen, he saw her control the conversation by not saying anything. He saw her smile more of her encouragement. He saw her nod more of her appreciation. He saw her question with the slightest of looks and accept his explanation with the smallest variation on it. He saw how she drew the conversation out of him. How she concentrated on what he said. Watching her listen, he wondered what that must feel like; to have someone's undivided attention, to have them want to know. When he finished wondering, he thought he saw her look over at him.

The man from legal affairs had finished speaking and one of the other older men in suits was talking to him now. She was listening, but not as actively; the focus of the conversation having shifted, her attention being less in demand, she seemed suddenly distracted. Every so often her eyes drifted from the conversation and glanced across the room. For a second time he thought she glanced at him. The third time there was no mistaking it. Her eyes went straight from the speaker to him and stayed there.

Instinct and embarrassment made him look away, try to pass it off as nothing more than their eyes accidentally meeting as he too glanced across the room. To himself he pretended that he'd been looking for Audrey all along and began searching the room immediately in front of him, but finding no sign of Audrey's black bob or luminous white skin, his eyes drifted back to the group of older men, and when they got there they found her gaze unmoved. She was still looking at him.

He tried again to look like someone casually surveying the room. Panic made him think of searching again for Audrey, but his eyes lingered on hers too long to be convincing. Finally dragging his focus away, he caught sight of movement in the crowd, a jostled parting of bodies, the black hair and pale features of a determined figure coming towards him, the beautiful sight of Audrey coming to his rescue.

Audrey was offering to introduce him to the new editor of the magazine's *Incoming* section, saying that he'd only been in the job a week and didn't know anyone yet and that if he got in there quick he could probably have his pick of work. As he listened to the reassuring sound of her talking he looked back across the room to see if he was still being watched by the woman he wanted to tell everything to, but when his eyes found the older men in suits their blond companion was no longer there. He looked to the left and right of them in case she'd moved to talk to someone else. He tried to see between and behind them, thinking that one of the older men in suits might be obstructing his view again. He looked along the bar and over to the toilets and everywhere in between, hoping to find her on her way to or from one or the other. He looked back to the older men in suits, hoping that he might previously have missed her or that she'd found her way back to them while he'd been looking to the bar and the toilets. All the time he tried to suppress the panicked thought that she might have left the party altogether.

Audrey was still talking, but by now he wasn't even trying to pretend that he was paying attention. He half expected to hear her say as much when instead he heard someone shouting her name. 'Audrey . . . Audrey.' By the time he turned to see who it was, Audrey had already replied with a shout of her own and was squealing and hugging the tall blond woman from across the room, shrieking questions at her – when had she got back from Paris, why she hadn't called, how long had she been at the party, how the hell was she – not giving her a chance to answer before pushing her away, looking her up and down and shrieking that she looked amazing. The tall blond woman from across the room was looking at him as Audrey hugged her again. She looked into him and held his stare until it wasn't uncomfortable or disconcerting any more; fixing his eyes in a way that wouldn't let him look away; holding them long enough so that he didn't want to. One. Two. Three. Four. Five. Six. Seven. She held his stare as Audrey broke away. She held his stare and smiled. An intimate smile. A smile of warmth and collusion. A smile that told him everything that he wanted to hear from her: she wanted to listen, she wanted him to tell her everything.

She smiled at him and he felt the sadness evaporate.

Audrey caught the look between them. She paused, trying to work it out, and then said: 'Do you two know each other?'

The tall blond woman from across the room, still looking at him, still holding his stare, shook her head and said with a soft yet sure voice that carried above the music's anonymous beat: 'Not yet.

You'd better introduce us.'

Another uncertain moment passed as Audrey looked between them, still feeling that she was missing something, then turning to him she said: 'In that case may I introduce one of the finest legal minds in London, a junior, soon to be senior partner at Fitzgerald Ellis, personally responsible for defending the magazine's good name against the countless threats of libel generated each year by misquoting hacks like you, who also happens to be another very, very, very good friend of mine, this is Sophie . . .'

'Carlson. Sophie Carlson. Hello.'

Chapter Three

He looks at the clock above the counter. It says 07:23.

He's already got himself a tea and a stool by the window. He's taken off his coat, his hat and his gloves. His scarf he keeps on, wrapped tight and high around his neck to stop what little warmth he has from escaping, until he's sure he's staying. It's still barely light. The pavement and road are still damp from the morning's frost and the air is still sharp and unwelcoming, the sun having not yet risen enough to take the sting out of it. The bitter cold of outside rushes in and hits him every time the door opens, but he needs to be by the window, he needs to be able to see across the street, to see who's coming and going while he sits and drinks his tea, which is why he takes the same stool each morning and arrives early to be sure of getting it.

He looks around as he adjusts his coat on the stool under him and tries to get comfortable. The coffee shop's almost empty, there are a few people queuing at the counter, but most are ordering takeaways; only two other people are sitting at tables. He could have any table he wants. He could sit all the way over at the back, in the corner far away from the cold of the glass and the draught of the door; he could sit at one of the tables by the side of the counter, next to the steaming hot coffee machine; he could sit along the far wall where there's a radiator that's probably warm and cosy. If he were here for any other reason he would probably move. He'd go for the far wall and one of the tables next to the radiator so he could properly relax and drink his tea in comfort. But that's not why he's here. He needs to be by the window. He needs to be able to see. If he wanted to be comfortable he would have stayed in bed.

He wipes a hole in the condensation on the window with his gloves. Through the clear wet circle he has an unobstructed view of the front of her office building. He can see the whole of the reception area, spanning the width of the ground floor, with its tall glass wall separating the cold grey of the morning and the warm neutral tones inside. On the left-hand side of the reception he can see the long desk and the backs of three computer screens which mark where each of the three receptionists will sit when they arrive to take over from the night security guard who's currently studying the screen of the middle computer. On the right-hand side of the reception he can see the low sofas and the three large canvases of modern art on the wall behind them. The centre picture, a multicoloured paint explosion in the shape of a skull, he recognises as a Damien Hirst. The glowing neon circles painted on the canvases either side are familiar too, though he can't be sure if that's because they're renowned works or because he's spent so long looking at them from his stool in the window of the coffee shop across the street.

He sips at his hot tea and watches the long hand of the sculptural clock that takes up most of the wall behind the reception desk as it inches towards seven twenty-five. People walk briskly past on both sides of the street. Occasionally someone opens the door to the coffee shop, letting the cold in as they do so, but no one troubles the revolving door of the office building across the street.

Sipping his tea, watching the hands of the clock and the head of the night security guard, he's suddenly hit by a sense of failure. Looking at the empty low sofas and the unobserved modern art he feels suddenly defeated. The revolving door motionless; the security barriers closed and unapproached in front of banks of lifts which have no one waiting for them; he feels the sudden realisation of the depressingly obvious.

The minute hand of the clock behind the reception says that it's seven twenty-six.

This is the earliest he's been here, yet now he's convinced that, once again, he's already too late. For no other reason than it's possible, he thinks that he's already missed her, just as he has all the days before. He thinks that she's already in there, already at her desk, already working. He has no way of knowing if she is or isn't, but now the possibility that she is seems more likely than not. She could have arrived a minute before he did. She could have walked through the doors, through the barriers and into the lift while he was standing at the counter, waiting as the cute, slightly goth barista with the fringe and big eyes, who used to smile when she saw him but now seems to view him with suspicion, discomfort even, made his tea. She might be getting into work earlier than she did when she used to leave him in the grey light of his bedroom in Peter's flat, leaving him with her tender instruction to go back to sleep. She might be getting in to be at her desk by seven, not seven thirty. She might not be, but the only way he could know for sure would be if he'd been there earlier.

He looks at the sign on the back of the coffee-shop door. It says that they open at six thirty every morning except Saturday and Sunday, when it's eight and nine respectively. He thinks that six thirty could be early enough, to be sure.

The disappointment he feels is only made worse by the thought of leaving. If he leaves now, he'll be giving up all hope of seeing her today. He doesn't know if she's already in there or not. He doesn't know if she's happily working away or running late; if she's making the most of the quiet before everyone else arrives or hurrying up the road from Barbican tube, thinking about all the peace and quiet she's missing. She could be in a cab somewhere or about to walk through the revolving door, her briefcase in her hand, a long tailored coat over her grey skirt and jacket, or she could be several floors above him, looking out of a window, watching him sitting at the coffee-shop window as he wonders where she is and why he never sees her. He wasn't here early enough to know for sure if she's in there or not, but he knows that if he leaves now, the only thing he can be sure of is he won't see her today. What if he hasn't missed her? What if she isn't in there? What if he leaves now before he's given her a proper chance to get there? Another half an hour can't hurt. He could leave now and miss her by a minute. Or he could wait, give it a while, and even if he has already missed her arriving, he might see her leaving, going for lunch, for coffee, going home. He knows he could wait all day and not catch sight of her, just as he has the last however many days, but at least he would know that he hadn't left too soon.

If not being early enough was a mistake, leaving too soon would be worse.

He looks up at the windows of the floors above him. He wonders which of the five floors she might be on. He thinks of her standing at a window, looking down at him. He thinks of her watching him sipping at his tea as she drinks a cup of her own. He hopes that this time she would be pleased to see him. He thinks about the two times he met her from work. How the first time she told him to wait for her, not on one of the low sofas in front of the modern art, but here in the coffee shop across the road from the office, and how uncomfortable and annoyed she looked the second time, when he'd decided to surprise her one evening by waiting for her in reception. She'd later apologised, saying that she was tired and had a lot of work to do and that she had been planning to go straight home, read some papers, have a bath and try to get an early night, and that while it was a sweet gesture and she appreciated the thought, maybe he should ask her first next time. There never was a next time.

Still looking up at the windows of her office block he imagines her spotting him and what she might think at seeing this once so important face from her recent past. He hopes that she wouldn't mind him being here like this. That this time she might like the surprise, be pleased to see him after so many weeks; that feelings might have softened, the hurt subsided, and she might be surprised by how happy she was to see him again. Thinking of her looking down at him, watching him, he smiles, partly at the thought, partly as a gesture of friendliness, to show her that he's there with the best intentions: because he wants to see her, because he misses her, because he can't be without her, because he's been lost ever since she stopped being there. He smiles because he wants her to know that he still cares about her and that the last thing he wants is to make her uncomfortable.

He smiles but he knows that she's not looking. His view into the offices themselves is restricted to the first two floors, with the top three angled out of sight and made impenetrable by the reflection of the grey morning sky, but he knows that she's not there. He knows she's not at the window. He knows she's not looking down at him, seeing his smile, feeling its meaning and returning it. He can't say why he knows, he just does.

The clock behind the reception desk says it's nearly eight.

The night security guard is gathering up his things and two of the three receptionists are now sitting behind their computers, concentrating on the screens in front of them, readying themselves to welcome visitors to the building, people with appointments, perhaps some with appointments to see her. He watches as people begin to file through the reception's revolving door, as they touch ID passes on the top of the security barriers and congregate by the lifts. He watches as they fill the empty lifts when they arrive. He watches the lift doors close on the men and women, mostly young, a few middle-aged, who stand patiently, waiting to be taken to their floor so they can resume their journeys to their desks above. He watches the process repeat and repeat. Men and women, mostly young, a few middle-aged, pass through the door and the barrier and congregate by the lifts. He studies each of them, the men and the women, trying to tell one dark winter coat from the next; trying to see trousers and skirts, gloved hands and briefcases, hair, faces, eyes; trying to find points of reference, distinguishing marks; trying to find signs of her.

He sips at his now cold tea and thinks about getting another, then he thinks about all the arriving men and women he might miss while queuing for it. He watches the doors close on another lift full of heavy, dark coats. The reception momentarily empty and the street showing no sign of the next wave, he turns to see how long the queue behind him is. Five people are waiting to be served. If he was at the counter now, being served, he might be back at the window before anyone new disappears into the lifts and off to the acres of unseen office space above. But not with five people in front of him.

He looks to the front of the queue, at the man being served: early to mid twenties, black coat, grey scarf, brown leather satchel bag across him, a big fur hat, Russian army style, with the ear flaps down and tied under his chin. He's got a takeaway cup in one hand and change in the other. When he goes the queue will be four. The cute, slightly goth barista hands him his receipt. She smiles. She asks him if he's got a loyalty card. He says he has. She asks if he'd like her to stamp it for him. He gives her the card, she stamps it. Handing it back she smiles and tells him that she likes his hat. He looks slightly embarrassed, blushes, fumbles for an answer. He thanks her. She says it looks warm. He says that it is. She smiles again. At this the waiting customers shift restlessly. The young man in the Russian hat thanks her again, although it's not clear what for, blushes again and turns to leave. During this exchange another four people have joined the back of the queue, making another cup of tea out of the question.

He turns back to the men and women outside, looking for signs that any of them might be heading towards the reception. He feels the need to pay extra attention, to concentrate on the men and women passing by his window, to register their faces and check them off one by one, to make up for being distracted by the cute, slightly goth barista's flirtations. He feels he needs to double-check the details: the coats, the gloves, the briefcases; to see that he hasn't missed anyone; to be sure.

Watching the men and women in the street, he sees the young man in the Russian hat standing on the edge of the pavement, cup in hand, looking both ways, waiting for a cab to go by so he can cross the road. He watches him cross the road and push through the reception's revolving door. He watches him lift his takeaway cup that little bit higher as he touches through the security barrier. He watches him waiting for the lift with two other people, a man and a woman. He watches the three of them step inside when the doors open, and the young man in the Russian hat check his watch as the doors close. Then, a minute later, he sees him appear again, on the first floor, at a desk next to the window. He watches as the young man in the Russian hat puts his takeaway cup on the desk, turns his computer on and hangs his coat, hat and scarf on a hat stand behind him. The young man, now in a grey suit and white shirt, sits down at his desk and opens a newspaper and starts to read. He sits at his desk, reading the paper and drinking from the takeaway cup for a couple of minutes.

As he finishes his drink the young man in the grey suit and white shirt looks out of the window next to him, maybe down at the street, maybe down at the coffee shop, maybe at the coffee shop window and the man sitting looking up at him. Perhaps he senses that he's being watched. Perhaps he's looking down at the coffee shop, thinking about the cute, slightly goth barista who liked his hat and made him blush. Perhaps he's thinking about what she meant by the smile and how he feels about it and whether or not he can picture himself going out on a date with a slightly goth barista from the coffee shop across the street from his office and how he would introduce her to his friends and what they might think of him going out with a goth from a coffee shop even if she is cute. Perhaps he's trying to think of something interesting to say to her tomorrow when he goes in for his pre-work coffee, something to make up for his blushes today, something to make him seem more like himself, more interesting, more like someone she might want to go out with, not just smile at, something to make her remember him and want to see him again. Perhaps he's already wondering if she will be there tomorrow morning, realising that if he goes in to get his coffee and she's not there he'll have no way of contacting her, he'll have no way of knowing if it's her day off or if she's left for good. Perhaps he's thinking about coming back down and giving her his number, to be on the safe side, worried that he may never see her again.

The reception's now busy with couriers dropping off packages and people waiting on the low sofas under the gaze of the painted skull and the two hypnotic neon circles, but since the young man in the Russian hat arrived at his desk and became the young man in the grey suit and white shirt, only a handful of people have gone through the barriers and up in the lifts, all of them men.

He looks up at the first floor again and the young man in the grey suit and white shirt is on the phone. He's talking and looking at something on the screen of his computer. He hangs up the phone but stays focused on the screen, his unbroken concentration suggesting that he's still looking at whatever he was talking to the person on the phone about. Looking up at the young man in the grey suit, he wonders who he was on the phone to. Maybe it was her. He watches the young man in the grey suit and white shirt as he looks at his computer screen; as he types, clicks and looks back at the screen again; as he leans in closer, almost squinting, trying to see something, trying to make sense of it; as he clicks and looks and types again.

He watches the young man in the grey suit and white shirt while keeping an eye on the reception: checking in the new arrivals, noting all the details he can; looking for, still hoping to see, hints of her; comparing heights and builds and hair colours and coats and gloves and scarves and skirts and shoes and briefcases to a mental directory of her personal possessions and physical attributes; looking, if not for her, then for something in their faces that might tell him that they know her, that they've seen her, that they've sensed what he has, that they know what he does, that they know more, that they know where she is. He looks from face to face, first to see if it's her, then to somehow divine if they're visitors or colleagues.

The young man in the grey suit and white shirt picks up the phone again and starts talking. This time he's laughing, not looking at his screen, not thinking about his work, not trying to make sense of anything. He's talking to someone else, someone he likes, someone he's pleased to hear from. He's talking about something that definitely isn't work. Watching the young man in the grey suit and white shirt laugh and chatter, he wonders who it is he's talking to. He knows it definitely isn't her this time. She wouldn't laugh and chatter like that, not during working hours, not with someone junior to her, not with someone as young as the young man in the grey suit and white shirt who looks like he's possibly a junior assistant or a clerk of some description. Not because she doesn't laugh, they laughed all the time together, and not because of any ideas of superiority or ego, but because she wouldn't have time, not during the day, not while at work. Her work is too important to her to allow for laughter and chatter. He knows that it's not her that the young man with the grey suit and white shirt is talking to on the phone. If he knows her at all, it's not in a way that would allow him to laugh and joke with her like that.

Watching the young man in the grey suit and white shirt as he laughs and talks on the phone, he wonders if he does know her. He wonders if he's happened to share a lift with her on occasion as he checks his watch and sips his pre-work coffee, or if they work for the same company, on the same floor. He wonders if he knows her by sight or perhaps to speak to. He wonders if they spend long hours together, going through documents, making sense of things, him fetching and carrying and copying and researching all the important papers that she was always so eager to get to each morning when she left him with the tender instruction to go back to sleep, in the grey light of his bedroom in Peter's flat. He wonders where her glass office is, if it's on that floor. He wonders if the young man in the grey suit and white shirt can see it from where he's sitting, if he can see her now. He wonders if he should speak to him tomorrow morning, once he's got his coffee and flirted with the cute, slightly goth barista. He wonders if he should ask him about her; ask him to give her a message; ask him to ask her for forgiveness; ask him to tell her that he's sorry, that he wants her back, that he needs to see her, to talk to her, to make her understand, to be near her, to feel her closeness, just for a moment.

The young man in the grey suit and white shirt hangs up the phone and goes back to his computer screen. Looking at him, he wonders if he'll ever see her again. As he thinks this he feels the sadness reach up and pull him down into it, pulling him down from the inside, rising up around him, filling his chest, pushing down on his lungs, forcing the air out, taking him over, becoming him, defining him, weighing down on him, overpowering him until he can't breathe, becoming a burden that he might never be able to step out from under.

Then he wonders if this might be the day that he sees her after all, and he starts to feel the load lighten. He reasons that he's got to see her eventually, that it is only a matter of time before he examines the coat and scarf and gloves and hair and face of a stranger pushing through the reception's revolving door and finds that it's her. He feels the sadness dull to an ache deep inside him. He's got to see her, eventually. If he stays here long enough, if he looks hard enough, if he refuses to let the sadness become him. He just needs to see her. He doesn't know what he'd do if he did. Nothing probably. He imagines shock and fear paralysing him; the sadness replaced by excitement and the frustration of not knowing what to do next. He knows that it wouldn't be enough to change anything, but it would be enough to keep him going, to keep the sadness as an ache rather than the wave that comes ever closer to drowning him every time another thought makes the tide turn against him. Today, seeing her would be enough.

The young man in the grey suit and white shirt is still looking at his computer screen. The reception is busy with couriers dropping off packages and people waiting on the low sofas under the wall of modern art, but few trouble the security barriers and the lifts, and those who do are leaving, not arriving. He senses that everyone has arrived for the day. Everyone who is meant to be there is at their desk, working away, answering phones, looking at their computers. Everyone who is meant to be inside is in there somewhere, hidden from view, tucked away in far corners, behind partitions, or maybe looking out at him, watching him sitting in the window of the coffee shop across the road, thinking that he's probably missed her, that she got there before he did and has been warm and working all this time. He doubts that he'll see her arrive now. He could stay though. He could wait to see if she leaves: to go to a meeting or to lunch or to go home. If she is in there, she'll have to leave eventually. All he needs is to see her. If she is in there, all he needs to do is wait and he will.

He feels the sadness sink back into its hole, quietly retreating into him, realising that if he chooses to stay, it will have to wait until later to pull him back into its depths.

The cute, slightly goth barista comes to clear away his half-drunk cup of tea. She asks him if he's finished with it. He nods and she puts it on her tray along with his empty packets of sugar and serviette. He thinks about going and then he thinks about staying, waiting for her to come out. He thinks about getting another cup of tea and looks at the queue at the counter, at the two people waiting to be served by the tall Italian barista with the beard and the glasses and the hair scraped back with an alice band.

He takes off his scarf and lays it across his lap.

He decides that he'll wait for her. What else would he do with the day?

Chapter Four

They went back to her hotel after the party. Just the two of them. She said she didn't normally do this kind of thing and he believed her. Neither of them knew how to act. Unsure whether it was better to be excited or coy, they found themselves nervous and awkward instead.

All of the magazine's important guests, even the ones who lived in London, had been booked into the K West, a ten-minute walk from the party. Its minimalist white reception and adjoining lounge mirrored the conspicuously conscious style of the bar they'd just come from, as did the handful of guests congregated around the lounge's open gas fire; a collection of figures in muted tones, which his heightened sense of self-consciousness wouldn't allow him to look at fully.

As they waited in the reception for the lift to arrive he tried to reorient himself. He studied the white wall in front of him. He examined the white marble floor under his feet. He glanced across at the thin double-height white curtains which softened the transition between inside and out. He followed the line of the sweeping white staircase down from the mezzanine restaurant until it disappeared behind him, out of reach of his peripheral vision. He followed it back up to where the neon glow of the K of the K West sign outside coloured the white curtains blue. He looked everywhere his eyes could scan without turning his head or making any obvious movement. He looked everywhere he could except at her.

He couldn't be sure, but he sensed that the awkwardness between them meant that she wasn't looking at him either.

He suspected that she too felt the attention of everyone around them: the night receptionist, the staff behind the bar, the other guests. Though no one had shown any sign of having noticed the couple waiting for the lift, after the anonymity of the dark bar and the seclusion of the walk over, the K West's clinical brightness, dimmed though it had been for the hour, felt harsh and exposing, leaving nowhere for a self-conscious couple to start to find each other.

In the minute that they waited for the lift to arrive and the doors to open he changed his mind countless times, but every time he decided that this was ridiculous, a mistake, not him, that he should apologise, make his excuses and leave before he embarrassed himself even more by trying to be something that she must already have realised he wasn't, every time he decided that the humiliation of leaving was preferable to that of staying, he felt the sudden pull of her again: the sense that this was right, that he was meant to find her, that they were meant to find each other. There was something about her that made him feel that he needed to be there, and, without asking, he knew she felt the same.

So they waited next to each other, so close that a stretch of fingers would have been all it would take for their hands to touch, and they said nothing. They didn't speak, they didn't touch, they didn't look at each other, they barely did so much as breathe as they waited and watched the countdown of the numbers above the lift doors. He tried to think of something to say to speed the moment and dissolve the tension building between them. When he couldn't, he looked instead at the white walls and the brushed metal and the hidden strip lighting and thought how much Peter would have liked it there.

Only as the lift doors opened and they stepped inside did he dare to steal the briefest of glances at her. He couldn't be sure, but in the flicker of the moment that he caught sight of her face he thought

33

he saw her smile.

There had been nothing awkward about them earlier as they'd walked from the party to the hotel. As they'd crossed at the lights and walked along the side of Shepherd's Bush Green, past the shabby hotels, the language school and the petrol station, it had been as if he'd known nothing and everything about her: her newness reminding him that there was so much he needed to tell and her familiarity convincing him that telling her was the most natural thing imaginable, as if he was filling her in on events which had happened since last they'd seen each other, in another life perhaps. More than that, he'd been convinced that she wanted to know every word of it. Her encouragement, like the encouragement he'd seen her giving the man from legal affairs at the party, but much, much more so, had been intense yet unconscious, lacking all the formality and politeness that normally came with strangers, immediately designating her not as a new acquaintance but as a co-conspirator, an old love, a confidante, a long-standing ally whom he happened to have only just met. If he had stopped to think for a minute, as they turned right down the side of the block of flats and then left a couple of hundred yards later at the Pizza Express, he would have been struck by how strange it was to consider her familiar at all, let alone recognisable and sympathetic, but she was. Everything about her had made him feel the closeness of a shared history that they couldn't possibly have had and the deep understanding that such a closeness brings. After only an hour in her company, his discomfort at talking to strangers had been all but forgotten.

He'd talked all the way to the hotel. Even as the words had left his mouth he'd been unsure where they were coming from or why he was saying them. She made him talk. She made him want to talk. It was as if he hadn't spoken to anyone in months and now he couldn't stop. She'd smiled and laughed and every time he'd come to the end she'd wanted to know more, prompting him for the next piece of information, for the next part of the story, then listening carefully to all his additional words, too busy absorbing him to offer

34

anything of herself. And he was too busy telling her. He'd wanted to know about her, he'd wanted to know everything about her, and yet the conversation hadn't gone that way. Not that she'd been evasive, just too interested, too busy listening and asking all the right questions and wanting to know more. The conversation's chaotic stream of consciousness, which had started from the moment Audrey had left them alone together at the party, had continued all the way to the hotel door, interrupted only by her suggestion that they leave the party together.

They'd talked about the party, and parties in general, and how neither of them saw what everyone else found so exciting about them. She'd assured him that if she made it look as easy as he'd suggested she did, it was only because she worked so hard at it and because she'd had plenty of practice: her work required her to attend lots and look interested; working the room and making clients feel important were part of the job – although *this*, she had assured him, *this* was not. *This* was something that she never did.

He'd told her about the magazine's previous Christmas parties. This had been her first, other years she'd either been working in Paris or at other clients' parties, otherwise she was sure they would have met before now, especially if Audrey had had anything to do with it. He'd assured her that, meeting him aside, she hadn't missed much, and that likewise, this was not what usually happened to him. Usually he arrived late and left early, always alone, having spent most of the evening that way. He'd told her that he didn't think he'd ever get the hang of them, no matter how much practice he got. He'd told her that parties were more Peter's thing.

He'd told her about Peter, about how he'd moved into the spare room in Peter's flat in the Barbican at the start of the year, about how surprised he'd been by the Peter he'd moved in with, about how much he'd changed, how unbelievably charming he'd become, how unexpectedly kind and thoughtful he was. So different to the Peter he grew up in the shadow of. He'd told her about how different they both were, how different they were together, how suddenly as adults they were the friends that as a child he'd always wanted them to be.

They'd agreed what a wonderful friend Audrey was; how she was always so kind and thoughtful, and so generous, and how to have a friend like her made them truly lucky, and at times they probably didn't deserve her – he'd added that he didn't think she had a bad thought in her head, and that it sometimes frustrated him how good she was and how bad her good made him feel.

He'd told her about his work and his disillusionment with it and how he couldn't get excited any more about churning out interviews with people no one, least of all him, cared about, giving importance to their thoughts and opinions for no other reason than there were pages to fill. He'd told her that they all said the same things and all had the same aspirational lifestyle to sell; a lifestyle that he'd never wanted, but which, through Peter's success and generosity and Peter's very single, very male taste in home furnishings, he now found himself almost living.

As they'd walked along the back of the old shopping centre, he'd told her how Peter had taken him in when things weren't going so well, how his always busy older brother, the successful businessman who worked so long and hard that he hadn't had time for a personal life of his own, had seen that his younger brother was struggling and had made time for him. He'd told her how good it was to have had a chance to get to know that Peter.

Surprised at how readily he'd told her about Peter, and remembering her mentioning Paris, he'd changed the subject and told her about the one time he'd been up the Eiffel Tower, and how he'd discovered his previously undiagnosed yet embarrassingly severe fear of heights halfway between the *premier* and *deuxième étage*.

As they'd walked and laughed they'd lit cigarettes and he'd told her how he'd given up smoking a year ago, but after moving into Peter's flat he'd started having dreams, vivid, real dreams where he'd sneaked cigarettes, and would wake up feeling guilty and defeated, and how it got to the point where the daily anguish of waking up to the guilt of his dreamed smoking failure was so unbearable that the only way to stop it was to start smoking again, much to Peter's amusement.

He'd told her how much he'd come to admire his older brother during the relatively short time they'd lived together, and how he'd come to want what Peter had, not the material things, not the flat and the clothes and the sports car and the villa in the South of France, but his sense of purpose, something to devote himself to, something he believed in.

He'd told her how much he'd admired Peter's sense of who he was, and how, in a way, he'd resented how lost that had made him feel. He'd told her that for a while after moving into the flat he'd been jealous of Peter, and how, after what had happened, he'd felt guilty for it ever since.

He'd told her all of this – stupid things, embarrassing things, things he hadn't himself realised he'd felt until he'd said them – in the time it had taken to walk from the party to her hotel. He'd told her everything he could think to tell and then he'd wanted to tell her more, and he would have done had they not rounded the corner and arrived in front of the K West. That was when the awkwardness had started.

Confronted with the bright white of the glass-fronted hotel, no doubt a warm and welcoming sight for most, the space between them had instantly opened up again, to a distance that had seemed to be almost that of strangers. As he'd followed her through the revolving door and stepped into the reception's glare, the awkwardness had turned to a tension so acute that it had threatened to bring the evening and the relationship that they'd yet to have – which only minutes earlier he'd been sure was the reason they'd been so drawn together – to an abrupt end. Only his inability to resist the pull of her had seen him stay there, counting down the numbers, waiting for the lift doors to open.

The awkwardness was gone as soon as the doors closed and they were alone again. In the pause before the lift jolted into motion he felt her little finger touch the back of his hand, grazing it so lightly that he wasn't sure if it was real or imagined. Feeling it again, he reached his hand to hers, grabbing it tight when he found it. As the lift moved off they were already pulling themselves into each other; his hands at her waist, hers either side of his face, their lips pressing them hard together and keeping them there in a fixed, breathless clinch that neither of them wanted to let go of, that got harder and harder as they pulled and tightened into each other. Their heads remained pressed together as they came up for air, rubbing cheek against cheek, mouth against ear, locking them together and holding them closer than before, both trying to lose themselves in the smell and sense of the other, not wanting to let go, not wanting to move, pulling apart only enough to find each other's lips again, for her to push her mouth into his, breathing in every bit of him as he kissed her back.

They almost didn't register the lift jolting to a stop or hear the bell signalling their arrival on her floor. They only just managed to pull apart as the doors opened, and then only managed to stay that way for as long as it took them to make it down the hall to the door of her room.

She was already gone when he woke up the next morning. His first thought was that she might be in the bathroom, having a shower, getting dressed, readying herself for the day; the bed next to him was still warm and he was sure that he could still sense her in the room. But by the time he'd fully registered where he was and listened patiently for the sound of running water or movement and heard neither, he'd already found the note propped against the clock on the bedside table. Without even touching it he could predict the content: a gracious yet firm brush-off; a thanks for the good time, nice to have met you, don't forget to tip the doorman on the way out note to make sure there would be no confusion or wrong ideas or awkwardness in the future.

Seeing his name, black on the white of the envelope, his heart stopped and the sadness flooded back to him in an instant, washing away all the flimsy certainties of the night before. All the things he'd been so sure of: that they were meant to meet, that they were destined to be together, that they had both been waiting all this time to find each other; all the things that he'd convinced himself of the night before, that had kept him standing there in the glare of the K West's reception as they waited for the lift to arrive and the doors to open, had all been a figment of his overactive and painfully romantic imagination. In the equally bright yet more penetrating light of day, it seemed ridiculous to think that there could have been any more to the previous night than a happy diversion; a fun distraction between consenting adults, not the start of something – definitely not the start of something as profound and meaningful as the chance meeting of future soulmates that he'd pulled out of the air like some adolescent fantasy.

Opening the envelope he found a folded piece of hotel letterhead and on it one line, in an elegant, romantic hand, which even as he read it made him feel the closeness of her and the excitement and significance of their meeting all over again. Little though it was, there on the starched white paper, in black ink and a few definite strokes, was enough to fill him with her sadness-quelling warmth and to reinstate every one of the countless possibilities.

Had to run. Will get your number from A. Will call you.
Sx

Chapter Five

She's standing in the window of the apartment in Paris.

Her back to him.

Sunlight pouring in around her. A halo to her outline.

He can see her only in silhouette.

Her legs, her hips, her waist, her arms, her shoulders, her hair flamed golden in the bright afternoon sun.

Swaying.

Swaying to the music from the stereo: a lively trumpet; a light, swinging beat.

Swaying to the noise coming in on the breeze: traffic, people, a late-afternoon Paris.

He watches her as she moves her hips, her waist, her arms, her shoulders.

Dancing in the window.

Leaning out over the little Juliet balcony into the sunshine.

Pressing up against it.

Swaying.

Leaning back into the dark of the apartment.

Shaking her hair and gently rolling her hips to the music.

Swaying to the lively trumpet.

Swaying to the light, swinging beat.

He watches her feeling the breeze, feeling the music,

*feeling the afternoon sun, feeling the stop and start of the traffic,
the echo and beep of scooters and their horns.*

The rest of the apartment's in shaded darkness.

*Everything's dim and in shadow save for the dazzling
floor-to-ceiling brightness of the window and her dancing in it.*

*The curtains flutter around her in the breeze. Brushing
against her leg. Wrapping around her arm. Waving new air into
the room, lifting the stale mustiness, bringing the sunshine of the
afternoon in, almost reaching him, but not quite.*

He breathes hard to smell it.

Extends every sense to feel it.

*Reaches out as far as he can without moving to try to
touch its lightness, to feel its freshness, to know its warmth.*

He watches her dancing in the window.

*Swaying to the lively trumpet and the stop-start of the
traffic below.*

*He takes deep breaths to try to smell the breeze that she's
feeling and the sweetness of the sun on it.*

To try to smell late-afternoon Paris.

To try to pick up just a hint of her.

*All he can smell is stale cigarettes and coffee and the
coolness of the room.*

*All he can feel is the distance between him and the
silhouette of her dancing in the window.*

He wants to touch her.

*He wants to feel the ripple of air coming off her skin and
the warmth of the sun on her bare shoulders.*

He wants to reach out.

To feel the softness of her skin on the tips of his fingers.

Taste its sweet saltiness.

Smell her soft perfume.

He comes up behind her.

*Puts his hands on the tops of her arms then slips them
under and round her waist. Pulling her back. Pulling her in. Pulling*

her close until he can feel the music through her.

She laughs.

A small, contented laugh. Full of happiness.

He feels her relax into him.

He feels her legs, her hips, her waist, her arms, her shoulders as they pick up the rhythm of the music again.

He feels himself start to move with her.

She leans her head back into him, into his neck.

She closes her eyes.

Her lips smile wide and she says: 'I love this music.'

She sways more.

Deeper. Firmer. Meaning it more. Affirming her love for the music. Wanting him to share it. To feel it.

He feels her hips against him. Rolling to the wandering bass. Banging to the cymbals.

He feels her shoulders roll to the drums and her head bounce and shimmy to the lyrical couplets of the trumpet.

He breathes in the smell of her neck and she laughs.

He breathes out into her ear and she shudders and laughs and she says: 'I could stay like this forever.'

He feels the warmth of the sun on his face as he moves into it. As he kisses her hair. Her ear. Her cheek. Her neck.

He feels the lightness of the breeze. The stop and start of the traffic. The echo and beep of scooters and their horns. He feels the rhythm of the music. Of a late-afternoon Paris. He feels her.

She says it again: 'I love this music.'

He kisses her neck. Her cheek. Her ear. Her hair.

He breathes in the smell of her and asks her what it is.

He gets up and struggles to the bathroom.

Staggering on tiptoes, he tries to keep his feet off the cold laminate floor of the bedroom and hallway. He stumbles as lightly as he can from the ball of one foot to the other like someone trying to be quiet, as if afraid of waking the rest of the flat even though there's no one else there.

In Peter's grey slate-tiled bathroom he runs the shower and

tries to regulate the temperature of the water, stepping under it once it's gone from cold to hot to cold to bearable.

He feels the water scald and sting and he tries to come fully awake. He wills it to make a difference: to bring him into the here and now; to exert its magical power on his tired and listless limbs and pour over him the energy he needs to leave sleep behind. He breathes in the steam in the hope that it will make him bright and alert and happy; that it will clear his head of the thoughts filling it and dissolve the residue of a night spent thinking of her.

He closes his eyes and tips his head back, offering his face to the water. He rolls his head forward, letting it work away at the back of his neck; wanting it to pummel and prod him into feeling something else, something other than her.

He feels the water rushing over and down him.

He feels it start to soothe the morning sadness away. He feels the hot pins and needles reach into him, trying to do their thing and drag him into consciousness, but she doesn't want to let him go. With every push and pull into the morning comes the flicker of a memory of the night before. The more he tries to bring the day into focus and let himself be revived by the shower, the more the dream comes back to him. The silhouette of her standing in the window. The taste of her neck as he kissed it. As the bathroom becomes airless with steam, he thinks of the soft, cooling breeze blowing in through the open window. As the smell of his shower gel tries to stimulate his senses, he smells her perfume and her hair. Rinsing his hair and neck, he feels her swaying to the music from the stereo. Closing his eyes and turning his face to the water again, he sees the golden bright sunlight flaming her hair and bare shoulders; the sound of the water replaced by the echo and beep of scooters and their horns and a late-afternoon Paris.

He turns the water off and steps out of the shower.

He towels himself off, rubbing his head as hard as he can to make sure that he's awake and to try once again to shake off any thoughts other than those of the day in front of him. He tries to think about what's there, not what's missing. He wraps himself in the towel and savours its warmth and softness. He pulls the towel tight around him. He embraces the feeling of contentment it brings. Then he takes a breath to steel himself for the cold floor and the run back down the hallway to his bedroom.

Bright and awake amid the bright white cupboards of Peter's tiny kitchen – made more for displaying beautiful machines and utensils than actual cooking – he fills and boils Peter's immaculate stainless-steel kettle and hums happily to himself. He twists and contorts in time to the light, swinging rhythm in his head. He takes a bowl from one cupboard and a box of cereal from another and places them, one after the other, accents to the beat, on the polished black granite counter. He takes a tea bag from the jar and spoons from the drawer, noiselessly mouthing a lively melody that's vaguely familiar to him, although he's not sure if it's real or if he made it up or if he dreamt it. He nudges the cutlery drawer closed with his hip as a cymbal crashes in his imagination, and spins 180 degrees to get the milk from the fridge as a trumpet begins to soar somewhere in the far-off distance inside his head.

And then he stops. The melody like everything around him disappears. Whatever's in his head – this morning a tune he's not sure if he remembered or made up, yesterday the need to hurry to be sure of being at the coffee shop in time, tomorrow who knows? – it's gone in the same instant every day.

He studies the fridge door before he opens it. As he does every morning.

His hand hovers over the handle while he scans the scene in front of him, taking it in, checking off the items, making sure they're all there, letting them sink in and feeling them as if seeing and feeling them for the first time. It's part of his breakfast routine now. In an odd way, his favourite part. He boils the kettle, he gets things out of the cupboards and then he stands for a long moment looking at the fridge. Looking at the collection of things pinned to the brushed metal door by a dayglo alphabet of magnets – his one addition to the flat and Peter's one concession to colour. Taking it in piece by piece, he runs his eye over the collage of clutter that's built up on Peter's beautiful fridge door now that Peter's not there to

44

police it: shopping lists, receipts, prescriptions, postcards, an envelope with Peter's writing on it, a gas bill on which Peter had written 'paid' in the top right-hand corner; reminders from the past of things to be done, reminders of happy times. He runs his eye over all of it, confirming all the pieces are in their place, as he knows they will be, but taking particular care to see the photograph, the Post-It note and the unfolded piece of hotel letterhead – the three things that he always saves until last and spends longest looking at. There's no reason for him to do this other than that he wants to. He knows what he will see, he knows how it will make him feel, but he does it anyway because he wants to feel it. Because he thinks it helps to feel it. Maybe it does. He can't be sure either way because he never fails to stop, he never fails to look and he never fails to feel all the happiness and sadness he's hoping to find there.

It's the same every morning.

He looks at the picture: a photograph of him, Peter and Audrey. He looks at Peter. He looks at the broad smile, the healthy tan, the patches of grey on the sides of his short, stylish haircut and the brightness in his eyes. He always finds himself fixed by Peter's eyes; by the way they stare, full of confidence and assurance, straight into the lens of the camera; by the way they look straight out of the picture at him. He never looks at himself or Audrey. He doesn't need to look to know that their faces are pasty and white next to Peter's and their eyes are scrunched and barely focused in tired, inebriated smiles. He never thinks about the occasion, where they were, why they were laughing. He never thinks about the three of them together; how Peter adored Audrey and treated her like a little sister and used to tell him how lucky he was to have someone who cared about him the way that she did, that he was jealous of them, that they were perfect together, that they were meant for each other and should get married. He does, occasionally, think of how Peter laughed every time they reminded him that they were just friends. The rest of the time, as now, all he can think of is the weight of Peter's arm on his weary shoulder, pulling him in, pulling him into the middle of the picture. He can remember exactly what that felt like, how tired he was and how heavy yet reassuring and welcome

Peter's arm was. Sometimes, when he looks hard enough into Peter's confident and alive eyes, he thinks he can still feel it.

He looks at the Post-It note: a reminder from Peter to buy milk. The last such note that Peter left him. He looks at the yellow square, but he doesn't see what's written on it; instead he remembers all the other Post-It notes Peter used to leave for him. For someone as in love with the minimalist aesthetic as Peter was, he left a lot of notes about the place. Sometimes they were tasks, things to do around the flat, things to keep him busy: clean the bathroom, water the plants, tidy your shit up. Sometimes they were more philosophical instructions, including Peter's favourite missive, 'Cheer up goth', usually stuck on the inside of cupboard doors, on the bathroom mirror or on the side of a jar in the fridge.

He looks at the piece of hotel letterhead, unfolded and held in place by a small dayglo orange S. He follows the elegant sweep and curve of the writing. He feels the sweetness and care and affection the writer intended it to convey. He feels the lightness and excitement of its *Sx* signature. There's a carefree romance and a want and a kindness and an optimism that he finds in each of the words as he reads them again and again, that he thinks he could restore to the person who wrote them, if only he knew where to look for her. As he does every morning when he reads her words, he thinks that that tenderness must still exist, and that more than anything he wants to feel it again from her, if only for a moment.

He hears the kettle come to the boil and click off.

Sitting at the table in Peter's black-and-white living-dining room, he eats his cereal and drinks his tea and purposefully concentrates on the bowl and the cup in front of him, not letting his eyes wander to the shelves that take up the whole of the wall opposite, or to any of the many things on them: souvenirs of Peter's life. Today is going to be different. He's going to make the most of it, not waste time thinking about all the things he can't change, so the last thing he wants is to sit and eat his breakfast looking at the spines of the coffee-table books and old vinyl records Peter obsessively collected, or the stereo Peter used to play the records on late into the evening, or the framed photographs of Peter: happy and smiling, standing next to his little white sports car; tanned and relaxed, reclining on a lounger by the pool at his house in the South of France; red-faced and excitable, laughing for the camera with a group of unidentified friends. He knows they're all there, on the shelves. He doesn't have to look at them to feel the empty presence they fill the room with. Today he's determined to do everything he can not to feel it. Today is going to be a good day.

Out on the terrace he smokes a cigarette and takes in the Barbican's acres of grey-brown concrete. He lets his eyes drift along rows of blank apartment windows, floor after floor of them. The patchy greenery spilling from window boxes and down over balconies is the only sign of life from any of the flats; the only break in the grey-brown concrete monotony and grey-white November gloom. Not stopping to focus on anything in particular, he looks out across the ornamental lake that runs the length of the estate. He follows it to the lonely-sounding fountains at the far end and back again, sweeping over the Barbican's rough surfaces and hard edges to the peaceful quadrangles and gardens slotted between the residential blocks. The gardens and quadrangles are all empty. The residential blocks surrounding them are similarly peaceful and deserted. Quiet. Unmoving. A menacingly protective network of low-rise bunkers, seven storeys tall but built high above the ground on concrete stilts to make them at least the height of fourteen, filled with hundreds of identical flats and joined together by mid-air walkways like some 1960s dream of a future where communities lived together in blissful peace and indestructible harmony in the sky. They feel unwelcoming but safe.

In another part of London the Barbican might be mistaken for a failed social housing experiment: a 1960s dream of future community living that turned out to be fundamentally flawed. But its location on the edge of the City of London, the ornamental lake, the fountains, the gardens, the arts centre it was built around and the iconic if brutal architecture all elevate it to something far more desirable: a safe haven for nice, successful people who don't want to be disturbed, particularly by each other.

He watches solitary figures make their way along the walkways, going about their solitary business, alone like him, keeping themselves to themselves, never knowing if the person they just passed on the landing was an outsider or their neighbour and not being particularly bothered either way.

He looks back over the residents-only gardens, the lakeside benches and tables, the quiet quadrangles; communal areas with no one in them.

He looks around the terrace at Peter's designer garden furniture and imagines bringing his laptop out and sitting there in the summer mornings, happily working away, rebuilding, getting on, feeling energised by the sun shining all of its possibilities down on him. He closes his eyes and breathes the thought in and is filled with a brief stab of excitement at the promise of it. The future is always summer. Summer is always a happy thought, no matter how unreachable it seems. Opening his eyes to the dense November sky bearing down on the Barbican, he finds it hard to believe that the summer will ever come again. But then he thinks of all the times he's thought that before and how every time he was proved wrong.

He finishes his cigarette and puts it out with all the others in the flower pot in the corner of the terrace. Peter used to hate him doing that and was forever on at him to empty it.

He stands for a moment, trying to enjoy the peace and ignore the sting of the wind on his face, before deciding it's too cold and going back inside.

Sitting back down at the table in Peter's black-and-white living-dining room, he opens his laptop and checks his email. There's only one new one. It's from Audrey:

Are you still alive?

Dare I ask if you've done anything for the January music special? It goes to bed the week after next, so I need copy from you by Monday. How likely is this?

Seriously, where are you? What are you doing? Why do you never answer your phone or reply to emails? I thought we were over this, so what's going on? Are you alright?

Ax

He immediately wants to go back outside for another cigarette. He would, but he's promised himself he's going to be productive, which means he needs to learn not to let things affect him so easily. He knows that she means well. He knows that he would miss her if she stopped. And he knows she's right.

He had been alright. Or at least he'd been better and on his way to being over it. After he'd come to terms with the fact that he wasn't going to see Sophie again, after it became clear that she didn't want him to, he had reluctantly accepted the situation as one he couldn't change and the sadness had started to fade again – the same sadness that had overwhelmed him when Peter died; the sadness that she had dissolved, or at least contained, during their five months together, which had then returned to swamp him when their relationship ended. Painful as it had been when she disappeared from his life, in time he had become used to the space she'd left.

After a month or so she had faded to something he thought about only in quiet moments, and Audrey did her best to make sure that he had as few of those as possible. He'd started to think that Audrey might be right, that there might be life after Sophie – just as Sophie had shown him that there could be life after Peter. If nothing else, Sophie had shown him that it was possible, that the energy and excitement he thought was lost forever could come back, and that all the things he was sure he'd be forever numb to could be felt again. She'd shown him that it was about being patient, staying calm and waiting for the right person to come along and lift the cloud and breathe new air in. Sophie had proved that it was possible to get over someone, and after a month or so of being patient and staying calm he was starting to believe that he could get over her.

He'd even started to find joy in work again. If his work had held little interest for him before Peter died and left him the flat and half his money – having no wife or children to leave it to, Peter had ensured that his younger brother was well taken care of, with the other half of the money going to their parents, along with his investments and the house in the South of France; the business he left to his longterm business partner – then after Peter died, with no need for the little he got paid for doing it, the idea of glorifying in print people who bored him in person seemed like a waste of effort and opportunity. As children, he and Peter had been told by their parents that they could be anything they wanted to be in life: Peter's generosity meant he finally had the chance to find out what that might be, and he was sure it wouldn't involve typing the tenuous thoughts of minor celebrities. But after Sophie, after the sadness had faded to a dull ache, he'd started to feel differently. He found work gave him a new purpose that it hadn't been able to offer him before or after Peter died. It gave him a focus and a sense of identity. It gave him a way to not think about her, a way to quiet the thought that he might never see her again, that he might never touch or smell her or even sense her nearness. It gave him something to think about other than all he'd lost. It might not have been much, but it was all he had. It was his and he was grateful for it. And then the dreams came and undid everything.

The dreams started two and a half months ago.

Seven weeks after he'd last seen her.

A year to the day since Peter died.

To begin with there was no pattern to them. They didn't come every night. Their intensity, like their resonance, varied. Sometimes he could remember minute details, sometimes all he was left with was the vague feeling that he'd been with her. Sometimes they were a clear drama of events, played out with him in a central role, sometimes they were more snapshots of a moment, sights and sounds captured by heightened senses working to capacity. No two were the same. The content, the actions and locations were always different, drawn from a seemingly random selection of episodes of him and her together, although when he woke he could never be sure if they were real memories or composites of all the things he longed to feel again with her.

As time went on they developed a rhythm. They became more regular. They became clearer. Their content crystallised and began repeating. They became less about plot and more about feeling, developing into a revolving catalogue of things seen and heard and touched in all the places they'd spent their time. Sometimes they'd be in her hotel room at the K West or in the lift on their way to it. Once or twice they'd been in her company's Paris apartment, more often than not they were in Peter's flat or in the back of a cab or in a bar or a restaurant or a club or a park. Sometimes it was a summer's day in London, sometimes it was a spring afternoon in Paris.

At first he'd tried to ignore them, but the more they came the more he found himself thinking of her. He started finding her in everything. Little reminders of her, of places they'd been, of things she'd said, started working their way into mundane everyday tasks. Cooking dinner, brushing his teeth, shutting the front door, opening the curtains, taking out the recycling, crossing certain roads, and then crossing all roads, walking around the supermarket, buying particular items, ironing certain clothes, eating specific meals, watching TV programmes, waking up: as the dreams became more regular, everything in his waking day started to come with flashes of a time when he'd done or crossed or worn or eaten or seen it with her. Then he started seeing her everywhere he looked. Every blond businesswoman in the street, on the tube, in the back of a cab or in a coffee-shop window suddenly became her until a detailed study of her hair, her clothes, her manner, her face, her eyes, her lips, the way she carried and held herself and the way he imagined she might feel to touch, satisfied him that she was in fact someone else. More than once he was aware of making the subject of his gaze uncomfortable, making her shift in her seat or pull her coat around her.

Then, instead of catching imagined glimpses of her out of the corner of his eye, he found himself actively looking for her in the street, on the tube, in the back of cabs and in coffee-shop windows. He found himself going to places where he thought he'd be more likely to see her; places they'd been together, places she'd talked about. He found himself in places where he had no business being other than to look for her. Then he found himself waiting for her across the road from the only place he knew she would always return to: her office.

Somewhere along the line the balance had shifted. Gradually the dreams had become more real, more satisfying; a happier place for him than real life. His dreams were all neon: bright, dazzling, seductive, exciting. They were beautiful and tempting. They were sweet and tender and filled with the togetherness of love. His dreams looked and felt a lot like love. Intense, bright, brilliant love. Radiant love. Overpowering love. Immersive love. Complete and forgiving and limitless love. Real life was never going to be able to compete.

He would wake up in the morning's greyness and wish he could be back there with her, deep inside their world which got more neon bright and seductive every time he fell asleep into it. As time went on and the dreams became more regular, he started to walk around his daily life as if he was asleep, knowing that it was only when he closed his eyes at night that he could hope to feel anything meaningful.

He started going to bed every night hoping to see her, hoping to feel her warmth or just sense her in the room. He couldn't wait to dream, even though he knew that when he woke in the morning he would have to endure the pain of losing her all over again. The certain knowledge that the moment he opened his eyes he would be confronted by the reality of another day without her, a realisation that would open the trapdoor in the bottom of his stomach and invite the sadness to rise up once more into him, did nothing to dampen his need for another moment with her or the fervour with which he clenched his eyes shut each night. Because as hard as it was waking up alone after a night dreaming of her, it was nothing compared to waking up from a sleep in which she'd failed to make an appearance. Then he would lie there in the greyness of the morning, searching the ceiling for the slightest memory of a dream, desperate to grasp anything that would prove that she had been there and that for some reason, in waking, he'd forgotten for a moment. But finding nothing to keep the possibility alive, he had no choice but to accept the disappointment that she hadn't been there and to give in to the panic that she might never be there again.

Two months after the dreams started, he stopped pretending to himself that there was anything accidental about the places in which he found himself passing his lonely daytime hours. He stopped trying to convince himself that he was getting over her, that things would get back to normal, that time was all it would take, and he accepted that to find the happiness he experienced in his dreams, he would have to find her. Two months after the dreams started, he started looking for her in earnest.

For the next two hours he sits at the table in Peter's black-and-white living-dining room trying to occupy himself with work, but he keeps thinking about Audrey's email and what he should say in reply. The first response that had come to mind was not the one he'd expected. Instead of placating her with a lie that they both knew she wouldn't believe – everything's fine, I'm on top of it: the work, Sophie, Peter – he'd thought about telling her how empty everything was and that, after weeks of wanting to do nothing but sleep in the hope of seeing Sophie, he was now spending his days – every day but today in fact – in a coffee shop across the road from her office in the hope of seeing her while awake. For the moment that he thought it, he'd wanted nothing more than to tell Audrey everything. He wanted her to know just how far from being over Sophie he really was. But then he'd thought again, which in turn made him wonder why it was that he was so determined to keep at arm's length the one person who wanted to help him. Finally he'd concluded that for all Audrey's shows of support and desire to help, she wouldn't help him find Sophie or support any attempt to restore their relationship – a relationship which he'd never felt Audrey particularly approved of, and which she certainly never encouraged.

After clicking Send on a reply telling Audrey that he'll do his best to get the copy to her on time, he closes his laptop and turns off his phone. Without knowing what time it is, he has the vague sense that the morning is over and he hasn't achieved any of his promised productivity. He thinks about eating. He tries to decide if he's hungry enough to make himself some lunch, and while he thinks about what he's got and what would restore his spirits and energy to the positive levels with which he started the day, his eyes start to wander the shelves in front of him.

He looks at the picture of Peter standing next to his little white sports car, a 1970s Mercedes soft-top. He thinks about how much Peter loved that car and how very him it was: a little bit flashy, but stylish. He looks at the picture of Peter by the pool, at the house in Cap Ferrat. He thinks about what a beautiful villa it was, in one of the best spots on the Riviera, halfway between Nice and Monaco. He thinks about how immediately happy and at home he'd felt the one time he'd been there with Peter; and how unbearable its peace and brightness had seemed when he'd returned on his own a few months later to collect Peter's body after the accident. He thinks about the pool and the afternoon sun scorching his skin as he floated around it on a lilo; Peter kicking water over him and laughing. He thinks about the view out across the bay of Nice, with the sun glinting off the water, and as he thinks about the soft air blowing in across the Mediterranean, in his mind he takes a deep lungful of it and feels the same endless calm as he did when he first stood there. He thinks about freezing out on the terrace late at night, when it was too cold to be outside in shorts and a summer shirt, because Peter wouldn't let him smoke in the house. He thinks about the little white Mercedes parked in the villa's drive, with Peter forever polishing and taking pictures of it. Then he thinks about the pictures the Nice police had shown him when he went to collect Peter's things, of what was left of Peter's little white Mercedes and of the coastal road between Cap Ferrat and Monaco where it had happened, just after the Cap Estel tunnel. He hears again the policeman telling him that the little white Mercedes had hit the barrier and rebounded across the road into the hillside wall, and he sees the concerned face of the doctor who said that Peter would have died instantly and advised against seeing him – advice that he had gladly accepted.

He looks at the picture of Peter, red-faced and excitable, laughing for the camera with a group of unidentified friends and he thinks about how going to the South of France to collect Peter's body had felt like the first grown-up thing he'd ever done.

He looks at the books and the records and the record player and he thinks about Peter here in his black-and-white living-dining room; sitting on the sofa reading, low melodic murmurs from the stereo filling the room; sitting on the other side of the dining table, enjoying his food, pouring more wine, smiling, laughing, asking him what he's thinking about and telling him to 'cheer up'. Whenever he thinks about Peter he's laughing. Peter was always laughing. That deep, warm, all-encompassing laugh which sometimes he thinks he still hears until he listens out for it and is met with the definite silence of Peter's empty flat.

He thinks about Peter and is immediately, predictably, struck by how quiet the flat is. Still looking at the shelves, at the mementos of trips and signs of the flat's former life, he feels compelled to leave for somewhere where he can be surrounded by the noise and warmth of others. Everything around him is a reminder that, far from bringing him back, constantly thinking about Peter only makes him seem more distant. For now he needs closeness, a realisation that immediately makes finding her seem all the more important.

He looks at his watch and decides that if he hurries he might be in time to see her come back from lunch.

Chapter Six

She didn't call for five weeks. He'd all but given up hope that she would, and at the same time couldn't stop thinking about her. He'd kept the note on the K West stationery promising that she would get his number from A, attaching it to the fridge door as much to prove to himself that he hadn't imagined or misinterpreted her as to extend the hope that her call might be imminent. Then as days turned into a week and one week turned into two he started to think that maybe the note had been nothing more than a polite brush-off after all. He'd thought about asking Audrey if she had asked for his number, and then thought better of it as he wasn't sure if Audrey even knew that he and Sophie had spent the night together, and for some reason he felt uncomfortable about bringing it up, like he didn't want to be the one to tell her.

Christmas came and went, the day itself passing off far more easily than he'd thought it would. It should have been sad and awful, their first Christmas without Peter. Peter who used to organise everything. Peter who provided all the energy and enthusiasm that Christmas needs. His parents' refusal to talk about anything or even mention Peter's name since the funeral – they never talked about the sadness, he could only assume from the awkward quiet that had defined them since Peter died that it was something that the three of them shared – should have made his absence all the more unbearable. It should have, yet all the time, all he could think of was her.

New Year also passed without incident. He spent it with Audrey and some of her friends in a bar in Hoxton, and while he could think of little to justify his feelings of optimism for the year ahead, he felt them nonetheless. He'd half hoped that she might be among the unnamed friends whom Audrey had promised he'd get on so well with when she was trying to convince him to join them. When she'd said where the bar was, he'd resigned himself to the fact that she wouldn't be there – he couldn't imagine Sophie, all understated and grown-up sophistication, seeing in the new year surrounded by try-hard hipsters, all thick-framed glasses and uniformly individual haircuts – but it didn't stop him watching the door all night, right up to midnight, in the hope that she might make an appearance.

Even after the barren first few weeks of the year, with the energy of the new start having inevitably dwindled and all optimism having succumbed to the anticlimax of January, he couldn't shake the feeling that there was more to meeting Sophie than one night together after a Christmas party. Even though her lack of contact told him otherwise, he still felt a cautious surge of excitement whenever he thought of her, and despite the advance of the weeks, he thought of her a lot. Every day he read care and excitement into the sweeps and curves of her writing on the note pinned to Peter's fridge door. Every day he smiled at, and reassured himself with, its clearly stated promise that she would call.

From time to time he would look for her online, first out of idle curiosity and then out of something more focused and determined. No matter where he typed it, 'Sophie Carlson' never brought up anyone he recognised. Even her law firm's website couldn't satisfy him with a photograph or a biography or a clue as to her current whereabouts and recent activity, listing as it did only news and details of senior partners. He tried again and again. Whenever his mind wandered from what he was meant to be doing, he would find himself using what little he knew about her to try to find out more. Again and again he was left wondering how it was possible, now that the internet had moved from optional extra to the place where life was conducted, to be invisible online, to not exist, to return nothing in a search, not to be in anyone's professional network. Then after a while he started to think that it probably wasn't so hard; were it not for his articles online he probably wouldn't exist either. The more he thought about it the more he realised that, for all of the friends and followers and connections, only Audrey ever seemed to notice his presence, physical or digital, or his lack of it.

After a while her nonexistence didn't seem so odd. In fact, he admired her for it. He respected the professionalism which saw her maintain a dignified silence about her life and how and where she lived it. He was impressed that she valued her privacy so highly and didn't feel the need to validate herself with the attention of strangers or mine them for contacts and opportunities. The more he thought about it, the more he felt that her invisibility was intentional, and the more he thought that, the more intrigued he became by her. The more he realised just how private her life was, the more he wanted to share in it with her.

Then after five weeks his phone rang with an *Unknown Number*.

When he heard the soft female voice say, 'Hello. It's me,' he knew instantly who Me was.

It was half three in the afternoon.

Tuesday 25 January.

She said that she'd been at a meeting and that it had finished unexpectedly early. She said that she was in a bar in South Kensington, the Firehouse, on Cromwell Road, opposite the Natural History Museum. She said she might be there for a while if he wanted to join her.

When he got there she was sitting at the bar reading a file of papers. She didn't see him come in, only looking up when he was next to her. She didn't say anything when she saw him, but smiled with an eagerness that said she was every bit as pleased to see him as he was to have proof that she was real and true to her word. They looked at each other for a long unawkward moment – him trying to read her conspiratorial look and be sure what it meant; her trying to say with a stare all of the forward and explicit things he guessed she might be thinking – then he looked at her empty glass and asked if she wanted a drink. Her smiled widened. 'Not really. Do you?'

He asked her if she wanted to go somewhere else instead. She said: 'Yours?'

They didn't speak again until long after they got to Peter's flat. In the cab they sat like an estranged couple, looking out of their respective windows, apparently ignoring each other, her slight smile and his flush of embarrassment as her hand circled the inside of his thigh the only clues to the true nature of the tension between them.

Once inside, before Peter's front door was even closed behind them, he was pushing her back against it, slamming it shut with the weight of him on her, forcing her to drop her briefcase as he grabbed at her wrists, pulling them above her head, pulling them up and together, pinning them against the back of Peter's front door, holding them there with one hand, grabbing at her face and hair and pulling her towards him with the other. He was pushing his lips into hers, kissing her mouth and not waiting to be kissed back. He was kissing her, and pressing into her, and not letting her catch a breath, forcing her to gulp for air in desperate gasps, and the more she gasped, the tighter he wanted to grab hold of her and the harder he wanted to press his mouth into hers. All the tension from the cab, from the walk to Peter's front door, from the five weeks of not knowing if he'd ever have the chance to touch or kiss her again, found its way to his mouth and hands and into her wrists as he pulled them back down by her sides and rolled her over, rolling her face first into the hall wall, pushing her up against it.

This wasn't how he had imagined it. Over the days and weeks that he had thought about her, all the times that he had imagined having her here, in the flat, it had never been like this. He'd imagined her walking around, looking at Peter's things, taking everything in, seeing the note on the fridge and realising just how important she was to him, understanding that he knew that there was more to their meeting than one night, that he had been thinking about her ever since. He'd expected, if he ever actually found himself here with her, that he'd be shy and unsure of himself, and that they would suddenly find themselves awkward together once more, the move from neutral space to Peter's flat putting them back on guard, forcing them to find each other all over again.

Pulling her back round, pulling her up straight, pushing her back up against the wall, he kissed her again, harder than before, and started to try to move her along the hallway.

They struggled and stumbled their way to the bedroom. Struggling and stumbling and falling over each other, they fell onto the bed, him on top of her, her face down, her face pressed into the sheets, her hands back above her head, him pulling at her shirt, pulling it up over her head, dragging the fingers of his free hand down her back from her neck to the top of her skirt, digging his fingers hard into the taut, firm flesh, dragging them back up to her neck, digging deeper and harder into her shoulders, into her hair, pulling it tight, tighter, pulling her head up, pulling it to the side until he could reach her lips, kissing her as she struggled to take a breath and kiss him back, her reaching, straining, trying to get her mouth to his and him pulling away and pushing her head back down into the sheets, his lips and free hand back to her shoulders, the tops of her arms and down to the small of her back. His hand loosened in her hair and slipped down onto the back of her neck as his mouth worked its way back up her spine to her shoulder blades, his free hand pushing ahead, stroking her skin, reaching for her neck, reaching around between her and the pillow, reaching around to her mouth and her lips, sliding his fingers between them, into her mouth and then sliding down to her chin and then again to her throat. He felt his fingers tighten, just for a moment. He felt all the tension in his body focus on them. He felt them tighten again, and tighten just a little more, digging into her neck and her throat with a soft and gentle firmness as he kissed and bit her shoulders. He tightened his grip, he pressed harder and harder and then, his fingers still firmly in place, with a practised ease, he used his knee and elbow to turn her over. When he did he found her smiling.

It was late when she left. He couldn't have been asleep for

long, but when he rolled over she was already up and dressing. He said she could stay if she wanted to. She said she had to get back, work was busy at the moment and she needed her sleep, plus she had an important client meeting first thing and didn't think turning up in yesterday's clothes would make quite the right impression. He offered to call her a cab. She said it would probably be quicker hailing one outside. She wouldn't even let him walk her out to the street. She insisted that he stay where he was, in bed, in the warm, that she would be fine, that he should go back to sleep. She kissed him softly, lingering for a second as their lips parted, and then she smiled and said she'd call him.

The next day she called to say that she wanted to take him to dinner, if he was free. She said she knew a nice place in the West End, very stylish, very intimate, very romantic, very discreet, with amazing food and views overlooking Regent Street. She said that she could be there by eight and would book a table.

He got to Cocoon at ten to eight, but when he was shown to the table he found that, again, she was already waiting for him. As soon as he saw her though, he noticed a difference. Her hair, her make-up, her dress: everything about her said she was out on a date. The previous evening she'd been smart and businesslike, straight from the office; even at the magazine's party she'd been dressed for a night out in a professional capacity. But now the softness that he thought he'd sensed when he'd first watched her across the room was there, patiently waiting for him in a quiet corner of the restaurant's dimly lit dining room. The gentle drape of her hair, pinned back, exposing her neck and the soft curve of her slim, bare shoulders, had her as tender and vulnerable, not the in-control Sophie she offered to strangers. All her self-assurance of twenty-four hours earlier was gone. She looked nervous. When she saw him making his way between the tables, a broad smile returned the confidence to her face, but it was the only thing about her that seemed familiar.

As he sat down she radiated an excitement that eclipsed her nervousness and had her smiling almost too much – apparently lost either for what to say or how to get it out, she left it to her beaming eyes and wide smile to express the importance of the evening. He understood immediately. This was not the Sophie he had met before, it was the Sophie he had been hoping to meet, the one who hid shyly behind the determined overachiever everyone seemed to like so much. This was not the Sophie he and everyone else knew, this was the Sophie he'd spent five weeks thinking about. She was letting him in. He'd made her feel safe, that the real Sophie wouldn't be a disappointment to him. He'd made her relinquish control, trust him, be vulnerable with him, and she'd liked it. She liked being the real her with him and she wanted to be the real her all the time now. So this was his formal introduction, their first proper date, the start of the something more he'd hoped for.

By the time the main course arrived they were already more comfortable and relaxed with each other than they'd ever been before, and the urge to tell her everything was back and strong and only overtaken by the need to know everything about her.

He told her about how Christmas had been more surreal than sad with his parents practically refusing to acknowledge that Peter wasn't there. He told her that even when he was alive his parents had been left slightly shellshocked by Peter; as much as they had been ambitious for their children, they had always been amazed by just how much Peter, their family's overachiever, had actually achieved. He told her about the mixed messages they received growing up, that their parents drilled into them the need to be ambitious, yet were themselves terrified by the risks involved in chasing anything worth having – Peter, he explained, had somehow only picked up on the message of ambition, whereas he had grown up to be fearful of just about everything. He told her things about his parents and his childhood and Peter, things that he himself had only vaguely thought and never put together, and suddenly it all made so much sense. In telling her, he suddenly understood himself.

In return she told him about her father, a lawyer like his father and his father's father before him. She told him that she was an only child and that as such it was expected, from an early age, that she would go into law too, her father had always made that absolutely clear. She said that far from being resentful, she was hugely grateful to him for refusing to entertain any other ideas for her future. She said that she loved the law and that thanks to her father and his passion for it, she had something in her life which meant everything to her, which she too could be passionate about and devote herself to.

Even so, she said that she knew that eventually she would disappoint him. His first ambition was for her to continue the family profession. His second was that she would one day practise at the same firm in which he and his father and his father's father had all eventually become partners, and this, she said, was never going to happen. She said she loved the law for different reasons to her father. He loved its intricacies and balance and the way it could be used to broker and finesse in the corporate world, whereas she loved the idea of its blindness to position and means, how it could protect those most vulnerable from those who might seek to abuse and exploit them. Her ambition, as far as law was concerned, was to prove that everyone is equal before it, which she knew would put her in conflict with her father in many ways. Her father believed that once she'd worked her way up through the firm she was at now, representing media companies and other high-profile corporate clients, she would be coming to work with him, not the charities and not-for-profits that she was actually already talking to. She said he wouldn't be happy, in fact she didn't think he was ever likely to forgive her, although she hoped that he would at least understand that it was what she wanted, and he must know by now that, ultimately, she always did what made her happy, no matter what the consequences.

By the time dessert came they had talked more than he thought he had ever talked to anyone. They had told each other things which, though not necessarily secret or sensational, were still deeply personal; things that affected them, which they rarely shared, or wanted to share, with others. Listening to her talk, he could feel her trusting him, letting him in on information which she would have held back in other company for fear of how she might be viewed. He was different though. He was privileged. He felt that. He knew that this was what real intimacy with Sophie felt like, and he liked feeling it with her.

Had he stopped to give it a moment's thought he would have noticed that the sadness, which in the last couple of days had already faded so far into the background that he had to actively think about it to know if it was still there, had now all but disappeared. But he didn't because he was too engrossed in the sound of everything she had to tell him, too excited by the confessional tone and conspiratorial glances. In the disbelief of having her there, telling him things like he was a confidant or a friend, or at the very least an equal, he found it hard to hold onto the individual pieces of what she was saying. It was as if he was catching every other word, absorbing only the broad sense of what they meant – enough to keep up, not enough to offer a meaningful response. Even as he struggled to pull all the strands of her conversation together, he found himself getting more and more lost in her; the candlelight dancing across her face as she tilted her head making him lose focus on everything except the dark centres of her eyes that seemed to grow wider as she leaned in to him. Lulled by the intimacy of her voice, he willed her to just keep talking.

He tried to insist on paying the bill when it arrived. She wouldn't let him, immediately offering the waiter her card – not as a grand gesture, but to deal with the intrusion as quickly and efficiently as possible. It was too late though, the moment was broken along with the conversation, and once the waiter handed back her card and thanked them, they were left alone with nothing to say and no clear idea of what would happen now. Would they go back to his as they had the night before? Or maybe back to hers, to continue his discovery of the real Sophie. The fact that she hadn't looked at him or said anything since he'd asked for the bill suggested that perhaps neither was appropriate, that perhaps getting to know the real Sophie might take longer than before, and this being their first date, he didn't feel he could assume anything.

Watching her, intent and silent, studying the tablecloth, a wave of nausea unsettled everything he thought he'd understood about the evening, like maybe he'd missed something vital or read too much into it all. He watched her not looking at him, not saying anything, and tried to decide if she was building up to something or just waiting for the next thing to happen.

After a full minute of her saying nothing and him trying to discern what that nothing meant, she spoke, still not looking at him.

'I have to go away for a while.'

Now he felt the sadness. He felt it rushing up to his throat, flooding his chest.

'I have to go to Paris to oversee a project I've been working on. A UK publisher we represent is buying a division of a French publisher and I'm going to work in our Paris office while it goes through.'

She looked up for a second, just long enough to meet his eyes and look away again.

'I'll be there for at least a month.'

She looked up again, holding his gaze this time.

'Maybe a bit longer.'

She looked into his eyes like she was looking to see what a month or longer without her might mean to him.

'So I was wondering . . .'

She looked into his eyes, like she was looking for a flicker of encouragement.

'I was wondering if you'd like to come with me.'

Chapter Seven

The coffee shop's busy with the lunchtime rush.

As he looks around for a seat, he sees all four window stools are taken: three by women, none of them her.

The only free table is all the way over at the back, next to the toilet; from there he knows he won't be able to see out of the window at all, never mind the comings and goings of the heavy-coated men and women through the revolving door across the street.

For a moment he stands in the middle of the coffee shop not knowing what to do, hovering indecisively as if trying to decide what his options are, even though he knows he hasn't got any. He tells himself again and again that this is why he gets here early, not just so he doesn't miss her, but so he can secure his place at the window, so he can be sure of a good view. Without it he knows there's no point being there, but he hovers because he doesn't know what else to do or where else to go. He hovers hoping that an answer will make itself apparent, that someone will move or leave or an appropriate course of action will somehow suggest itself. He hovers until the queue from the counter extends and grows and snakes its way to where he's standing, and people start joining behind him having assumed that he's part of it, deciding for him that he's staying after all.

From his place in the queue he can just about see most of

the reception across the street. He can see two of the three receptionists sitting behind their computers, he can see the modern art on the walls, but not the low sofas below or anyone who might be sitting on them. When the women on the stools in the window move their heads a couple of inches this way or that, he can intermittently see the reception's revolving door and a couple of men, one of whom may or may not be the young man with the Russian hat from yesterday, who are standing just to the side of it smoking. Seeing them smoking makes him want a cigarette. He thinks about leaving his place in the queue, leaving the coffee shop, running across the road, asking one of them for a light and striking up a conversation with them: maybe making a comment about the weather, about how they must all be desperate to be smoking outside when it's as miserably cold as this and then asking them if they work in the building, what they do there, who they work for, if they work for her, if they know her, if they can tell her that he's here. He decides against it, reasoning that there's no way to make such questions sound casual and natural, and watches the men finish their cigarettes and go back inside. He looks back at the queue to find that it's moved on a couple of places without him.

From his new position in the queue he can see significantly less of the reception, his view obscured by the heads of the woman and man to the right of the window and by a window sticker advertising a new range of winter drinks. The queue moves quickly. Both the slightly goth barista and the tall Italian barista with the beard and the glasses and the hair scraped back with an alice band are behind the counter, working independently of each other, serving their own customers rather than operating their usual, frustrating cashier-and-coffeemaker double act. They're being uncharacteristically efficient, thinning the queue two customers at a time, accelerating his progress along the counter, speeding him towards the point where he won't be able to see the reception at all. Keeping one eye on what he can still see through the window and one on the baristas, he tries to work out which of the two will serve him. He's hoping for the tall Italian. He's now convinced that the slightly goth barista, who he used to think was cute before she

67

started looking at him the way she has been the last couple of days, has taken a dislike to him; that she disapproves of his extended daily presence and is actively trying to discourage him from returning: where once she was smiley and friendly and chatty and welcoming, now she looks at him in a way that suggests she wants him to know that him being there makes her uncomfortable. The next two customers take their drinks and his view of the reception is finally obscured by a column and then the wall.

The tall Italian barista takes his money and hands him his tea as the goth girl takes the next customer's order while fixing him with a stare that confirms that he is indeed unwelcome. Moving back around the counter, he sees that all four window stools remain taken, with none of their occupants looking like they're about to leave. The table at the back next to the toilet is still the only table available, and with a hot cup of tea and no other options, he goes and sits at it.

At his table at the back next to the toilet he tries to make himself comfortable. He tries to just sit and enjoy his drink. He tries to occupy himself with looking at the people around him, but instead of the students and shoppers and mothers with children in pushchairs who fill most London coffee shops, he's surrounded by men and women in suits who all look like they work in offices exactly like hers. He tries not to think of all the similarly attired people in the street outside. He tries not to think about everything that he's missing by sitting in a dark corner of the coffee shop, not being able to see out of the window. He tries not to picture her among them, passing by, stopping outside the coffee shop, within touching distance, just the other side of the glass, with him not there to see her as she waits to cross the road on her way back to her office from lunch. He tries to think of other things he could do and places he could go, of a better way to spend the rest of the afternoon. He tries not to think about the look that the slightly goth barista gave him. He tries not to read into it things that aren't there, something he knows he's good at, that he knows he does all too often.

He stirs two packets of sugar into his tea. He keeps stirring his wooden stirrers long after the sugar has dissolved, more to occupy himself for a few seconds longer than because he's lost in the deep contemplation that anyone watching might assume. He doesn't want to think about why he's here any more than he wanted to stay in Peter's flat thinking about Peter, but with nothing to see and no one to watch or look out for, he inevitably starts to go back over all the times he tried to call her, how her phone would ring and ring and how he would leave messages and then one day it didn't ring at all. He thinks about how there was no discussion, no debate, no accusations, no anger or heavy exchanges or bitterness or name-calling or visible signs of emotion, she just never spoke to him again. She walked away and then she turned her phone off. He thinks about how she didn't give him a chance to explain and how he left countless messages trying to, and how he had no way of knowing if she ever got or listened to them or heard anything he had to say. He didn't even know if she'd ever heard him say that he was sorry. For everything.

He looks at the surrounding tables, at the middle-aged men in suits, with their pens and notebooks and coffees and muffins, having meetings with other middle-aged men with all the same hand gestures and laughs, and he tries to think about other places he could go to look for her before coming to the same conclusion he always comes to, that this is the only place he knows to look, that it's the only place she gave him.

He thinks of all the places they went together and all the things they did in them, of the bars and the hotels and the parks and the coffee shops and the restaurants, in London and in Paris. He thinks about Peter's flat and all the times she stayed over and left before he was awake enough to really see her go. He thinks about all the times she kissed him goodbye, all the times he felt her warm breath on the side of his face and her cheek on his, he thinks about all the times he felt her warm lips pull away and the cold morning air replace them, he thinks about the sound of the front door closing behind her and the smell of her perfume that lingered like part of her for minutes, maybe hours, after she'd gone. He thinks about all the times he kissed her and she kissed him back. He thinks about all the times she touched his face or stroked his hair or held his hand or smiled or laughed and he knows that no matter how hard or how long he thinks about them, none will ever tell him where to find her. They were always where she said they should be, and that was always Peter's flat, not hers – Peter's flat being easier for her for work, so she said; being there meant that they got more time together, that she didn't need to leave him quite so soon. And if not at Peter's flat then it was restaurants that they only ever went to once, or bars he'd never heard of before and could barely remember, or parks and coffee shops which like the restaurants and bars were at all ends of London, scattered far and wide across the city, always of her choosing, but never giving any clue as to where she really existed. Not that he ever seemed to take in the details anyway. She was the memory, not the places they went. The touch and warmth of her, the things they'd said, not the wine they'd drunk or the food they'd eaten.

He sips his hot tea and thinks that, at the time, he didn't realise how little of her he had to go on. It wouldn't have mattered if he had. He didn't need the details of *her* life, he was only interested in *theirs*: what they did together, what they said, how she looked at him, how she made him feel that she was there for him and always would be, how she'd started to feel like home to him. Her dominance of the relationship, her direction of everything they did, that it was always her suggestion of where and when they should do it, was part of the fun. It was exciting. It made the relationship feel illicit, like a secret. It ensured that they, their relationship, their time together, their illicit, secret little existence, had nothing to do with the ordinary world and everyday life and all the mundane and tiresome things that happen during its long, slow hours. It was a secret escape. Their secret escape. All rendezvous and stolen moments that had nothing to do with anyone else. That she told him where and when and how was one of the best things about the relationship, until her phone stopped ringing.

He sips his hot tea and thinks that the only thing that he knew really mattered to her was her work and the office was the only place of hers he'd ever been to, and even then he wasn't welcome. Again he thinks about being told to wait for her in the coffee shop the one time he arranged to meet her from work, and then of her look of discomfort at finding him in reception the one time he had acted on his own initiative and surprised her. It was the only time he'd set foot in the reception. The memory of her reaction to finding him there then is the only thing keeping him out of it now. He thinks about how he's wanted nothing more than to go through the revolving door, to walk up to the reception and ask to see her, to have one of the three receptionists call her and tell her that he's there, waiting for her, in reception, but the thought of how she might react has so far stopped him. He thinks that the only thing he wants more than to find a way to reach her and talk to her is to find a way to reach her and talk to her and have her pleased to see him. He knows that turning up unannounced at her office and demanding an audience isn't the way to do it, but at the same time he needs to know that she really is there, because after all the days and weeks of watching and waiting and not once catching a glimpse of her, he's starting to wonder if she actually is. He's starting to think that he imagined that she worked there. He's thinking that he might have imagined her and them and everything they did together. He must have done, otherwise he would have seen her by now. He thinks about the office that he can't see from his table at the back of the coffee shop next to the toilet, and he tries to imagine her in there, but he can't. He doesn't believe he'll ever see her, and now he needs to see her more than anything, even more than he needs to have her be pleased to see him. He needs to believe that she's there because if she isn't, he doesn't know where she is or how to find her and he might as well have imagined the whole thing.

She must be there, so why does he never see her? He's there every day. He's there all day. Apart from today he's been getting there earlier and earlier and he's been staying later and later. He's spent days there, looking out of the window, never taking his eyes off the reception, searching the face of everyone going through the revolving door, tracing their outline, trying to decide if it's her or not, if it could be, if it might be, if in a different light they might look more like her. It's no wonder the slightly goth barista looks at him the way she does, wondering why it is he sits there day after day, wondering what it is he's looking at, who he's waiting for, what he's waiting to see, why he hasn't got better things to do, other places to be, wondering what's wrong with him, why he's there, why he won't go somewhere else, why he won't leave them alone. He's spent so long there, looked over so many strangers, he's starting to worry whether he would be able to pick her out of the constant stream of people who come and go through the security barriers and the lifts. What if she's been there, every day, and he just hasn't recognised her? What if he's remembering her all wrong: her shoes, her skirt, her briefcase, her gloves, her coat, her hair, her face. What if he doesn't recognise her expression, having never seen her full of the purpose and place-to-be determination that all of the strangers he's watched come and go over the last few weeks have had? He only ever saw her with affection in her eyes and a gentle openness in her smile; he thinks, for the first time since he's been coming here to try to see her, that this is not the face she would be wearing if he were to see her now, coming or going. She would be harried and focused or lost in faraway thoughts of the day ahead or the day that's been, and he never saw her like that. The Sophie he knows is full of kindness and patience, things none of the faces he's seen have offered.

Or maybe she's not even in the office. Maybe she's working from home, wherever that is. Maybe she's on holiday. Maybe she's away on business. Maybe she's left the company. Maybe she's gone and he'll never find her again.

He tries to think again of all the other places he could try to look for her, and again, he can't think of any. He tries to think if there are any other clues, any other leads, any other searches he could have done, any other keywords he could have entered that he might have missed or overlooked, which might have given him the slightest something to go on, which might have led to another search and another site and another link which might have led him to somewhere else to go, somewhere else to sit and wait and watch, somewhere else to try to find her. He thinks of all the searches, all the sites, all the social networks and all the links that he's already tried, and how Sophie Carlson is never there. Not the Sophie he knows anyway. Not the quietly determined yet elegant and tender and caring and sophisticated Sophie that he's looking for. It's not an unusual name. There are plenty of Sophie Carlsons out there and he's looked at all of them, at every news story, every link, every profile picture. Some of them are younger than her, some are older, some are plump and homely, some are thin and neurotic-looking, some are attractive, some incredibly so, some border on beautiful, but none of them is her. Every time he looks he finds lots of people in her place, but even before he starts going through them, he knows she's not there. The lack of online presence, the carefully maintained privacy that he once admired her for, is now a painful frustration, an absence that feels more and more like a conspiracy, orchestrated just to keep him away.

No, she must be there, in her office across the street. He has to believe that she is. Otherwise where else can he go? Where will he spend his days? In Peter's flat, thinking about Peter? Thinking about her? Searching again and again for her online, even though he knows there's no point?

Finishing his tea he repeats again the one piece of solid information he has to go on: that work is the thing that matters to her most and the office is the one place where she will definitely go. And again he is left with the same disturbing afterthought, that now he's not even sure about that.

Looking at his empty paper cup he thinks about all the emails and texts that he sent that were never replied to. He thinks of all the messages he left that he has no idea if she listened to. Messages saying that he missed her, that he needed to see her, that he was sorry. Texts saying that he loved her, that he wanted to make it up to her, that he needed to be with her. He thinks of all the days that he's sat here, in his coffee shop across the street, waiting for her, like he did that time, like she told him to, sitting here waiting for her to come, growing more sure by the day, by the minute, that she never will. He thinks about all the texts and messages and calls gone unanswered, he thinks about all the days of waiting, and he feels her slipping away, slowly fading into the background. He feels the sadness swell and rush up inside him, propelled by a new sense of panic into his chest and throat. He thinks that if he doesn't do something soon, there'll be nothing left to find, she won't even be a memory.

He looks at the surrounding tables, at the middle-aged men in suits, with their pens and notebooks and coffees and muffins, having meetings with other middle-aged men with all the same hand gestures and laughs, and he remembers that there is a real world for him to come back to; and then he wonders if there's really still a place for him in it. He did rejoin it once. When her phone had stopped ringing, he'd understood; she'd made it clear that it was over, that she didn't want to see him and he had, reluctantly at first, then with surprising ease thanks to work and Audrey, picked up his life where he'd left it, almost like *they*, him and her, had been a dream, something passing, something that never actually was. But then the dreams had started and she had pulled him back to her. She had decided that she wasn't done with him yet.

Sitting at his table at the back of the coffee shop, next to the toilet, he thinks that she probably won't ever be done with him now. He looks at the surrounding tables, at the middle-aged men in suits, going about their lives, free to come and go as they please, free to choose what comes next, and he's not sure he'll have another chance to join them again. Not unless he does something. Now. Something to end it or start it properly. Something this instant. Something to end the waiting. He looks at the surrounding tables, at the middle-aged men in suits, having meetings with other middle-aged men with all the same hand gestures and laughs, and he realises that it's the waiting he can't take, and that he can't wait any more.

Chapter Eight

Their month in Paris was like nothing else he'd known. Like being taken out of himself to a world he had only ever imagined and then being immersed in it to the point where he felt he could disappear completely. And he liked the feeling.

Paris seduced him with its contentment with itself and lack of interest in him. It seduced him with indifference. He liked the sense of being apart from everything that came with being a stranger, the lack of connection to the people and places around him that made everything seem fresh and interesting and that made him a tourist, but more than that he liked the elegant way Parisians ignored him. It wasn't the same as being invisible in London, it was something altogether more romantic and inclusive; a hard to define but palpable sense of being watched but not seen, of being there but not.

He fell instantly in love too with the romance and elegance and sensuality present in the stonework and windows of every building; with the secrecy of the tall doorways and gated courtyards; with the literary and artistic allusions of street signs; with the arrogance and allure of the wide boulevards and the narrow side streets; with the love and laughter and promiscuity and pretension that seemed to spill out of every bar, restaurant and cafe, crowding every street corner and filling every pavement. But most of all he fell in love with the company of strangers so used to being on display in parks and pavement cafes, so used to watching and being watched, that they never gave those around them the satisfaction of noticing. He quickly found Paris to be a city of disinterested voyeurs, and being there on show among them the perfect way to hide. Within days he began to crave the anonymity they conferred on him. Being alone in Paris – which he was for much of the time, with Sophie busy overseeing her takeover – he found was a very sociable experience, and what it lacked in contact and conversation, it made up for with the constant visual and auditory stimulation of all the other people passing their time with him. In Paris, he found, it was almost impossible to be alone in being alone.

The apartment wasn't anything like he'd imagined either. Not the high ceilings, long rooms, brilliant white walls and endless parquet flooring that he'd always associated with Paris and money. The floor-to-ceiling windows were narrow and squat like the rooms themselves. Instead of ornate mouldings and grand period features rendered tasteful by monochromatic interior design, it was shabby and plain and warm. Lived in. Stylish but, for want of another more Parisian word, cosy. He'd envisaged a business residence in Paris, one used by employees of a large law firm like Sophie's, to be impressive and quietly overstated: an airy, minimalist shell, tastefully furnished with modernist design classics, chosen for their universally recognised style, not comfort. Somewhere Peter would appreciate. But the tiny apartment on the Rue Quincampoix couldn't have been further from it. The small combined living room-dining room-kitchen was made even smaller by a large sofa, designed not just for comfort but for long cosy evenings together, with the rest of the limited floor space taken over by a magazine-strewn coffee table, a variety of house plants and an extendable kitchen table which stood with a chair either side of half its surface and nowhere for its other half to extend to.

The company's apartment wasn't a chic pied-à-terre, it was somewhere they could pretend was home. The low ceilings and compact floor plan, like the two-ring electric hob and microwave in the kitchen and the tightly packed toilet-sink-shower of the bathroom, were about what was needed and nothing more. The apartment made no concession to appearances, it offered only functionality. It wasn't about impressing those who worked for the company, it was about giving them somewhere comfortable and welcoming to come back to at the end of the working day, and he was grateful for it. The bedroom, like the living room-dining room-kitchen, was big enough only for the pieces of well-worn furniture that had been crammed into it – a large bed, a wardrobe, a dressing table, a bookcase with nothing on it and a high-backed, low-seated chair, the apartment's one real luxury – but they would have made do with half the square footage for all the freedom it gave them. The apartment wasn't cramped, it was secret; a hidden place two flights up a tight, twisting staircase. It wasn't dark and claustrophobic, it was intimate; a cosseting safe house, shading them from the glare of the outside world. Its air wasn't musty and stale, it was thick with atmosphere and anticipation. But most of all the apartment was neutral ground; a place where they could find peace from who they were and who they had been and who they might still be if they were somewhere other than there, with each other.

Likewise, from the first moment they had turned into it, the Rue Quincampoix felt like a refuge. A narrow side street in the 4th arrondissement, tucked behind the Pompidou Centre, it was a short walk and an aesthetic world away from the tall rooms and wide opulence of the Avenue de l'Opéra, which, based on a childhood memory from his only previous visit to Paris, was what he pictured when Sophie said her company had a place they could use on the right bank. Surrounded by streets full of tourists and teenagers who massed around the Pompidou and moved between the bohemian boutiques of the Marais on one side and the fast-food outlets and chain stores of Les Halles on the other, the Rue Quincampoix offered instant quiet and calm. Little more than an alley, the five-storey buildings cast its bars and offices and art galleries into near-permanent shadow, giving the whole street the feel of somewhere that only those who lived and worked on it knew existed; a feeling that soothed him every time he stepped into the coolness of its shade and filled him with a childish excitement every time he entered the key code on the street door.

At first they lived the romantic vision of Paris living. They arrived late on Thursday evening, and with Sophie not due in the office until Monday morning, had three whole days of being a couple escaping to an apartment in Paris and doing all of the things that couples escaping to Paris do. Each morning he went down to the boulangerie at the end of the Rue Quincampoix and bought croissants and bread to have with the coffee he brewed for breakfast, after which she took him on guided tours of Sophie's Paris – taking in the Marais and Les Halles, Saint-Germain and the Latin Quarter, the Avenue de l'Opéra and the department stores of the Boulevard Haussmann. They stopped for lunch in her favourite brasserie one day, ate ham and cheese baguettes in the Jardin des Tuileries another and wasted a couple of hours in a quiet bistro she knew off the Rue de Rivoli when the warm February sun failed to arrive on the last. After lunch they spent afternoons wandering up and down the grand avenues: the Champs-Élysées, the Boulevard Saint-Michel, the Avenue George V, the Boulevard Saint-Germain. They immersed themselves in the untouchable and unabashed glamour of the designer boutiques of the Rue Saint-Honoré, and she showed him her favourite quiet places: the hidden squares and gardens of the Place des Vosges and the Palais Royal. They walked arm in arm along the Seine, crossing back and forth between the right and left banks, stopping to take pictures at Pont Neuf, and then heading down into Saint-Germain with Sophie pointing out galleries, cafes, bookshops and bars as they went, and the cinema where she'd watched American films dubbed in French. They stopped for coffees along the way, ate crêpes from a crêpe stand and read restaurant menus and bar cocktail lists, making mental notes of places to spend what seemed like an endless supply of evenings. In reality though, after hours of wandering and exploring, with the bright spring sun having set and the crisp air having turned cold, they were happy to spend those first evenings, like many that followed, in the apartment. They went to a restaurant one night and to a bar the next, but they didn't stay long in either, so excited were they to get back to the warmth and privacy of their very own piece of the city. For all the exploring and seeing of Sophie's favourite sights that they did during those first few days, it was the evenings alone in close isolation on the Rue Quincampoix, and the sudden domesticity that it forced, that felt like the real adventure. Like newlyweds setting up home together, they found the deepest pleasure and the most excitement in doing nothing, but doing it together and alone.

Once Sophie started keeping office hours they quickly settled into a natural routine, the domestic rhythm of a couple whose lack of a combined past or meaningful knowledge of each other was outweighed by the reality of sharing such intimate space. During the week Sophie left the apartment at half seven in the morning, and when she returned at half six in the evening he would prepare a simple meal, something that could be cooked using only a two-ring hob and a microwave, or they would go to one of the French, Chinese or Korean restaurants in the surrounding blocks for something quick to eat and then head straight home. Friday nights they headed over to either the Marais or Saint-Germain for dinner and drinks, and maybe a walk along the Seine if it wasn't too cold – making sure they were well placed to witness the hourly spectacle of the Eiffel Tower exploding into life; its thousands of randomly flashing lights making it sparkle from root to tip, like something otherworldly and unimaginably beautiful; a display which never got any less magical or romantic, no matter how many times he saw it. At the weekends they did as they had done those first three days: walked, talked, went to Sophie's favourite places and to places he'd discovered on his days alone, ate, explored, laughed, forgot, got lost and enjoyed being together.

Their being together didn't seem strange to him at all. He didn't question what he was doing there, or why she'd asked him to come. He didn't stop to think about all the things he didn't know about her, because he already felt he knew so much. She'd never felt like a stranger to him, just someone he was excited to meet and know more of, and every day he spent with her felt like the fulfilment of something he'd been waiting for. Something fated. There was never any trepidation about being with her, never any uncertainty, only an eagerness to get on with it, to get past the preliminaries and on to the point where they were just together. He didn't question the reason behind her invitation, because it was exactly what he wanted.

As they settled into their routine, they settled into each other. They stopped explaining who they were and who they'd been and who they might still be if they were somewhere other than there, with each other. They stopped talking about the past. They spent every day in the now and the immediate future, in Paris, thinking only of the things that affected them in their small apartment in a quiet side street in the 4th arrondissement, and nothing else. She stopped talking about work, or at least she didn't discuss it beyond replying to his nightly enquiry as to how her day had been; she was more interested in what they were eating, if they were going out for drinks, what they might do at the weekend. And he stopped talking about Peter. He stopped telling her about his life with his brother, because he stopped thinking about it; he was so swept up in being with her that he couldn't have been further away from Peter's flat and Peter's things and the life he'd lived with him.

With Sophie out all day, their time together was filled with an urgency that moved everything at double speed and made moments of closeness feel stolen. Weekends were a luxury, a wide open space, hard to quantify but big enough to get lost in, where time slowed to the point of stillness and they could gorge themselves on each other. The rest of the time they snatched what they could. Before work, after work, fresh from the shower, unpacking the grocery shopping, cooking, dressing, changing to go out to dinner, stumbling in the stairwell on their way back. When she woke him in the morning to kiss him goodbye, her kisses would multiply and linger until she was back on the bed with him, protesting but only half attempting to pull away and regain her composure, insisting that she had to get to work, that she had time for one more kiss and nothing more, except maybe one more kiss. The pattern the week followed was one of growing need and lessening resistance: starting with the contentment of having just spent two whole days together, and ending with the frustration of five days predominantly spent apart. Monday morning she would successfully stick to one more kiss and nothing more; by Friday she would be the one looking for excuses to postpone her departure, less concerned about him disturbing her skirt and blouse, less convincing as she told him to go back to sleep.

Once she finally left for work, and the last of her perfume had faded after her, he was free to pursue his own daily agenda. Loose as it was, in a matter of days he had constructed a roster of activities – places to explore, errands to run, new regular haunts to return to – which occupied his time to such an extent that he easily lost track of it, on several occasions returning to the apartment to find her already back from the office and missing him.

He spent a lot of time sitting outside cafes, smoking, watching Paris go by. He found cafes he liked in Saint-Germain, Montparnasse, the Ile de la Cité, the Marais, Bastille, and Montmartre. He would sit inside with the students in a cafe on the corner of the Rue du Bac and the Rue de l'Université when it was raining. He would sit under the gas heaters outside the Café de la Mairie on the Place Saint-Sulpice and eat croque-monsieurs and omelettes and Salade Parisienne and watch the comings and goings in the square opposite when it was dry.

After cafes, he was next most likely to be found in the Carrefour supermarket on the Rue de Seine. To begin with they did the grocery shopping together. They walked along the narrow aisles stacked high with exotic packets and unrecognised, unpronounceable brands, guessing at the contents of individual packets, choosing meals and ingredients, learning each other's likes and dislikes; him using his knowledge of the bottles in Peter's kitchen and the limited culinary skills his brother had impressed on him to pick out wines and devise menus; her loading their basket with all her favourite French delicacies and treats. But Sophie, being more accustomed to Parisian grocery shopping and particularly to the small Carrefour squeezed between the bars and bistros on the Rue de Seine, moved efficiently between the shelves and the freezers, the cold cabinets and the vegetable sections, picking up what they needed and spending no longer studying a shelf than it took for her to find what she was looking for, whereas he wanted to browse, to look at everything, to take it all in. He wanted to savour the foreignness of the produce, to appreciate all the alien sights and sounds of what to him seemed the most Parisian of experiences. He was used to the small, lightly stocked Express or Metro supermarkets that surrounded Peter's Barbican flat, or the suburban supermarkets with their vast car parks and wide aisles, modelled after the American love of large-scale choice set to a large-scale floor plan. The Carrefour on the Rue de Seine was every supermarket he'd ever experienced, inverted: a local mini-mart, with a frontage equal to no more than two of the bars and bistros either side of it, but with an inventory to rival the choice and selection of the most impressive of out-of-town French hypermarkets. For him this small space, full of riches and delights and all manner of sumptuous things to stimulate the senses and excite the mind, came to symbolise Paris more than anything else, the Eiffel Tower included, and he could spend hours in it. Unable to recalibrate her view of Carrefour to anything other than a supermarket, Sophie soon suggested that he do the shopping while she was at work.

And so he did, going at least twice, sometimes three times a week to collect basic supplies and to browse the shelves – familiarising himself with all the curious things so as to be at home among them and therefore at home in Paris, but also worrying that one day he would walk in and, recognising all the packets and names, would feel that Paris was normal, commonplace, just like everywhere else, and that the city he was falling in love with would have lost its magic and charm.

That he walked there and back necessitated regular trips as he could only carry so much on his own, and while they regularly ate out like most Parisians – their tiny kitchen's limited resources made the preparation of anything more extravagant than a salad a major undertaking – their desire to make the most of the isolation the apartment afforded them meant they ate in often enough to make Carrefour on the Rue de Seine the highlight of his Tuesday and Thursday mornings.

Every Tuesday and Thursday the anticipation that filled the

walk down the Boulevard de Sébastopol, across the river and along the Rue Saint-André des Arts, was edged by the quiet fear that this might be the day his supermarket in Paris lost its appeal. It never did.

When he wasn't gazing at Carrefour's shelves he was wandering the streets, gazing in shop windows, closely studying items that in London probably wouldn't have caught his attention. He took to browsing through the racks in entertainment shops, looking at records by artists he'd never heard of and DVDs with titles that meant nothing to him. Daily he seemed to find himself loitering outside yet another bookshop, admiring and sifting through the piles of books he couldn't read.

He was adept at keeping himself occupied, spending little to no time in the apartment on his own. He ate lunch in sushi bars and Lebanese restaurants, he strolled through the Jardin du Luxembourg, he took the Métro to the far reaches of the city to see what was there, walking all the way back to the apartment to get a sense of where everything was and how it all fitted together. He preferred to be out, exploring, finding new places, making himself at home, mingling with all the Parisians who spent their hours watching each other pass by. He twice went to the cinema and watched American films dubbed in French, finding their familiarity and foreignness and his inability to understand them comforting, confirmation that he was alien to what was going on around him and therefore couldn't be expected to take part in it.

But mostly he sat on his own outside cafes and bars, smoking, watching, content. He was happy. Disquietingly so. Almost the moment he stepped off the train at the Gare du Nord he'd felt the sadness, what little there was left of it, slip to somewhere deep inside him, somewhere out of reach of his conscious thoughts. Now, for the first time in a long time, he was actually, definitely, happy. Happy to be somewhere outside of himself, away from his life and all the memories of it. Happy to be someone else, somewhere he didn't belong.

He spent most of his time alone, but it was different to being alone in London. It wasn't lonely. He thought at first that it was Paris that was the difference, that it was the company of these disinterested strangers, who watched but didn't care if he was there or not, who let him be alone and lost among them. But after the first few weeks he knew that it wasn't Paris, it was Sophie. He knew that the truth was that he wasn't alone, not really. He was alone only for the moment, only for the day, only as he sat there drinking his *café crème*, smoking one cigarette after the other, watching and pretending not to be seen. He knew that his being alone would end that evening, when either she would be there to welcome him back from his day of being alone on the streets of Paris, or he would be there to welcome her home from a day of overseeing whatever it was she was overseeing, and they would cook and talk and enjoy the simple pleasure of being together. He knew that someone would be expecting him, waiting for him, looking forward to seeing him at the end of the day, and that made all the difference. He knew that even without Paris, as long as he had Sophie he could be alone, but never lonely.

Chapter Nine

The reception's bigger than it looks from across the street, bigger
than he remembers it being the last time he was there. He stands for
a moment in the middle of it and tries to make sense of the wide,
high space around him. The revolving door behind, the security
barriers in front, the lifts beyond them. To the right the low sofas
and the modern art that seem so familiar. To the left the reception
desk with the three computers and three receptionists that he's so
used to looking at from across the street. He looks from one to the
other, trying to get used to the new scale, to the size of the sofas and
the canvases above them, to the length and height of the reception
desk and its distance from the seating and the art and the security
barriers and the lifts. He looks from one to the other, trying to get
used to not being able to view the whole of the reception as one. He
looks up and around, trying to equate the depth and angles with the
letterbox view he's used to from his stool in the coffee-shop window.

    The change in perspective and atmosphere, from the
compact and oppressive grey of the street outside to the airy-triple
height expanse, is so great, so disorienting and unexpected, it makes
him forget for a moment his reason for being there. For a moment
all he's aware of is the space, not the noise or the people in it. Slowly
he starts to sense the movement of those around him and with it the
panic that picked him up from his table next to the toilet at the back

of the coffee shop. As the murmured sound of greetings and enquiries starts to seep through, so does the need that brought him across the road and through the revolving door to this side of the reception's glass – the need to ask for her by name, to have it confirmed that she exists, that she's there, that he can see her if he wants to, the need *to* see her and put an end to the waiting. The voices reverberate around the marble and glass walls, multiplying to a polite din that brings him to and reminds him of his purpose and all the possible implications of it, that tells him to act before he loses his nerve and turns back to the revolving door and his stool in the coffee-shop window.

He looks to the three receptionists. He tries to decide which one to approach, which one is the most helpful-looking. Two of them are on the phone, the other is talking to an older, rounder man who's got his briefcase on top of the counter of the reception desk and is rooting through it looking for something. The receptionist is smiling, being patient, her smile not faltering as he shakes his head and laughs and pulls paper after paper out of his briefcase and deposits them on the counter. Looking at the older, rounder man with his briefcase on the reception desk, and at the three receptionists sitting on the other side of it, he suddenly wishes he was wearing a suit. The older, rounder man with the briefcase, the people coming and going through the security barriers and in and out of the lifts, the three men sitting on the sofas under the modern art are all wearing suits under their dark winter coats. They're all wearing suits and long dark winter coats and smart black shoes. If he was wearing a suit he might look more like someone who would have business there, someone who would have good reason to be making enquiries about a woman who works in the building, someone whose reasons for wanting details of a junior partner in a corporate law firm would be considered legitimate. Looking at the people coming and going and the three men sitting on the sofas he starts to think that he looks a lot like a dumped ex-boyfriend come to cause a scene. He looks around the reception again: from the desk to the lifts to the sofas. He thinks about all the time, all the hours and days, he's spent watching the comings and goings of the reception and tries to think if he's ever seen a security guard there during office hours. If he has he doesn't remember them. Looking around the reception again, from the sofas to the lifts to the reception desk, he tries to find one now, but there's no one he can see; no one in uniform, no one on guard, no one keeping watch over the reception area which anyone can walk off the street into, no one making sure that everything is as it should be, that everyone there is someone who should be there. He can't even see anyone who looks like they're particularly paying attention, not even to him. He thinks that they must be there, somewhere, in another room, hidden away, watching the images from all the security cameras that he can't see either. He wonders if they're ever needed, if there are ever scenes for them to deal with. He wonders if Sophie will make a scene when she sees him.

The two receptionists are still talking on the phone, but the one dealing with the older, rounder man with the briefcase is pointing him in the direction of the low sofas and smiling as he collects up his papers. He wonders if she will smile and send him to sit on the low sofas while he waits for Sophie. He thinks for the first time about actually seeing her. He pictures the lift doors opening and Sophie stepping through them, and he knows almost for certain that she won't make a scene. She never would. She'll be calm and together as she always is, her expression inscrutable to everyone but him. He'll know. If there's happiness or relief or anger or disappointment anywhere on her face he will see it, just like he did before when he saw her panic at seeing him sitting there. Anyone else would have seen her smiling a businesslike and professional smile, as unfaltering and practised as the receptionist's to the older, rounder man with the briefcase. But he could tell, he could see it, the anger, the panic, the embarrassment maybe, the discomfort at him being there, he read it in an instant and then everything else made sense – her previous request that he wait for her across the road in the coffee shop, her insistence whenever they met for lunch that they ate near him, not her, and that he didn't walk her back to the office. He'd leaned in to kiss her as he'd stood up, but she'd pulled away, made it into a two-cheeked continental kiss of polite acquaintances, apologising as she did so, very quietly, saying: 'Not here, it's not professional.' No, he knows that Sophie would never make a scene, not here, not in front of everyone, not at work. He knows that he's safe in that respect, but thinking about her coming out of the lift and seeing her for the first time since that night, the night it ended, seeing her here of all places, suddenly doesn't seem like such a good idea. He suddenly thinks that he would be better to wait, to go back to the coffee shop and wait for her to leave, and to try to talk to her when he sees her, as he no doubt will, at some point, if he waits long enough. He wishes he was back on his stool in the coffee-shop window, watching the scene from a safe distance. He hears the thump-thump of the revolving door behind him and he thinks about turning around and stepping into it.

The older, rounder man passes in front of him, still pushing papers into the top of his briefcase as he makes his way across the reception to join the three men on the sofas. He hears the thump-thump of the revolving door and looks again at the reception desk. The two receptionists are still on the phone, but the one who was dealing with the older, rounder man with the briefcase is now available and looking and smiling in his direction. He hears the thump-thump-thump-thump-thump of the revolving door and he thinks about turning around and stepping into it, but already his stare has lingered too long on that of the now available and smiling receptionist, acknowledging that he's seen her and that he is indeed in need of the help that her encouraging smile appears to be offering. He returns her smile and watches it broaden into a professional welcome as he approaches the reception desk.

As he reaches her she says: 'How can I help?'

He looks at her smile, he reads the encouragement in it and thinks about the right thing to say. He goes to ask if Ms Sophie Carlson works there and then thinks better of it. He smiles, looks the receptionist in the eye and says: 'I'm here to see Ms Carlson.'

As with the older, rounder man with the briefcase and the papers which he fumbled around with and deposited all over the reception desk, the receptionist's smile never flickers or falters, she merely turns it to the screen in front of her and says: 'And who's she with?'

After a moment she turns her smile back to him and, sensing that an answer isn't imminent, tries again.

'Which company is Ms Carlson with?'

He laughs with the realisation that it wasn't a trick question.

'Sorry. Fitzgerald Ellis. She's with Fitzgerald Ellis.'

The receptionist turns her smile back to the screen. He listens to her mouse clicks as she studies whatever's in front of her. He hears the thump-thump-thump of the revolving door followed by more clicks from the receptionist's mouse. He hears the light acrylic tap of her nails as she types on the keyboard. He hears the click of her mouse and then a pause and a click and a pause and more light acrylic tapping. He watches the receptionist's smile dissolve into concentration, he watches her eyes focus and narrow and her eyebrows knit as concentration gives way to curiosity and then confusion.

Without looking up she says: 'Did you say Ms Carlson?'

'Yes.'

'I'm afraid I don't have a Ms Carlson listed.'

She continues looking at the screen for another couple of seconds as if double-checking, then looks up at him with disappointment and apology where her unfaltering smile was.

He thinks for a moment that it must be his mistake. He tries to think of a logical reason why the receptionist wouldn't be able to find Sophie with the information he's given her, and then apologises and says: 'I must have got the name wrong. Maybe it wasn't Fitzgerald Ellis. It was Fitz something, Fitzroy, Fitzrovia . . .'

'No. Fitzgerald Ellis is right. They're on the third floor,' she says, looking back at the screen to be sure of what she's saying. 'But there's no Ms Carlson.'

'Well, maybe that's not who she's with. Maybe I misunderstood. Are there any other law firms here?'

'There are two,' she says, still looking at the screen. 'But she's not with them either, I'm afraid.' She looks up and offers him an apologetic smile, smaller, less encouraging than any he's seen her previously use, which she then quickly turns back to the screen. 'I've looked by company and by floor and I've done a general directory search and I don't have a Ms Carlson anywhere on the system.'

'You must have. Ms Carlson. Ms Sophie Carlson.'

She looks up again, her smile now flat with resignation.

'Carlson. C-A-R-L-S-O-N. Or maybe C-A-R-L-S-E-N.'

She shakes her head.

'I've tried both. And K-A-R-L-S-O-N.'

She studies his face for confirmation that he's understood, and then for clues as to what happens next and how she can help him further, but he doesn't offer her any so they both just look at each other until her happy-to-help smile returns and she says: 'Maybe you could call Ms Carlson. Do you have a number for her?'

For a moment he can't quite focus on the receptionist, her smile or anything she's saying. If he could he would probably know what to ask next. Instead he says: 'Yes, thank you, I'll do that,' and turns away.

He walks to the centre of the reception and stops for a moment to try to think. He can feel the receptionist watching him, no doubt as confused as he is about where Ms Carlson is and what he's going to do now. He thinks about leaving. He thinks about going back and asking the receptionist to check again, because it doesn't make sense to him that she's not there; she must be there, she has to be there, otherwise where is there for him to look for her? And then he thinks that it all makes perfect sense, that it at least explains why he's never seen her after all his hours and days of waiting. Suddenly he's convinced that she's left and she isn't coming back, that she's gone and so has his reason for being there. He hears the thump-thump-thump of the revolving door and heads towards it.

Chapter Ten

The second two weeks in Paris were much like the first, following the same routine of him amusing himself in the streets and parks and cafes while she was at work during the week, and the pair of them getting lost together at the weekend. By the middle of the third week though, he'd sensed a change in her, a restlessness that hadn't been there when they first set up home together in the company's apartment in the Rue Quincampoix.

The purchase of the French publisher had progressed faster and more smoothly than anticipated, which had the unexpected effect of leaving her surplus to requirements and bored as she waited for the court hearing to formalise the deal. She started getting back to the apartment at five instead of half six, and by seven she would be wanting to go out, suggesting restaurants and bars and places for early-evening walks and late drinks. Always new places, always somewhere different for them to try. She would say that after the boredom of the day she needed some excitement, something to wake her up, to make her feel something. In truth, she didn't care where they went just as long as they were out, among people, enjoying Paris. Most evenings, after she'd suggested half a dozen new and exciting possibilities, they'd find themselves somewhere comfortable and familiar where they could be alone together, it being the confines of the apartment that she'd grown tired of, not his company.

Three nights in a row they went to Bar du Marché on the Rue de Seine, a few doors up from his favourite Parisian supermarket, where they ate chicken wings and frites and drank French 75s – the mixture of champagne and gin going to their heads as they talked about all the places he'd been that day and plotted future adventures together. One evening they went to Brasserie de la Grille Saint-Germain, where they sat at a table in the corner by the kitchen, surrounded by the wood panelling and grainy black-and-white photographs of the '68 student riots that she found romantic, and ate a sharing platter of steak, followed by dessert and coffee and then a nightcap around the corner at Café Mabillon, where they ended up drinking cocktails and shots until the early hours.

They talked more when they were out than they did curled up on the apartment's sofa, and as they spent longer evenings in quiet corners he was reminded what a good listener she was: marvelling and laughing at the breadth and width of his wanderings around Paris, asking interested questions instead of just waiting for her turn to speak. In fact, she rarely actually said anything. He talked and she replied with wide eyes and encouraging smiles. Yet while it was his voice that dominated the conversation, she was always the one in control of it, dictating the subject and the pace with her questions and nods, managing to be an active participant while saying little more than the occasional 'why?', 'where?' or 'really?'

Several times he felt suddenly self-conscious, suddenly aware of the sound of his own voice and how much he'd used it, and once he went so far as to apologise for the amount he'd talked even though he was sure that it was what she wanted. She laughed and told him that she liked listening to him. She told him that she talked all day long, to the point where she couldn't stand the thought of having to talk any more. She told him that listening to him was a relief and that she loved that he wanted to tell her things, that his excitement was infectious and she didn't want him to stop. Then she leaned in and gave him a slow, lingering kiss and told him again that she really, really, really didn't want him to stop. So he didn't. Every night he talked and talked and she nodded and smiled like everything he had to say was all she wanted to hear. Twice, first at the bustling Café Hugo on the Place des Vosges and then at a quiet bistro on the Rue de Richelieu, they found themselves the last customers in the restaurant, a couple so wrapped up in each other that they hadn't noticed everyone else leaving and the staff clearing up around them. Both times he'd talked and she'd listened intently, but neither of them if asked could have said what they'd found so engrossing, only that whatever it was, they weren't finished with it when they were finally interrupted with the bill.

They stayed out later and later and she started going into the office for nine instead of eight, and then ten instead of nine. Some nights they stayed up talking when they got back, others they fell straight into bed, their return to the apartment having been prompted by a look or a touch or one of the sudden public displays of affection which caught them off guard and quickly escalated to a level which at home, in London, would have made both of them uncomfortable.

The night they went to the bistro on the Rue de Richelieu they didn't make it back to the apartment until nearly three. After they left the restaurant they wandered down to the Seine and along to the Pont des Arts to sit and watch the Eiffel Tower put on its last light display of the night, and ended up staying for another hour, wrapping themselves up in each other, pulling together against the cold, starting a new conversation which picked up the closeness where the one in the restaurant had left it.

They talked about Paris and where they felt most at home and where they'd like to live if they lived there. He told her about a family he'd seen unloading their car in the Rue du Bac. The dad was getting bags and cases out of the back of the car, the mother was leading two children, a boy and a girl, both about five or six, into their building. The street door was left open for the dad to bring the bags in, and through it he could see the most beautiful courtyard, surrounded on all sides by high-windowed apartments with balconies and impressive architectural plants; an expensive oasis of calm and money and good taste that was completely hidden and secret once the street door was closed. He said that he stood and watched for a moment as the dad locked the car and took the last of the bags inside. He looked at what he could of the apartment windows overlooking the courtyard to try to catch a glimpse of the mother and the children, to see if he could spot where they lived and pick up any clues as to the life they enjoyed there. From the way they were dressed, with that casual old-money elegance that Americans who have houses in the Hamptons try so hard to replicate – both parents in pressed jeans and slip-on shoes, wearing blue blazers with jumpers under them and scarves tied so nonchalantly around their necks it was clear that even bitter spring winds couldn't affect their sense of style – he was sure that they had the perfect life, with their two perfect children dressed as smaller versions of themselves and their perfect apartment on the Rue du Bac with its tall windows overlooking a beautiful secret courtyard. They probably had a house in the country to go with it, where they went at weekends to ensure that their idyllic existence was as perfect as their old money could make it. That's probably where they'd just come back from, their beautiful, perfect weekend house in the country. When the dad closed the street door behind him and the courtyard was hidden again, he looked up to the apartment windows which overlooked the street to see if he could catch a last glimpse of them there, but there was no sign of his perfect little French family, and after another minute of waiting he carried on up the Rue du Bac.

As he told her about them, his perfect little French family and the perfect little life he'd imagined for them, Sophie pulled herself tighter into him, burying her face in the shoulder of his thick coat, only looking up to kiss the side of his face and say, 'Sounds lovely,' into his ear.

He said with Peter's money he could probably afford to come and join them. He said that the house in the country was probably beyond him, but if he sold Peter's flat he might be halfway to an apartment on the Rue du Bac, and with everything else Peter had left him he was sure he could come up with the rest and have enough left to eke out a comfortable life bumming around the left bank, drinking coffee and smoking all day. He said that maybe that was what Peter had wanted him to do with the money: start a new life. It was the first time he'd mentioned Peter since they'd been in Paris. He told her it was the first time he'd thought about Peter since they'd got there. He said it must be because it was almost time to go back to London.

She pulled herself in tighter again, working her face into his tightly wrapped scarf, burrowing into the side of his neck and breathing deep and heavy. He asked her if she'd like that, an apartment on the Rue du Bac with a secret courtyard and two perfect little children and a wardrobe where everything was meant to be worn with pearls. She laughed and looked up just long enough to say again: 'Sounds lovely.'

They sat for another moment, not saying anything, staying wrapped up in each other, sharing their warmth, and then he said, 'I think I'd like it. I think I could be happy here, living like that. I think I'd like it better than what I've got now. I'm dreading going back. What about you?' He nudged her head up with his shoulder, just far enough so he could see her face. 'What's waiting back in London for you? I don't even know . . . what's your place like? What and where do you call home? I don't know, maybe you already live in a swish apartment with high ceilings and a balcony and a view.' She laughed and said, 'No, that's you. You live in the swish apartment. You've got a terrace and a view and a desirable address. I live somewhere much smaller and far less exotic, and I really don't want to think about it. I don't want to think about London and going home. I just want to enjoy being here, with you.' She rested her head back on his shoulder and changed the subject.

'There's so much of Paris you haven't seen yet,' she said as they watched the last of the night's tourist boats pass under them. She said it with a regretful tone as if she felt she'd been lax or a bad host or somehow let him down. 'There's a whole other Paris that I wanted to show you. We'll have to come back and I'll take you to all the places that you'd never find, that someone's got to take you to for you to know they even exist. There are lots of them in Paris. It's not like London where everyone knows everything and they make a point of telling everyone that they know about it. Nothing's ever secret or hidden in London. Paris isn't like that. People like keeping things to themselves. They like to know and to know that you don't. If you want secret places, Paris is full of them. Next time I'll take you to some.' She looked up from his shoulder, considered his face, then pressed her nose and her lips into the side of it. He felt her smile and then he felt her breath on his ear say, 'Maybe we could still go to one. I could take you to one of my favourites. We could go tomorrow night if you like, give you something to savour until we can come back.'

The club was hidden away in plain view, like everything and everyone in Paris. An anonymous doorway in an anonymous backstreet, possibly the Rue Fontaine or the Rue Duperré or one of the other roads off the Place Pigalle, he couldn't tell which and was too concerned with what came next to think to ask her. There was no sign above the door, just a black facade, a brass plaque bearing the word *Privé* and a buzzer which buzzed and clicked the street door open when she pressed it.

Once inside they followed a trail of lights in the floor to the end of a dark hallway and up two flights of stairs to another, shorter hallway and a set of leather-upholstered double doors. He could hear and feel the low throb of music coming from beyond them and made himself ready for the wave of volume and lights and colour that he expected when they opened, but it never arrived. Instead the sound was clearer, deeper and richer but no louder, and the curtained area they entered was only very dimly lit by a small table lamp with a red shade. A smartly dressed female maître d' was waiting to greet them. She smiled a smile of recognition and welcome to Sophie, and one of knowing and welcome to him. Neither Sophie nor the maître d' said anything. The music, though not deafening, was loud enough to require a raised voice or extreme closeness and from the way the maître d' carried herself it was clear that she would never contemplate either. Instead, she took two menus from the table with the lamp and, without looking at either of them again, led them through the heavy curtain into the main room.

The main room was even darker than the hallway. The

walls, like the carpet – which felt thicker under his feet than the carpet on the other side of the double doors – he would have guessed at being black or dark red if he could have seen them. As it was he could barely see Sophie an arm's-length in front of him as she followed the maître d' to a semi-circular booth with tall sides and a small knee-high table in front of it. The maître d' smiled as she presented the booth to them. She put the menus down on the small table, smiled again, and almost bowed as she took a step back and faded into the blackness.

As with the room itself, it was impossible to tell exactly how large the booth was in the dark. Perhaps as deep as it was tall; two people sitting apart could probably lose each other in it, so he and Sophie sat as close as they could, not talking, trying to adjust to the lack of light and the space around them. He ran his hand over the plush velvet of the seat and followed it up the tall back of the booth as far as his arm could casually manage. He looked in the direction of the small table until he could make out the menus the maître d' had left on it and the outline of an unlit table lamp with what could have been a brass switch next to it. He looked up from the table and out into the darkness to try to find the rest of what he assumed to be a lounge bar, and although he couldn't see anything of any consequence, he thought he saw, or at least sensed, movement. The booth's tall sides meant that there was no left or right, only straight ahead, and as he concentrated on the room in front of him his eyes started to penetrate the darkness and see what he thought was another identical booth and table facing them from what he guessed to be the other side of the room. The more he concentrated the surer he was of the outline of the opposing booth getting clearer and clearer and he thought he started to make out shapes which might have been the booth's occupants, but then the lamp on the table at his knee flashed on and even though it only offered a dim redness, it was enough for him to lose the shapes across the room which he'd just begun to get hold of.

Sophie had turned the lamp on by pressing the switch next to it. It was the same small table lamp, with the same red shade, as the lamp on the maître d's table, but lit it had the added effect of summoning a waitress to their booth. Sophie ordered drinks without looking at the menu, he couldn't hear what. The waitress, who wore a fitted white uniform dress with poppers all the way down the front that made her look like she'd come straight from working on the perfume counter of a 1950s department store, bent low to listen to Sophie's request, nodded twice and returned a couple of minutes later with a tray bearing two French 75s. As she put napkins and then their drinks on the table, he noticed that the bottom two poppers of her dress were undone, extending the view of her black stockings up to her inner thigh. She saw him noticing and smiled, then flipped the switch to turn the table lamp off again.

Back in the dark he began to see other faraway lamps go on and then off again. He caught sight of the occasional faint white uniform moving about in the dark, but never the booths' occupants, each lamp being only bright enough to illuminate the very centre of each table. For all the darkness though, there was no doubt that the room was full of people. The lamps and the movement of waitresses told him so and after a while he could hear them, a tense hum of voices rising and falling with the pulse of the music and gradually rising above it. He could sense their growing restlessness, he could feel them waiting in the darkness for something to happen and he was sure that, unlike him, most of them already knew what that something was.

He turned to Sophie and found the faint features of her face smiling at him. He leaned in to her, close enough to see her ear before whispering into it, 'So, what now?' Still smiling, she put her finger to his lips and said, 'For once, don't talk. Just watch. You'll see.'

He sat back in the booth and returned to searching his narrow field of vision. He thought he saw the darkness move. He thought he saw outlines and shapes which moved and made new outlines and shapes and then disappeared into the darkness again. He felt Sophie's hand on his thigh and then he felt the anonymous Parisian house music getting deeper and louder and louder and louder still until it had the full attention of the room.

With the music having become a deep hypnotic pulse, a

single light came on in the ceiling. It cast a white beam down into the empty middle of the room, highlighting a small round platform which had previously been hidden by the darkness of the floor. From somewhere out of the blackness around it, a girl stepped onto the platform.

She was young but not too young. Slim but not in an unhappy way. The first thing he noticed about her wasn't that she wasn't wearing anything other than a light-coloured silk slip, it was that she wasn't wearing any shoes. Her feet were bare. As were her legs and her arms and her shoulders, and by the time he'd taken in all her smooth pale bare skin, the fact that she was wearing so little seemed perfectly natural to him.

She stood in the middle of the platform for a moment, taking in the pulse and rhythm of the music as it began to build again around her, and then she started to sway to it. She swayed slowly at first, and then deeper and wider, her head rolling on her shoulders, changing direction with each beat, leaning further back and further forward with every bar. The whiteness of the light bleached her already white skin and focused all the invisible eyes in the room on her. She swayed, she didn't dance. Hers was an indulgence, not a performance. Like she was doing it for herself. Her eyes closed and her head back, she swayed and swayed and swayed and showed no sign of being aware there was anyone else in the room, let alone that anyone was watching her. She didn't take anything off. She just swayed, conscious of nothing, letting the music move her, letting it pull and push her, soothe her, caress her, make all her decisions for her. She seemed so distant as he watched her, so unreachable. So perfect.

For the first time he felt the music, her movement making him aware of the regularity of the beats and circles of the bass, details previously unheard even though the anonymous soundtrack had hardly changed since they'd entered the room. His awareness of everything was heightened, and more than anything he was aware of an intense feeling of beauty in what he was watching, that and a feeling of sadness that he felt in watching it.

As he watched her move and he felt Sophie's hand on his

thigh tighten, he thought for a moment that he knew what the girl on the platform was feeling. He felt her relief at being all alone in the darkness. He felt her longing to be lost there in that single moment, and her desperation to hold onto it and stay there and make it last, like she was holding her breath, and enjoying it. He thought he could imagine the freedom, the lightness of feeling not thinking.

He lost track of how long he was watching her. When she was finished or had had enough, it was hard to tell which, she stepped off the platform and back into the darkness. None of the invisible eyes clapped or made any move to acknowledge her or what they'd seen. For some reason he didn't feel the need to either. The white light dimmed and the music quieted to a background murmur for a few minutes. The noise of conversation grew in the darkness around them, but he and Sophie didn't say anything to each other. He kept looking at the platform as if hypnotised by what he'd seen and before the spell could be broken the music grew louder and the light came on above the platform again. This time two girls stepped out of the darkness together. Both naked and holding hands.

They were both good-looking with good bodies, more natural and artful than strippers, but their movements weren't as subtle or sensual as their predecessor's. The overt sexual intent of their nakedness and the conscious way they caressed and touched each other was meant to arouse, not seduce, and he felt slightly embarrassed at how effective it proved to be on him. He felt Sophie's hand on his thigh tighten and start to move, almost imperceptibly, back and forth, kneading deeper and harder with each stroke.

He watched the two girls dancing. They moved almost together, almost in each other's arms, almost connected, almost feeling the music. They stroked each other's shoulders. They ran fingertips along lips and down necks and touched the backs of hands to the outlines of breasts and hips, coming to rest on each other's waists to slow dance together for another few bars, before they stroked and caressed and ran their hands all the way back to their faces and hair. He watched their hands moving. Their skin was pale, not white like the girl before them. He watched them touching each other and despite himself he liked it, but he didn't want to touch them like he did the girl before. He didn't want to feel what they were feeling because from looking at them he could tell that they weren't feeling anything. He watched them sway and dance and he wanted the girl with the white skin back, not that Sophie would have been able to tell from where her hand was sitting.

The girls moved closer, retracing the path of their hands with their lips and tongues. Sophie leaned in to him and ran her hand all the way up the inside of his thigh in one long motion from knee to crotch, following it with her knee and her thigh as she started to climb onto him. She pushed him into the tall back of the booth and pulled herself up into him. Closer. Closer. So close he could almost taste her breath and the gin and champagne on it. When she spoke she said it quietly and firmly, breathing the suggestion into his ear, wanting the words to be felt, not heard. Pulling herself up and into him she said, 'Now why don't you fuck me.'

Chapter Eleven

'What are you thinking?'

He feels the weight of her head on his chest. Her hand stroking his stomach through his shirt. Her fingers finding his skin between the buttons.

He feels the breeze on his face, taking the heat out of the sun as it breathes across him.

He knows that if he opened his eyes the sky would be blue and cloudless.

He knows that if he could see her face she'd be smiling.

He can feel her smile.

He doesn't say anything.

He doesn't respond to her question.

He ignores it.

He pushes his head back into his rolled-up jacket of a pillow and runs his hand over the grass next to him, the tips of it tickling his palm.

'What are you thinking?'

He feels her fingers playing with the hairs on his stomach. Circling around and around, working their way into him.

He says nothing, listening to the sounds around him, a plane above, a dog barking, the voices of other people, other couples, conversations carried on the breeze along with the distant

sound of cars running along the bottom of Primrose Hill, and then
after a moment he says, 'Nothing.'

   He feels her fingers stop circling.

   He feels her smile.

   Curious.

   'What?'

   'Nothing.'

   He feels her lift her head to look up at him.

   'No, go on. Tell me.'

   He can hear the smile in her voice.

   He knows that if he opened his eyes and looked down at
her she'd be smiling at him.

   'There's nothing to tell.'

   She digs her fingers into the hairs on his stomach and
pulls them.

   'Tell me.'

   'Ouch.'

   'Tell me.'

   'No.'

   'Tell me.'

   'No.'

   She pinches his arm and lands her head heavily back on
his chest forcing the air out of him.

   He feels her take a deep sigh and fidget to get herself
comfortable again.

   He feels her put her hand back on his stomach. Her fingers
find their way back into his shirt. They wind themselves around the
hairs. Tighter and tighter. They stop as if about to pull, then she
goes back to stroking him. Stroking and circling. Alternating
between the two. Quiet. Contented. He can feel her smile again.
Stroking and circling, her fingers mirroring her breaths, her
breaths mirroring his. Slow. Relaxed. Quiet. Contented.

   He pushes his head back into the rolled-up jacket of a
pillow and runs his hand over the grass next to him.

   He feels the breeze on his face, taking the heat out of the
sun as it breathes across him.

The inside of his eyelids red against the sun, he knows that if he opened his eyes the sky would be blue and cloudless.

'What are you thinking?'

He says nothing, listening to the sounds around him, a plane, a dog, conversations, distant cars, the breeze, and then he says, 'That I think I love you.'

He wakes up on the sofa in Peter's living room. The sofa where Peter used to fall asleep listening to his records or pretending to read his coffee-table books. He doesn't know what woke him. For a second he's convinced it was the receptionist telling him that there's no Ms Carlson here. He can still hear her. Like she only just said it. Like if he listens hard he'll still be able to catch a faint trace of it somewhere in the dark of Peter's living room. The moment he opens his eyes to the darkness he knows that he's alone, in Peter's flat, on the sofa in the living room, but he still thinks he can hear her. The residue of her voice. Her words the sudden jolt that brought him to.

He lies in the dark, searching the ceiling and the wall and the bookshelf for clues, knowing he won't find any. Clues as to what time it is and how long he's been asleep. Clues as to how he came to fall asleep on Peter's sofa and why there was no Ms Carlson there. The darkness doesn't tell him anything. Instinctively, though, he knows it's late.

He reaches for his phone on the coffee table, wakes it to look at the time.

It says 23:59.

He watches it.

Waits.

One. Two. Three. Four. Five. Six. Seven. Eight. Nine. Ten. Eleven. Twelve. Thirteen. Fourteen.

00:00.

Somewhere he has a vague memory of getting back to Peter's flat, that it was still light in the living room when he sat down on the sofa, that he was still wearing his coat. He feels for the back of the sofa and finds the coat and scarf where he thinks he knows he left them. He thinks that he must have been asleep for hours. Maybe

104

seven or eight. He thinks that he can't remember how long it's been since he's slept that long. He wonders if it's the resignation that comes with knowing that he's lost her, that he won't find her, that she's definitely not there. He wonders if that's why he slept so long and so well.

Hard as he tries not to, he remembers leaving the reception, going out through the revolving door into the street, standing there for a moment, wondering where to go and what to do. He remembers looking back at the coffee shop across the street and thinking that there was no point going back there, that there'd never be any point going back there, not now he knows for certain that she isn't going to walk past the window, that he isn't going to see her across the street, going through the revolving door he'd just come out of. He remembers turning back up the road and starting to walk. He remembers not knowing where he was walking to, just that he started moving and then the next thing he remembers is dropping his keys and phone onto Peter's coffee table and himself onto Peter's sofa. The living room was grey then. Not light, not dark. He remembers sitting there, the light getting less and less and then he woke up with the sound of the receptionist reminding him there's no Ms Carlson here.

He rolls over and tries to get comfortable. He pulls his coat off the back of the sofa and drags it over him. Pulls it tight up under his chin and tries to think himself warm and not think about her. Where she is. Where she's gone. Why. How long for. How he might try to find her. The reality that he probably never will. He looks at the shelves, running his eyes over Peter's things, and tries to think about his brother, tries to think about him sitting on the sofa, in the flat's warm late-night glow, listening to his records, reading his books, drinking a large glass of wine and telling him to get himself one and join him. He tries to think of Peter laughing. He tries to hear the music, to see the photographs in the book on Peter's lap, to smell the wine. He thinks he should put some lights on. Maybe put on one of Peter's records and open one of his bottles of wine. He pulls the coat tighter around him, trying to get warm, trying to feel the warmth and the sounds and smell that used to fill the living room.

He fixes on the shelves. In the dark he picks out Peter's things, tries to remember the pictures in the frames, tries to remember the order and titles of books and the names of bands and songs and the shapes of trinkets and mementos that he can't quite see and all the time all he can think is that there's no Ms Carlson here.

He rolls onto his back and tries to focus on the ceiling.

There's no Ms Carlson here.

He tries to focus on the empty blackness and the distant grey of the white ceiling above him.

There's no Ms Carlson here.

He thinks about going back to sleep. He thinks about getting up and going to the kitchen and getting a drink. He thinks that she's gone and that he has no idea of where to start looking for her. He thinks about how close he felt to her the moment before the receptionist told him that there's no Ms Carlson here.

He thinks about going to the kitchen and getting a drink and bringing it back and drinking it in the dark. He thinks that he wants to stay in the dark, that he's not ready to turn the lights on, like turning on the lamps that Peter used to read by will fill the flat with a warmth that he can't bear the thought of. Like it will make things unavoidable. He wants to stay in the ambiguous dark just a little longer. Until he can accept it. Or until he knows what to do.

He looks out at the terrace and thinks about going outside for a cigarette, and then he thinks about going to bed, and then he thinks about how he felt while the receptionist was still smiling, looking at her computer screen, searching her system, still thinking she was going to be able to help him, and he knows that he won't be able to sleep. Not now. He can almost still feel the excitement that the sadness then drowned out: at the thought of seeing her again, at knowing that she was near, that the receptionist was looking for her, about to call her, about to tell her that he was here, in reception, waiting for her. Even now, with the sadness filling him to the top of his throat, making it difficult to breathe, he can still almost feel the happiness of thinking that she was close. And he can still see the smile on the receptionist's face falter and fade and make way for confusion and then disappointment and apology as she realised she wasn't going to be able to help him after all. He knew before she did, the sadness having already reached from his stomach to his chest as she looked to double-check before telling him what he thought he already knew, there is no Ms Carlson here.

He pulls himself upright and sits on the edge of the sofa, looking at the coffee table and the books and the keys on the key ring that she bought for him, next to the wallet that she bought for him and his phone. He wakes his phone to see the time again.

00:07.

He sits looking at its screen until it goes off, returning Peter's living room to darkness.

In the dark he sits on the edge of the sofa looking at the black shape of his phone on the coffee table and wills himself to think of something, anything, to change the moment, so he doesn't have to spend the whole night like this. He wills the phone to ring or new thoughts to occur to him so he doesn't have to think the same ones over and over: that he has no way of contacting her and he's never going to see her again, that there is no Ms Carlson here.

He looks at the phone and nothing happens.

He's tired yet painfully awake, his head filled with the heavy throb of thoughts that keep repeating themselves. He tries to focus them, along with the tiredness and images that he knows will keep him from sleep, on the black shape of his phone, if not to make something happen, then at least to stop the cycle long enough to give him actual space to think. To consider his options. Or to give him time to invent some.

And it starts to work.

The repeated phrases slow and then quiet themselves enough for him to hear himself over the top of them. His first thought is again of sleep and his certainty that he won't be able to go back to it tonight. His second is to wonder what would happen if he did. He wonders if he would see her. Will she still come to him when he closes his eyes? Or has she gone from his dreams too? Has losing his last hope of seeing her in the real world taken with it the possibility of seeing her in the other?

He tries to think back to minutes ago, to before he opened

his eyes to the dark of Peter's living room, to the sleep that the receptionist's voice woke him out of. He tries to remember if she was there. He closes his eyes and searches for a memory, for evidence, for the slightest fragment or sense or feeling of her. Then he catches a glimpse of a summer's day on Primrose Hill, of the two of them lying on the grass, her head on his chest, her fingers playing with the buttons on his shirt, stroking his skin, knitting into the hairs on his stomach, and brief as it is, it's enough. He can't be sure, he never is, but it tells him enough of what he wants to hear to make him believe that she was there, that she did come to him and that he still has the promise of at least that much of her. It gives him hope and makes him think again about sleep and makes him want more than anything to be back there. Now.

Focusing on the black shape of his phone on the coffee table, trying to hold onto the warmth of a fragment of a summer's day on Primrose Hill, he thinks about the bliss of sleep, of the possibility of seeing her, of being with her, of feeling her and touching her, of hearing a voice that he thinks sounds like hers – although he knows that the sound of her is the thing that he's least sure of now, the weakest part of his recreation of her, perhaps the reason she now says so little in his dreams. He thinks about the bliss of sleep and the possibility of finding her there, and then he thinks about what comes next. The morning after the night. He tries to imagine coping. Waking up to the realisation that there's no way of making everything he's just experienced in his sleep a reality. He tries to imagine being alright about it. Not being completely overwhelmed by a sadness so much greater than the sadness he has experienced every morning on waking up without her. At least with the disappointment of waking he's had the hope, however small, that he might be able to make amends, win her back, and that one day he may yet wake to find the bed warm next to him. Not now. Not now there is no Ms Carlson here.

He tries to imagine opening his eyes tomorrow and the next day and the day after that. He tries to imagine lying in the grey morning light knowing what he knows now. He tries to imagine opening his eyes and realising, and not caring. Not being affected.

Not feeling that all he wants is to be asleep again. Not wishing that he never had to wake up ever again. He tries to envisage waking up, getting up, going to the bathroom, showering, eating his breakfast in Peter's black-and-white living room, smoking the first cigarette of the day out on Peter's terrace. He tries to see himself sitting down at his laptop to work, concentrating on what he's doing, losing himself in whatever it is and not being dazed and listless and consumed by loss and overwhelmed by the sadness. He tries to imagine not being a mess. He tries to imagine being better. He tries to imagine it being easier. He tries, but he can't. He tries to imagine a future without her, without the hope of her, but it isn't there. It doesn't exist. He's sure of it.

He focuses on the black shape of his phone on the coffee table and thinks about the rest of the night, the hours between now and morning, and then tries to think about her telling him to go back to sleep. He can hear a voice, but he's no longer sure that it's hers. It sounds almost like the receptionist, and before he can do anything about it, he can hear her telling him again that there is no Ms Carlson here.

He closes his eyes to try to see her, straightening her skirt or putting on her jacket, leaning over him to kiss him goodbye or looking back and smiling at him from the bedroom door. He closes his eyes and all he can see is the smile of the receptionist with its welcome and disappointment and regret and pity.

He closes his eyes tighter. The receptionist smiles and asks if she can help him.

He closes his eyes tighter still and wishes that she could.

He opens his eyes, refocusing on the black shape of his phone on the coffee table. He wakes it.

00:09.

He watches.

Waits.

One. Two. Three. Four. Five. Six. Seven. Eight. Nine. Ten. Eleven. Twelve. Thirteen. Fourteen. Fifteen. Sixteen. Seventeen. Eighteen. Nineteen.

He picks it up and goes to Recent Calls.

Twenty. Twenty-one. Twenty-two. Twenty-three. Twenty-four.

There's only one phone number in the list. The same number repeated again and again.

Twenty-five. Twenty-six. Twenty-seven. Twenty-eight.

Each entry of it marked as incoming.

Twenty-nine. Thirty. Thirty-one.

He calls it.

Thirty-two.

It starts to ring.

Thirty-three. Thirty-four. Thirty-five. Thirty-six. Thirty-seven. Thirty-eight.

'Hello.'

She sounds sleepy, like she's just woken up.

He listens and says, 'It's me.'

There's a pause at the other end filled with the sound of awkward movement and more moans of waking.

'What time is it?'

'Sorry, it's late. I shouldn't have . . .'

'No. It's OK. What is it?'

'No, I'm sorry, go back to sleep. I'll call you tomorrow.'

'I'm awake now. What is it?'

There's a pause, from him this time. A blank moment and then:

'Where is she, Audrey?'

'What?'

'Where's she gone?'

'Who?'

'I need to know where she is. I need to know where she's gone, Audrey. Please.'

'Oh for God's sake.'

'Please.'

'We've talked about this. I thought you were over it. You said you were.'

'Please, Audrey.'

'I don't know. I don't know where she is. I don't know where she's gone.'

'But you know she's gone somewhere.'

'No. I didn't say that. I'm just saying what you said. What makes *you* think she's gone somewhere?'

'I went to her office today.'

'You went to her office?' She's suddenly awake. 'Why?'

'I wanted to see her.'

'Why?'

'Because I wanted to talk to her. Because I couldn't wait any more. I've been waiting and waiting. And I couldn't do it any more, so I went to see her. I wanted to talk to her. I wanted to tell . . . I don't know what I wanted to tell her. I just wanted to see her. Say I'm sorry. Try to make her talk to me. Make her listen. Make her see that it didn't mean . . . I just wanted to see her.'

'And what happened?'

'She wasn't there.'

'How do you know?'

'Because I asked for her. I asked for her but she wasn't there. She couldn't find her.'

'Who couldn't?'

'The woman on reception. She looked her up on her computer, and she wasn't there. She looked a couple of times.'

'What did she say?'

'"There's no Ms Carlson here."'

'Oh.'

'So where is she? Tell me where she is.'

'I don't know.'

'I don't believe you.'

'Fine, don't, but as I've told you God knows how many times, I haven't seen her since . . . since the two of you stopped seeing each other.'

'But you must have spoken to her.'

'Only for work.'

'So you must know where she is.'

There's another pause at the other end, this time filled with the sound of a heavy breath and resignation.

'Not exactly. There was an email, a while ago. It was just an internal email saying that there'd be someone else looking after the magazine's legal affairs for the foreseeable future while she was on secondment to her company's Paris office. Honestly, that's all I know. I don't know where she's staying or where the office is or what she's doing or how long she's going to be there. I just know that she's in Paris. And that she doesn't want to see you.'

'And how do you know that?'

'Because she told me. She sent me a letter. When you were calling all the time and wouldn't leave her alone. She and I weren't talking, so she sent me a letter asking me to tell you to stop calling her. To leave her alone. That she didn't want you to keep ringing and texting all the time. That what you were doing was harassment, that you were starting to frighten her, that I needed to get you to stop. That it wasn't normal. I tried to tell you that she didn't want to know, but you wouldn't listen. You kept at it. You kept chasing her. You wouldn't leave it. Which is why she changed her number. Didn't that tell you anything? It's probably why she jumped at Paris.'

'Did she give it to you?'

'What?'

'Her new number.'

'No. For God's sake, we were barely speaking. I'm the last person she would have given it to, and even if we had been talking, she probably wouldn't have trusted me not to give in and give it to you. Which I wouldn't, even if I had it.'

'You have got it, haven't you?'

'No. For fuck's sake. What is wrong with you? Stop. Just stop. Forget about her. Please. She's not worth it. And I'm sick of this. I'm sick of hearing about her. I'm sick of watching you do this to yourself. Please, please, please, just leave it.'

'I can't.'

There's a final pause on the other end, this time filled with an empty silence long enough for him to know that she's given up.

'You don't see what she's really like. You don't see what she's doing to you. What's happening to you. It's all because of her.

She's done this. She does this. And worst of all, you've no idea what you've got. What's there for you if you want it. What you could have, if only you'd let me in. You need someone who will really love you. Who cares. Who's there for you. Who wants to be with you. Someone who wants you. You need to get on with your life like she's getting on with hers. She won't have you back, even if you do find her. She won't forgive you. She won't forgive either of us. So why not stop now, leave it all where it is? Leave her where she is in Paris, and us here. You don't need her. Neither of us do.'

Chapter Twelve

He opened the door of Peter's flat to a small pile of post and the beep of the answering machine. He dropped his keys and the post, bills and junk mostly from the look of it, onto the hall table next to the phone. Five messages. He knew before he listened to them who they'd be from. He pressed Play anyway and listened to Audrey getting progressively more agitated and angry and then concerned and panicked. As Audrey told him that she'd been calling and texting and emailing, and that she didn't know why he wasn't answering but it wasn't very nice, he picked up his mobile from the hall table and turned it on. He'd decided to leave it behind just as he was walking out of the door on his way to St Pancras to meet Sophie. Out of habit he had packed the charger and put the phone in his pocket, but then at the last moment he decided that there was no one he wanted or needed to talk to, not while he was there, in Paris, with her. He didn't want anything, particularly Audrey and work, to intrude on his month in hiding and remind him of Peter's flat and everything it was missing, so he'd turned it off and left it on the hall table. True to her word, Audrey had been calling and texting and emailing. To the five messages she'd left on Peter's answering machine, she'd added another five calls and messages to his mobile, and almost as many texts and emails.

Her voice still chastising him in the background, he started going through the post. Sorting the bills from the takeaway menus, he found a folded piece of paper, lined, torn from a notebook, with his name written on it in a blocky, practical hand that he immediately recognised.

He unfolded it and read:

Call me.

If I haven't heard from you by the end of the week I'm coming back with the police – just in case you've done something stupid.

A.

At any other time he might have reacted to Audrey's obsessive interest in his welfare with his usual stiffening and resentment at never being left alone. But four weeks in Paris, away from Peter's flat and the sadness that lived with him there, had lifted a weight that even Audrey's tendency to overbear couldn't replace. Between being away and being with Sophie, he'd found everything he needed: escape, closeness, affection, solitude, the indulgence of another person, the promise of something different. Disappointed as he was to be back, he couldn't shake the feeling that he'd never been happier. Now he knew the sadness had limits, and in Sophie he felt he'd been gifted a future. Sophie felt like the only future he had ever wanted, one that wouldn't come his way again, one that he knew he had every intention of grabbing with both hands and enjoying. Now he had her he suddenly felt he had everything, and everything she said and did only made him surer that she felt the same. As he stood by the hall table, reading Audrey's note and listening to her messages, he read and listened with the benefit of a happiness that was as light as the sadness was oppressive, yet that for all its lightness was no less overwhelming. For once he could see Audrey's attentions for the kindness they really were. For once he was grateful for all that her attentions had brought to him.

Without bothering to read any of the texts or emails, he dialled her number from the Recent Calls list. Smiling, looking at her note as he waited for her phone to start ringing, he thought about how lucky he had been to have her there, cajoling, insisting, obsessing, making sure that he was safe and thought of, making sure that he wasn't left behind. As her phone rang and he waited for her to answer, he smiled at how grateful he now was that she'd insisted on him going to the Christmas party, and how different things could have been if she hadn't.

'So you're alive then?' she said as she answered.

'I'm sorry. I didn't mean to worry you.'

'Well you did. Did you get my note?'

'Yes.'

'I was serious, you know. I thought you'd topped yourself. I was coming back at the weekend with the police so they could break in and find you and cut you down or whatever. I couldn't even bring myself to look through the letterbox when I put the note through the door, I was too scared what I might see. That's how worried I was about you.'

'Really, I'm sorry.'

'I don't believe you. You think I'm overreacting.' She stopped and waited for him to jump in and correct her, but carried on before he'd properly had a chance to. 'You're probably right, but I can't help it. The way you've been since Peter. What am I supposed to think when you don't reply to emails or texts and you don't answer your phone for weeks? That everything's fine? That you're off somewhere having a good time? Having too much fun to answer your phone? That's not you, is it, not now anyway. And it's not like you're always busy working, well, not for me, and you barely leave the flat, so if you're not answering the phone and you're not answering the door, something's not right.'

He waited before replying, to show himself suitably chastised and to give her a moment to compose herself. Audrey had never been an angry person and even now her ire felt more like relief at hearing from him or embarrassment at worrying and leaving the note in the first place. He listened to the distant sound of her, to her breath against the mouthpiece, listening as it softened, the anger slowly dissipating, and then he smiled and, taking care not to sound defensive, said, 'Well, in that case, you'll be pleased to know that having a good time is exactly what I was doing. In Paris. With Sophie.'

He waited for her reaction, knowing that however pissed off with him Audrey was, curiosity and her need for details would always get the better of her. He listened and waited. He waited for a 'No!?' or a 'Really?' or a 'How?' or an 'I didn't even know you were seeing her, when did this happen?' He waited for her to be shocked and excited despite herself. He waited for her to drill him for answers, to regress to her teenage self and demand that he 'spill', as she invariably did whenever he gave her anything she could construe as gossip, or at least as she used to back when he had gossip to give. He waited and then he looked at his phone to check that it hadn't dropped the call, so definite was the silence in his ear.

'Hello?'

'Well, what do you want me to say?'

He hesitated, not sure if he'd heard her right or what she meant by it if he had.

'I don't know. I thought . . . I don't know.'

'What? You want me to say, "Well that's OK then, as long as you were off having fun, don't worry about it." OK. Fine. Great. Don't worry about it. Not a problem. You go off. You and Sophie, the pair of you, you go off together and have a lovely time and I'll just sit here, worrying myself stupid because you can't be bothered to pick up the phone or ever talk to me or tell me anything. That's OK. That's fine. But when the two of you are done having a good time, or more to the point, when she's had enough of having a good time with you, don't expect me to listen to it, because I'm not going to. I won't be here for you, like I always am, because I won't be interested. From now on, I will give you just about as much thought as you give me, which is none. Nothing. I won't bother you any more. I won't chase and harass you all the time, because you know what, I've had enough of doing it. It doesn't get me anywhere, and it clearly isn't what you want or for that matter need. I knew I was being a pain in the arse, but I thought you could at least see that I was doing it for all the right reasons, because I care about you and because I worry about you and because since Peter died you've been an impossible-to-reach mess, or at least impossible for me to reach. Sophie obviously has something I don't. A magic touch that means she can just click her fingers and pull you out of it, and make you all happy and fun like I can't. Who knew? All you needed was a little attention from Sophie and a quick trip to Paris to pull you out of it and make you forget, literally forget, everything and everyone, including me. Well, that's great. I'm thrilled for you. I'm so happy that she's been able to sort you out just like that. I'll leave you to her. My best efforts and intentions obviously weren't what you needed, or they weren't enough. I don't know. Whatever. She can look after you. She can make sure you're OK all the time. OK?'

He waited before replying, to make it clear that he had listened and heard and knew he was in the wrong and wasn't about to argue against anything she'd said.

'Are you finished? Look, I said I'm sorry. I promise it won't happen again. Honestly, I . . .'

'No, it won't, because that was it. That was the last time. I'm not doing it again.'

'Honestly, I didn't mean to worry you. I understand you're upset. I understand why you're upset.'

'You can say that, but I don't think you have the first clue. I don't think you can even begin to know what I feel or why, but you will, eventually, you'll know exactly what it feels like. To be forgotten about.'

'I do know. I do and I'm sorry. I didn't think. In fact, no, I did think. What I thought was that you'd be happy. You should be happy. You're always saying that I need to get out, to engage, see people, mix with people. You're always so worried about that, about me being at home, alone, never seeing anyone, never talking to anyone, never being "out with the living" as you put it, you're always so worried, I just thought you'd be pleased. I should have talked to you. I should have known that you'd be worried and I should have told you, but I also thought it would be a surprise. A good one. I've not just been out, I've been away, having an amazing time, having fun, actually enjoying myself, not thinking about all that other stuff, not thinking about Peter. Not once did I think about him. I didn't feel sad. I didn't feel, whatever, I actually felt happy. Properly happy. Like I can't remember the last time I felt that way. I still do, I still feel happy. I know I maybe didn't go about it in quite the right way, but if nothing else, at least it shows that I have been listening. I do take it in. It does mean something, all the worry you put into me, I do feel it. It does get through. I am trying. I just wish I'd told you before rather than now, that's all.'

He waited for her to say something. He waited and waited. He listened and waited and tried to think of something else to say to break the stalemate and make them friends again, and after a minute of waiting and listening he said, 'I'm sorry. I just want you to be happy for me. Pleased for us, both of us. I think I make her happy too. I really do.'

'I am. I'm pleased for you. Really. It just wouldn't have hurt you to tell me.'

'I know. I'm sorry. I didn't think.'

'No.'

'Next time I promise I will.'

'Yes, well. Anyway, I can't talk now. I'm in the middle of something. I'll call you. I'll . . . I'll call you.'

'No, wait. Let me make it up to you. Let me take you to dinner. Tonight.'

'I can't. I've got things to do.'

'No you haven't, you're just saying that to make us both feel bad. Don't. Let me make it up to you. Let me take you to dinner by way of an apology. I'll take you to La Perla. Come on, no one's ever too busy to go to La Perla, least of all you. It's your favourite. Come on, you can't say no. Please.'

He waited for her to say something. He waited and listened and the longer she didn't say anything, the more sure of himself he felt. A deep sigh broke over the mouthpiece, filling his ear with submission.

'Great,' he said. 'I'll pick you up at eight. Look gorgeous.'

'I'll think about it.'

Gorgeous didn't begin to describe how she looked that evening. She looked as he'd never seen her look before, as he didn't know she could look.

All the tomboy practicality that he had come to think of as Audrey had been replaced by something altogether more feminine. Not feminine in a soft and delicate sense, but focused and efficient. He didn't know who she was, but she wasn't dependable Audrey. She was someone wearing a little black dress because she wanted people to notice the gym-toned body underneath. Someone wearing make-up to draw attention to her eyes and lips because she wanted someone to get lost in them.

For the whole of the taxi ride from her flat in Hoxton to the restaurant in Covent Garden he tried to understand what was so different about this new Audrey. It wasn't the fact that she was wearing a dress and make-up. Although not things he usually associated with her, there had been plenty of occasions when he'd seen her forced out of the comfort of her jeans and Converse, when she'd been required to at least entertain the idea of dressing up. It wasn't the dress itself either. He'd probably seen it before, at the Christmas party perhaps, maybe several years running. But if he had, he'd never noticed it. Tonight he noticed it. That was the difference. It wasn't the dress, it was that it was worn without her normal reluctance and discomfort. Tonight this was who she wanted to be and he noticed because she wanted him to.

He tried not to react or behave as if anything was strange or amiss or out of the ordinary. As they sat in the early-evening traffic he tried to follow her surprisingly chatty conversation like it was regular Audrey speaking it. He watched her mouth, her lips parting and coming together, puckering and rounding into the shapes of words he couldn't quite hold onto. He watched her eyelashes flicker and flick the fringe of her black bob out of her eyes, and the sharp points of its ends glance and stroke her pale cheek as she moved her head when she spoke or when she smiled or when she looked at him. Her movements were playful. So unlike Audrey. When he wasn't watching her face, he was looking at her thighs through her thin black tights, following their firmness from under her dress, down to the bend of her knees and on to her delicate ankles. He tried to think if he had ever actually noticed her legs before. The curve of her calves. The shapeliness. The fleshy smoothness of the back of her thighs as he followed them all the way back up.

Dinner was just as pleasing and unexpected. He had prepared himself for the fact that she would be difficult and as annoyed as she had every right to be, that she would make him work for her forgiveness for going to Paris for a month, with Sophie, without thinking to tell her first. This after all was how they did things: he would let her down and she would eventually find it in her heart to stop making him feel guilty about it at exactly the point where to wait any longer would force an argument and things to be said that neither of them would mean. Not tonight though. Later, much later, when he looked back on it, he would be surprised by how little space she gave the subject. There and then he was just relieved.

As soon as they were seated he started to apologise. He wanted to do the right thing, clear the air, show her that he was sincere when he told her that he understood and was sorry for his thoughtless behaviour. He wanted to show her that whatever she might think, upsetting her was the last thing he had wanted to do. But she didn't give him the chance. When he started telling her how sorry he was, she looked away embarrassed and told him to forget about it. When he tried to pursue the point, she cut him off, looking for the one and only time that evening like the pissed-off Audrey he was expecting to have dinner with, and told him that she didn't want to talk about it. Any of it. Him and Sophie. Paris. She told him that she didn't want to argue with him, she wanted to make the most of this new happy him, now that he had finally stopped moping. Unfair as he thought 'moping' was as a description of his previous emotional state, he conceded that if anyone deserved the better part of his company, she did.

He watched her study the menu. He watched the points of her black bob fall across her face and poke at the edges of her mouth and tease her red lips. He followed the pale skin of her cheek down to her neck, to her shoulders, to her chest, and he thought about the taxi and this new Audrey. Sensing his gaze on her rather than the menu, she lifted her eyes slowly to catch him looking and then crossed her arms over her chest in feigned discomfort. 'What?'

'You seem different.'

'In what way different?'

'I don't know,' he said, looking over her face. 'I've been trying to work that out. You look different.'

'You mean I'm wearing make-up. And a dress. It has been known, you know. In fact, I'm pretty sure you've seen me look exactly this gorgeous before.'

'I really haven't.'

'Thanks. I think.'

'No, I mean, I haven't seen you look like this before. You seem . . .' He wanted to say determined, confident, self-aware in a slightly flirty way, or at the very least less eager to please, but he thought better of all of them because none seemed either right or appropriate, so he opted for '. . . happier. You seem happier, and more together.'

'Mmmm. Not sure how I feel about more together. Not sure how I feel about happier either. I'm always happy.' The smile she flashed gave him no clue as to how sarcastic she was being, if at all.

'I don't know, I don't think either of those is really what I mean.' He looked at her eyes and mouth and tried to find a way of saying that she looked less needy and more like someone who actually wanted something, someone who had a good idea of how to get it.

He tried to think of a way of saying that, for the first time in all the years he'd known her, he was thinking about her in a way that he was sure he shouldn't be comfortable with. He imagined Peter laughing, that deep, mischievous laugh, and saying he told him so.

'I don't know. You just seem different.'

'It's probably more you than me,' she said, returning to her menu. 'You're the one who's suddenly happy. I'm just me, no different.'

She was flirting with him and it didn't feel in any way awkward. But then this was a different Audrey. This was a sexy, confident, determined Audrey. He liked this Audrey, more than he knew he should.

The rest of the meal passed in a blur of flirting and happy

reminiscences. For the first time in a long time, he enjoyed the fact that they shared a history. That they knew each other. That she knew him from a time before things became so impenetrable. He wanted to be reminded of it. They talked about their teenage years and all the arguments and fallings out that featured in their conflicting memories of them. They glossed over her going to university and what he had done in her absence, and settled instead into their increasingly interconnected professional and personal lives since – including a detailed examination of her past relationships and exes, and his reasons why they had been unsuitable or unworthy of her.

They talked about his relationships, or his lack of meaningful romantic involvement in recent years, which he assured her, contrary to what she might have believed, was not by choice – with a social circle numbering only her and whoever she was seeing at the time, and no physical workplace in which to meet anyone, his options had, until very recently, been limited. They talked about work and his current lack of motivation, and his disillusionment with it even before Peter left him the flat and the money. They talked about Peter's flat and the fact that he still couldn't bring himself to do anything with it – he didn't really want to be surrounded by Peter's things constantly, but he couldn't shake the feeling that they belonged there more than he did. Not that he had anything to put in their place anyway – he couldn't actually remember ever buying a piece of furniture in his life, now he came to think of it, so wouldn't know where to start with replacing Peter's very definite, very Peter taste. She said she could help him if he wanted. They could pick some things out together if he liked, she was sure that there was a perfectly liveable flat, maybe even a home to be had there, if only he could find a way to soften Peter's manly monochrome.

They talked about Peter – *he* talked about Peter – a lot, and he didn't once feel sad or sorry. He was able to talk about him with all the varying degrees of fondness that had marked their relationship over the years. He told her stories about his childhood with him, and how the age gap always kept them slightly apart, how they were close but not inseparable, or not as inseparable as he had always thought they should have been. She reminded him how close they'd become, all three of them, over the months that he'd shared a flat with Peter. She reimagined nice meals in Peter's favourite restaurants, fun evenings in his favourite bars and drunken nights at his flat, turning them into momentous occasions and treasured memories, and he was happy to let her; happy to share in her exaggerated, super-vivid version of their past. More than anything he was happy to be able to talk like this, to her.

They were like they used to be. Like they hadn't been in ages. He felt close to her in a way that hadn't seemed possible since Peter died. Peter had become a reason or an excuse for shutting her out and undoing a closeness, a dependency, which wasn't healthy between friends.

Until meeting this new Audrey, he'd never acknowledged thinking of her in any way other than that of a friend, but in the brief gaps and pauses in the evening's conversation he began to wonder if at some point, deep down, he hadn't already considered other possibilities. He began to wonder if that was why he'd pushed her away: to get over the pain of losing her as he knew he inevitably would if he ever did anything about it. Not that it made a difference. Whatever he had or hadn't thought in the past, he was thinking it now and the more he thought it and the longer they talked, the more he realised how much he'd missed her and that he wouldn't risk losing her again.

He was relieved also that he could still make her laugh. So much of their relationship since Peter had been either tense or evasive, with him so pitiful and sorry for himself, it would have been understandable if she couldn't quite have brought herself to humour or indulge him again. But instead she laughed and laughed, like everything he said was the funniest thing she'd ever heard and he was the best company she could ever have asked for. Generous as he suspected she was being, he knew that this *was* the best company he'd been for a long time.

As the evening wore on he got more and more comfortable with being him again, and as he listened to Audrey rewrite another memory of Peter, this time a windswept day by the sea which she filled with all the sunshine and carefree happiness of a long weekend in a heatwave, he was suddenly overwhelmed by the fact that she'd waited for him at all. How lucky he was. He'd done nothing but dismiss and abuse her. He'd not so much taken her for granted as actively attacked her for being loyal. Every time she'd reached out to him, he'd slapped her attention away, taking it as a personal insult, and yet she'd persisted and waited for him to come back to her. He wasn't sure why, but he was grateful that she had.

He watched her eyes brighten and her smile grow wide when she talked about Peter and in that instant the sadness seemed so far away; he couldn't even think what it had been like to have it filling all of the spaces inside him until there was no room for anything else. He couldn't bring to mind what it felt like to carry it around with him every day, to wake up and suddenly remember Peter and have the sadness flood from his stomach to his chest and throat and force all the morning life straight back out of him. Watching how happy she seemed remembering Peter and the three of them together, seeing how she remembered only the good and how it nourished her, he couldn't imagine how he could ever feel that lost or broken again. He watched and listened and felt closer to Peter, closer to her, closer to being his old self. Only being with Sophie made him happier, and that was different because with her he was someone else entirely. He watched and he listened, and he thought about Peter and about her and the three of them together, and he felt happy and grateful, and then somewhere between coffee and the bill a pause in the conversation found them looking deep into each other's eyes, more like a couple at the end of a successful date than one old friend apologising to another for thoughtlessly running off to Paris with his new love interest. The look lingered longer than perhaps it should, yet neither of them felt awkward or uncomfortable. They didn't say anything. There were no smiles or laughs to imply nervousness or embarrassment. Then, for no reason other than to share another part of their joint Peter history, he said, 'Peter always said we should get married.'

She didn't say anything. Her expression didn't change. She didn't laugh or smile at the ridiculousness of Peter's suggestion. In fact, he thought he saw in her eyes a conscious effort not to react, which he read as containment of something: approval, interest, pleasure at the way it sounded? Instantly he wished he hadn't said it.

When she got out of the taxi she stood there in her little trench coat and heels, holding the door open, eyeing him coyly and perhaps a little drunkenly, and asked him if he wanted to come in. 'Just for a drink,' she said, as if either their relationship or her intentions needed clarification. He let the suggestion hang in the air for a moment while he turned the possibilities over in his head. 'Just for a drink,' she said again, a reassurance which only confirmed his suspicion that it was a bad idea.

'I don't think so. I've got an early start in the morning.'

'No you haven't,' she smiled.

He didn't say anything.

'Well, if you're sure,' she said.

As she went to close the door of the taxi he reached out to stop her.

'I wanted to say thank you.'

'For?'

'Everything.'

Audrey motioned for him to save any drunken declarations of love and friendship. 'OK,' she said, making to close the door of the taxi again.

'No, I'm serious. You've been amazing. Thank you for putting up with me and with the way I've been and for not holding any of it against me. I can't think of anyone else who would have kept on at me to sort myself out, or waited for me while I did, and it's appreciated. You always keeping on at me, always pushing. And thank God you did otherwise I'd never have met Sophie, and she's the best thing to happen to me in a long time. And thanks for introducing us and getting the two of us together. That too is very much appreciated.'

Audrey's smile thinned and drew tight. She made to close the taxi door again, then stopped and stuck her head back around it. 'Trust me, that's the last thing I did.'

...ide of the lift.

...drail.

...nd her waist.

His mouth pressed against her lips, pinning her head back against the mirrored glass.

His eyes closed, he feels her hands either side of his face. Pulling him to her. He feels her pressing her lips into his. Holding him there. Trying to get closer. Trying to get more.

She forces an arm around his neck. Wraps herself tightly around him. Into him. Her fingers digging into his hair. Pulling at it. Pulling him into her and her into him.

He pushes harder into her.

Pushes her back, up, almost onto the handrail.

Her head back against the glass.

He opens his eyes and sees her staring back at him, trying to read his eyes, trying to know what he's thinking, what he's feeling, what this means to him, trying to tell if he wants this as much as she does.

He closes his eyes and her arms tighten around his neck. Pulling his head down. Pulling his mouth to her neck. To her soft, flushed skin. He closes his eyes tighter and kisses harder at her softness, breathing in as much of her perfume as he can, trying to smell the real her behind it.

He feels her neck tense. Feels her hold her breath. Absorbs the shudder as she releases it.

He feels the tightening of her fingers in his hair. Her hands pulling him in closer. Pulling his head back up. Pulling him back to her lips.

He feels the movement of the lift. He feels the jolt and sway. The pull upwards and the drunken effect of it and her kisses.

He feels the side-to-side movements forcing them into each other and pulling them apart. Making them reach for each other. Making them hold onto each other.

He wants to reach into her. He wants to hold onto her tighter and harder.

He wants to smell her.

To taste her.

Her skin, her lips, her mouth.

He wants to touch all of her. To feel every part of her. To be part of her. To be inseparable from her before the lift stops and the doors open. Before he has to let go of her.

He presses himself into her as hard as he can.

He doesn't want to let her go. He wants to feel her in his hands. He wants to remember the tips of his fingers pressing into her. Feeling her skin, her clothes, her hair. His lips against hers. He wants to feel all of it, remember all of it, before the lift doors open.

He feels the lift slow.

He feels it shudder.

He anticipates it stopping.

His hands grab at her. Trying to find her skin. Trying to bury deep into her hair.

His hands try to feel as much of her as there is to feel before he has to let her go.

His lips press into hers. He feels the wetness of her mouth. He tastes champagne and cigarettes. He feels her reaching into him, trying to taste and savour him too. Trying to hold onto him before she has to let go. He feels her pushing herself into him.

The lift jolts to a stop.

128

He opens his eyes.

He looks at her. At the faded lipstick. At the little O of her
mouth.

The floor sinks and settles.

The voice of the K West lift announces the second floor.

The doors open.

He wakes up in Paris. The awareness of movement above and
around him opens his eyes as the Gare du Nord quietly slides into
place through the Eurostar's window. His fellow passengers pull
bags from the overhead racks and queue in the aisle to be among the
first off the train when it finally comes to a stop and the doors open.
He doesn't move to join them. He straightens himself and looks out
of the window. Still half asleep, he watches the platform as it slows
to a halt. The pillars, the litter bins, the security cameras, staff in
their grey SNCF uniforms, the reassuringly unfamiliar station signs.
His heart swells at the sight of them, and at the whiteness of the sky
over a damp winter morning in Paris. They force the sadness back
down inside him, soothing and exciting the longing that lives next to
it. He sits for a long moment, looking out of the window at the
station and the platform and the sky. Not wanting to move. Not
wanting to think of anything other than that this is Paris, and he is
here and so is she.

From the train he heads straight for the Métro and RER
Ligne D to Châtelet-Les Halles, which will take him to the Rue
Quincampoix. On the escalator down he finds himself looking for
her, searching the faces heading in the opposite direction, already
looking for signs of her presence, like anyone and everyone in Paris
might know her and somehow he'll be able to tell by looking at them.

Waiting for the RER his eyes wander from person to person
along the platform. An old man sitting silently on the green plastic
seats with a woman who could be his wife sitting next to him, a
group of teenagers listening to tinny French rap music on a phone, a
young mother with two small, dazed and well-behaved children, a
selection of the poor and unseen working men and women of Paris –
immigrants and refugees of all nations, unmistakably Parisian yet

vividly at odds with the cafe society above ground – on their way to jobs as cleaners or toilet attendants, a couple of stray businessmen and tourists, and two women who he puts in their early twenties and guesses to be office workers or students. He looks at them all, all worn or wary under the unforgiving yellow-green of the platform's fluorescent light, the opposite of the romantic version of Paris he's been working on all these months since he was last here with her. He thinks that none of these people would know Sophie. Then he looks again to the twentysomething office workers and wonders if they could be the exception. If they work in an office, who's to say it isn't Sophie's. Then he looks to one of the women he thought to be a cleaner and wonders if it's possible that she might have cleaned Sophie's office or the company apartment in the Rue Quincampoix, if she might have touched her things or seen her in passing.

Looking along the platform again, he thinks of all the time he spent in Paris and how rarely he ventured down onto the Métro. On his own he preferred to get his bearings above ground, on foot. Together they walked or got taxis. The Métro was not Sophie's natural habitat. Looking at the faces waiting with him for the Ligne D RER, he knows that none of them know her, but he studies them all the same. To be sure.

When the RER arrives, he gets on and stands just inside the doors. He looks up at the map to check that it's one stop to Châtelet-Les Halles. One stop and a two-minute walk to the Rue Quincampoix. He smiles to himself. He smiles at how close he is now. How close he's about to be. One stop until he finds her again. Just to know that he's near her again makes him happy. Makes his heart swell again. Forces the sadness deeper inside him.

He's only been in Paris for half an hour and already he feels at home. Relieved. The smell, the noise, the pleasing female voice announcing Châtelet-Les Halles as the next stop, even the Métro itself, somewhere they seldom went together, all remind him of her and make him feel closer to her than he's felt since that night in Peter's apartment, the last time he was with her.

As the RER clatters and jolts, he actually feels that he's being taken to her. Propelled towards her. To where he's meant to be. With every metre travelled he's surer that this is where he belongs. That this is how things were supposed to happen. That these last months have been a test to be passed, to be endured and overcome to bring him to this point, to here, to her. With every flicker of the half-empty carriage's yellow-green light, he's more certain that when he finds her he will be able to make her see that he never meant to hurt her, that he can make her understand that everything that happened, what he did, it was a mistake and he would never do it again.

He closes his eyes for a second, lets the carriage rock him gently and lull his heart, which he can feel is racing in his chest. Now he's here he knows that he has to make her believe that losing her once was enough. That now that he's found her, he has no intention of letting her go again.

He feels the RER slowing and hears a distant sound of brakes.

He opens his eyes and thinks that when he can make her see that this was how things were meant to be, that what happened will make them stronger if only she'll let it, when he can make her see what is now so obvious to him, then he's sure that Paris will be once again be theirs, that they will be happier there together than they've ever been. He's already decided that they don't ever have to go back to London, unless she really wants to. He can sell Peter's flat and get them an apartment on the Rue du Bac with tall windows and a balcony overlooking their own secret courtyard. They can start a new life there together. They can put the last months behind them. They can make Paris home. They can be anything they want to be in it.

He turns into the Rue Quincampoix and all his certainty is immediately gone.

He stops at the corner, in front of the boulangerie where he bought croissants and bread for their breakfast. He sees the narrow street with its overshadowed shop fronts and shaded doorways, more alley than road, and he can't think what he was meant to be doing there. Everything is familiar. Everything is exactly as it should be, exactly as he left it, as he's remembered it all these months. Everything except for him standing there, alone and uninvited. The Rue Quincampoix used to be their shared secret. Suddenly it feels like a private place into which he has no right to intrude.

Since Audrey told him that Sophie was there, he's thought of nothing else but coming to reclaim her, of proving his love by following her to Paris and not taking no for an answer. He's thought of all the things he would say to win her back. He's thought of how she might react and what he might say to finally convince her that he's sincere in everything he says and that he won't fail her again. He's imagined their embrace, their happy reunion, their whole future life together. He's imagined everything except what happens before all of that. Between arriving in Paris and reminding her of everything they were to each other. He's imagined everything except for what happens now.

He breathes in the damp air and thinks about walking away. Walking somewhere else. Finding somewhere to think about what to do, now that he's there. He looks to the boulangerie and the cafe on the opposite corner. He looks to the Korean restaurant where they ate a couple of times and to the wall opposite with its street art picture of a girl with the bandana over her mouth that one night he kissed her against, and he wonders what he's doing there. Everything looks the same, but it isn't and it can't be and suddenly he feels more alone than ever and doesn't want to see any of it.

He looks again to the far end of the Rue Quincampoix, and because he feels exposed and doesn't want to stand where he is any longer, he starts to walk towards it. The collar on his coat turned up, his chin buried low in his scarf, he can hardly bring himself to look up. He walks with long strides, with purpose, to get to the far end of the Rue Quincampoix as quickly as possible, to turn the corner and keep walking until he's gone far enough that he won't be afraid of meeting her coming the other way. As he walks he looks only for doorways to step into and places to hide should he need them, should he look up and see her coming towards him, should she step out of one of the bars or restaurants and into his path. As he walks he looks for places to disappear into now, and places where he might see but not be seen later, if he decides to come back, if he can find it in him to come and wait for her. He passes the street door to the apartment without looking at it. He gets to the end of the Rue Quincampoix and the only thing he feels is relief.

He walks eight blocks, zig-zagging his way up towards République, before he's able to think of anything other than getting away. He waits to cross the Rue du Temple and feels his heart racing in his chest again and realises with it that he's been holding his breath and still is. He breathes as hard and deep as he can. He tries to focus on where he's going and what he's doing.

He thinks that he should check into his hotel. He thinks that he needs to dump his overnight bag that's barely filled with toiletries and a change of clothes, have a shower and get something to eat. He needs the time to think that having a shower and something to eat will give him. He needs to start again.

Waiting to cross the Rue du Temple, he thinks about his hotel in Saint-Germain and realises that he's heading in the wrong direction, that he needs to go back the way he came.

He decides it's safer to continue up to République and to get the Métro back down to Châtelet and walk from there. He decides the Métro is the only place he can be sure he won't look up to find her there, staring at him with that look in her eyes, wanting to know what he's doing there and what he was thinking, turning up uninvited. Wanting an explanation before he's thought of one that won't make her angry or threatened or harassed like before. That's what Audrey had said, she'd felt harassed. He'd harassed her. He'd told Audrey that he hadn't, or he hadn't meant to. He'd told her that he'd just wanted to explain, to say sorry, to try to make it right. Audrey said it hadn't felt that way to Sophie, and he'd wondered who this new Sophie was, the one who could feel harassed and threatened by him.

As the lights change and he starts to cross the Rue du Temple, he feels the panic subside and the sadness crawl up inside him to take its place. For the first time since he stood in the vast white reception of her London office, his main feeling at the thought of seeing her is fear. Not of what to say and how she might react, but

133

of being near her and what to do when he is. Walking up to the Place de la République he realises that he's only imagined how the conversation ends, not how it starts, and that saying all or any of the things she's found so compelling in his head requires knowing how to approach her without making it worse, and he's not sure that's even a possibility now. All he knows for certain is that he needs to see her before she sees him. He needs to be prepared. Ready. He knows that if he has to chase her she won't hear anything.

As he hurries down the steps into the safety of the Métro he feels relief at last to be out of sight. He takes comfort from the warm machine air and in the familiarity of the sadness as he relaxes into it. As he tries to find a map or a sign or something, anything, to tell him where he needs to go, he feels grateful to have the sadness to hold onto, to have something so undeniably his to keep him company. As he follows the tunnel to what he hopes is the right platform, somewhere in the back of his mind he wonders what he would do without it, if he might not be too attached to it, if he's actually started to look forward to feeling it. He wonders if sometimes he doesn't encourage the thoughts that make it rise up and fill all the spaces inside him, if he doesn't think certain thoughts expressly to have it overwhelm him.

The platform's empty when he gets to it. The display says it's three minutes until the next train. He wanders halfway along, taking in the lights and the tiles and the tracks worn to a shine and the smiling faces of the happy families advertising banks and mobile phones and department stores on the walls, and he wonders how it's possible to be scared of seeing someone you've loved.

By the time he gets back to the Rue Quincampoix it's already starting to get dark. He feels instantly happier, more willing to wait and see what happens. He walks to just beyond the apartment's street door and steps into a doorway on the opposite side of the road. He lights a cigarette and pulls the collar on his coat up around his ears, doing his best to look like someone sheltering from the light drizzle that's started to fall. Like someone waiting for someone, which he is. He repeatedly glances up to the second-floor windows, trying to remember which ones belong to their apartment, while trying to look like someone casually looking up at the darkened windows above, not like someone waiting in a darkened doorway watching a specific apartment for signs of life. He feels less conspicuous than he expected, certainly far less exposed than he did earlier. It's early evening and there are plenty of people using the Rue Quincampoix as a shortcut or standing outside its handful of bars and restaurants, smoking cigarettes, just like him.

After checking into the hotel he'd showered and eaten and thought of all the ways he could go about approaching someone who'd accused him of harassing them. He thought about and discounted both casually bumping into her in the street and putting a note under the apartment door – the first for being implausible and impossible to control, the second for giving her the chance to disappear before he'd said his piece. He didn't want to confront her, but he couldn't risk wasting an opportunity. The conclusion he came to was that the only thing to do was to buzz the apartment's buzzer. To corner her, without having to do it to her face. Letting himself into the building and knocking on the apartment's door felt too confrontational, too threatening. Even though he still remembered the code for the street door and could picture the tightly twisting stairs behind it that they'd drunkenly stumbled and fumbled on so many times, to have used either would have been too intrusive, too unsettling, as much for him as for her. For some reason he thought that the distance that the intercom and two flights of stairs would put between them might make it feel safer for them both, while still forcing her to accept that he was here and she needed to talk to him. It allowed her to retain the gift of granting him an audience, while allowing him to insist that she give it.

Watching the windows, smoking his cigarette, looking about him casually so as not to be too obviously interested in one particular window, he notices a fellow smoker sheltering under the awning of the bar opposite. Early to mid twenties, with long black hair and a fringe where her eyebrows should be, she's wrapped up in an oversized cardigan, shivering, looking at him. Even in the red glow coming from the bar's neon window sign he can see how pale her skin is. The black fringe and the pale skin make him think of Audrey, so much so that he thinks she could almost be Audrey's younger, more bookish sister. She smiles between drags and exaggerates her shiver when she's sure that he's looking at her too. He smiles back before he has a chance to pretend not to have noticed her.

He finishes his cigarette, throwing it in a puddle, and looks up to see Audrey's bookish little sister scowling and shaking her head – if he were closer he thinks he would hear her tutting. She nods to an ashtray on the table next to her, gives him a disapproving look and then smiles to show that she's joking. He smiles back in acknowledgement and apology, and with it her smile widens to the point where he's suddenly sure that she's about to come over and start talking to him.

He fumbles in his pocket for his phone. He takes it out, looks at the blank screen as if checking the identity of the imaginary caller, puts it to his ear and says hello. He smiles and nods, for the benefit of his audience, and asks the other side of the nonexistent conversation how they are. He mimes listening. He nods again. He mimes laughing and deep conversation, hoping it's deep enough to make Audrey's bookish little sister lose interest and go back inside once she's finished her cigarette. Audrey's bookish little sister shivers and smiles and smokes and pulls her oversized cardigan tight around her. He laughs again and raises his eyebrows in interest at something the person he's pretending to talk to might have said. He glances up at the still dark apartment window and back to Audrey's bookish, still smoking little sister.

A smartly dressed man with white hair and black-framed glasses walks past. Audrey's bookish little sister takes him in as he passes, his long black coat, black leather briefcase, black umbrella, his black glasses and the high contrast of his thick white hair. She smokes her cigarette and stands statue still in her oversized cardigan, only her eyes moving to follow as he walks past and into the doorway next to the bar.

Still deep in imaginary conversation, still focused on Audrey's bookish little sister, he watches her watching the white-haired man switch his umbrella from one hand to the other so he can punch in the code for the street door of the apartment building. Their apartment building. Almost too late he shifts his attention from her to him, and watches the smartly dressed man press the buttons in the familiar pattern of the code he punched in every day, the same code he'd decided back at his hotel not to make use of. He watches the street door open, the smartly dressed man with the white hair step inside and the door close behind him. He looks at the closed street door, not laughing, not nodding, forgetting that he's meant to be in conversation with his phone. He looks at the street door, then he looks at Audrey's bookish little sister, who's almost finished her cigarette. She smiles at him and he remembers his phone at his ear and he smiles and laughs and looks up to see the window of their apartment light up.

He looks at the window and then at Audrey's bookish little sister, who's stubbing her cigarette out in the ashtray on the table next to her. She drops the butt into the ashtray, looks up at him and smiles. He nods along to the conversation he's having with no one and returns her smile and watches her turn and head back into the bar.

He looks back up at the lit window. He tries to think if he's mistaken, if one of the other windows could be the one that he used to watch Sophie dance at, the one that he used to lean out of and smell the crisp spring Paris air. He tries to fit the other, darkened windows to his memory but he can't. He looks at the lit window and he can already picture the inside of the room and the lamp by the sofa that's giving the window its warm orange glow.

He looks at the lit window and then he looks back to the bar. He checks that Audrey's bookish little sister has definitely gone inside, puts his phone back in his pocket, steps from the shelter of his doorway and crosses over to the street door. He moves with the speed and decisiveness of someone who's been waiting for exactly this to happen. He doesn't stop to think about it. He acts. Unexpectedly and out of character. It's like he's watching someone else. Like he's watching himself. He's not party to his actions or what comes next. He has no sense or feeling about either. He sees his hand reach for the intercom and find the apartment number. He watches his finger press the button without hesitation.

The noise of the buzzer brings him suddenly back to himself. He feels a flicker of panic, immediately overridden by the relief that it's too late now not to go through with it.

He hears a click on the intercom and a voice that could well be that of the man with white hair and black-framed glasses answer, '*Oui.*'

He hears himself say '*Bonsoir*' and ask in his awkward French if the person on the other end speaks English. The intercom replies, slipping easily into a rounded international accent, the product of a good Scandinavian or Swiss education, that yes, he does.

He hears himself ask if Ms Carlson's there.

There's a pause and then the voice asks in its soft Americanised English if he can repeat himself. He hears himself ask again if he can speak to Ms Carlson and then after another pause he hears the voice say that he's sorry, but he doesn't know a Miss Carson, and then after a moment add that he must have the wrong apartment. He hears himself ask if this is the apartment belonging to Fitzgerald Ellis, the London law firm. The voice on the intercom says that it is. He hears himself say that Ms Carlson works for the firm, that she's here in Paris, that he thought she would be staying at the apartment. He hears himself ask again if the voice on the intercom knows Ms Carlson, Ms Sophie Carlson.

He waits, unsure if the intercom is still listening. He repeats that Ms Carlson, Ms Sophie Carlson works for the company, that she's here, in Paris, working in the Paris office, is he sure he doesn't know her? The intercom stays silent.

He leans into the small round speaker. He listens and then says hello. He listens again and waits. He thinks he hears someone move or breathe in the static, and then he hears the voice say, '*Je suis désolé,*' and then repeat in English, 'I'm sorry,' and the intercom click off.

He leans into the small round speaker and listens but there's no movement, no breathing, no static.

He steps back from the street door and looks up at the lit window two floors above and sees the man with the white hair and black-framed glasses come to the window, look down at him and draw the curtain.

Chapter Fourteen

A month after they got back to London he still hadn't heard from her. For the first week the afterglow of Paris had been enough to carry him, giving everything a lightness and certainty that allowed him to fill her absence with the still fresh sense of them together. By the end of the second week certainty had given way to doubt, and he suddenly felt the helpless vulnerability of not being able to reach out to touch her whenever he wanted to. She had never offered her phone number and he had never asked for it, and as ridiculous as that fact seemed to him after two weeks of waiting alone in Peter's flat for her to call, he wasn't convinced that if he had her number he would actually use it. Their relationship and everything that excited him about it had been defined and determined by her. He liked and wanted the thrill that being subject to her whim brought to it. Her secrecy, her aloofness, her sudden grand gestures and conspiratorial glances offered escape, not the promise of domestic bliss, and he wanted to keep it that way. He didn't want her phone number because he wanted to call her, he wanted it to know that he could.

At the beginning of the third week he called Audrey to ask her for it. As he would have predicted had desperation not already started to infect his logic, she refused to give it to him, stating the obvious fact that if Sophie had wanted him to have her phone number she would have given it to him herself, and when he tried to suggest that her not having done so was more an oversight than her intention, Audrey told him that it wasn't her place to correct it. He would have accepted her point if she hadn't made it so angrily. Perhaps it was resentment at being put in an awkward position, but he chose instead to seize upon the other, to him more likely option; that her anger was annoyance at the suggestion that she aid a relationship which she had already made clear she neither endorsed nor encouraged. Claiming disapproval as her true motivation, he began alternately pleading with her to change her mind and accusing her of being mean-spirited and jealous until eventually she hung up. He immediately regretted taking his frustration out on her and called back to tell her so, only to find himself apologising to her voicemail.

A week later Sophie called. It was eleven in the morning. As before, his phone told him it was an *Unknown Number*, but he knew it was her. When he answered though, he wasn't so sure. She sounded strange. Hesitant. Her usual assured tone, clear and precise in its seductiveness, had been replaced by nervousness. Even before she spoke he could hear in her breath a tension and doubt that didn't belong to Sophie, not to the Sophie he knew. It wasn't the same as the night in the restaurant when she asked him to come with her to Paris. Then she was shy and girlish, nervous with the excitement, hesitant with the hope that he might say yes and at the possibility that he might say no. It took him a moment to realise what it was that he heard in the pause between her 'Hello' and the afterthought 'It's me'. It took him a moment, but after then hearing her go to start, then stop, and then apologise for not being in touch, and then, as another afterthought, promise to explain why when she saw him, he was sure that what he was hearing was fear. She was scared. Perhaps that she might have left it too long, that he might not want to hear from her, that after so many weeks without her he might have lost that sense of them together, and having finally overcome the absence that she left him with he might not be so willing to reinstate her this time. The other option, the only one that occurred to him, was that something was wrong. That she had something to tell him. That something had happened, that she was in some kind of trouble, that she needed help and had no one else to turn to. That she was turning to him.

She said she needed to see him. She said that she was sorry and she'd missed him and that she needed to see him now. She said she had to see him, that it really couldn't wait. To his ears at least, there was pleading to the urgency in her voice as she said it. When she said, 'Will you come?' he heard a desperation that he couldn't help but respond to.

He went straight to the hotel in West London that she'd given him the address for. In the cab he tried to concentrate on the reasons why she would need to see him so urgently. He tried to keep his mind on the gravity, on her vulnerability, on what he could do to help and how he could make her feel safe and loved. He tried to concentrate on the worry he felt for her, while trying not to admit to himself that he was excited, pleased even, that she'd come to him, that he was the person she trusted to be there for her. As he hurriedly paid the driver he almost convinced himself that his fumbling with notes and loose change was out of panic, not eagerness to be needed.

As instructed, he crossed the lobby to the hotel bar, where he asked for Ms Carlson. The barman smiled and nodded and handed him an envelope which had been propped against a bottle behind the bar. 'Ms Carlson' was written on the front in her familiar, romantic hand. Inside, a piece of hotel stationery, blank except for '342' written in the same romantic hand. He thanked the barman, who nodded and smiled and showed no sign of disappointment at not having the contents of the envelope shared with him, and made his way back through the bar to the lobby and the lifts.

The third-floor corridor was dimly lit, giving the impression of three o'clock in the morning even at lunchtime. Room 342 was at the far end, a long soundless walk on thick carpet from the lift, and with each soft footfall his heart raced faster and his stomach tied in tighter knots of excitement and anxiety. He stood and looked at the door. He checked the 342 in front of him against the 342 on the paper in his hand. He checked it again and thought about how to explain himself if it wasn't her who answered. He raised his hand and then stopped to listen for signs of life on the other side of the door before knocking three quick, quiet knocks and listening again. He waited and listened for the sound of movement, of feet on carpet, of a glass or cup being put down on a hard surface, of someone approaching the door. He listened and after what felt like longer than necessary he knocked again, the same three quick knocks, but louder this time, louder and harder than he'd intended. The sound made him instantly self-conscious and uncomfortable in the empty corridor, and the longer the door stayed closed the more uncomfortable he became and the more likely it seemed that knocking again would only cause the doors of other rooms to open, not hers. So he tried the handle. The door opened into a bright, airy, oversized living room of high ceilings and low sofas, the entertaining space of a suite, not a room. As his eyes made the transition from the 3 a.m. of the corridor to the sun streaming in through the floor-to-ceiling windows, his insides made the transition from the urgency of a crisis to something altogether more unexpected and decadent. Rounding the corner of the living room he found himself in the doorway of the bedroom, and there, ready and waiting for him, naked except for the bed sheet tucked under her arms, already drinking champagne and holding a glass out to him, already laughing, was Sophie.

Later, when he got out of bed to use the bathroom, she lit a cigarette for him and asked if there was anything sexier than 'screwing in the afternoon'. She handed him the cigarette as he got back into bed and told him that she didn't think there was anything quite like it, and that they should do it every time one of her meetings got cancelled. She told him that next time she'd just text him the room number. He took a drag on the cigarette and lay back against the headboard and asked how he was meant to know it was her as he didn't have her number in his phone. He pointed out that it could be awkward, the text could be from anyone, it might not even be for him, and without knowing it was from her the room number could be anything, a time, a price, the number of a bus. He said that if she wanted to make a habit of screwing in the afternoon, she probably ought to think about giving him her phone number. She agreed and pulled the cigarette in his hand to her lips. She exhaled and told him that the only thing sexier than afternoon sex in a hotel would be afternoon sex in a seedy hotel by the seaside. She told him that she'd always wanted to go to Brighton for a dirty weekend, but she'd never had anyone to take her on one. She said that just thinking about the smell of chip fat and sea air did it for her. That there was something about the idea of going to the seaside for no other reason than to have sex, and the fact that everyone would know that's why you were there, that made her want to have sex even more. He said that if she gave him her number he might arrange it for her as a surprise one day. She leaned in and kissed him and told him that he didn't have to do that, but it was very sweet that he wanted to.

They stayed like that for a while, propped up in bed together, her head on his shoulder, enjoying the silence while he finished the cigarette and she played with the hairs on his stomach. Once he'd put the ashtray on the bedside table she snuggled down and put her head on his chest and her arm around him and said that she was sorry for not having been in touch. Without looking up she told him that work had been insane and she hadn't had a minute to herself. She told him that even so, she'd been desperate to see him and that she'd done nothing but think about them together, and all the things they could be doing. She said that they would have to have plenty of afternoons in hotels to make up for it. She said they'd need a lot of afternoons in hotels to do all of the things that she'd been thinking about doing with him. She rubbed her cheek into his chest and took a long, pleased breath of him and said that she loved hotels. She said that they were made for afternoon sex. She said that people only went to hotel rooms in the daytime for one reason.

He didn't say anything and the way she was talking didn't invite him to. It didn't feel to him like she intended it to be the start of a conversation, it was more something she felt she needed to say and which he felt he was meant to listen to. Like something she'd been thinking about. Something she'd prepared. She told him that she knew she'd been rubbish, but that she'd make it up to him. She told him that she would make time for them, proper time, not just hurried assignations in hotel rooms when meetings got cancelled, fun though they were, but whole days when they could do things and be together and enjoy being together properly. She told him that she had some time off coming up and that she wanted to spend as much of it as she could with him. She said that there were lots of things she wanted to do that she hadn't had the time or the opportunity or the company to do in years. She said she wanted to go to London Zoo, that she hadn't been since she was a child and for some reason it was something she really wanted to do even though she'd heard that they no longer had any of the animals, the lions and tigers and giraffes, that she was sure she remembered seeing when she was little. She said she wanted to go to museums and galleries and parks, not because she wanted to see anything in particular but because those were the kinds of things you did with someone else, and she'd never had anyone to do them with and for some reason she could really imagine doing them with him. He felt her smile as she told him that she would take him shopping for some new clothes, that he could do with something a little less disinterested, that he dressed like a depressed person who never went out and that if he was going to have half the fun she had planned for them, he'd need a whole new wardrobe and she wanted to buy it for him. He watched the back of her head on his chest as she talked. He watched his hand stroking her hair, neither of them really noticing that he was doing it. She said they'd have proper time together, not like today, and with that she rolled back onto her side of the bed and looked at the time on her phone on the bedside table and told him that she had to get back to the office. Pulling the sheet off the bed and wrapping it around her to go to the bathroom, she said that, who knows, one of those days they might even have time to eat together at lunchtime.

When she came out of the bathroom, tucking her white shirt into the skirt of her grey suit, she told him that the room was paid for for the night if he wanted to stay for a while. She said he should have something to eat in the restaurant if he was hungry, he could put it on the room and the hotel would charge it to her card. She said that the restaurant was very good, a bit pretentious maybe, but worth trying. She said she would love to join him but she really

145

had to get back to the office. Still sitting propped up in bed, he motioned to her to throw the bed sheet back over him, and once covered up again he lit another cigarette and told her that he wasn't hungry. He said that he'd see her back to the office if she'd like. Without looking away from the mirror and the lipstick she was reapplying she said, 'I don't think that would be such a good idea, do you?' He thought about asking her to stay, to cancel whatever she had on and spend the rest of the afternoon and the evening and the night in the bed in the room that she'd already paid for, but he knew what her answer would be so he asked instead when he would see her again. She said soon. She would call him, she promised. She'd call to let him know about her time off, just as soon as she knew for definite what her plans were. He thought again about asking her to stay and then went with another question to which he thought he knew the answer: 'So what about your phone number? Do you think that maybe you ought to give it to me, in case another meeting gets cancelled and you want to text me a room number?'

He watched her adjust her jacket and straighten her skirt and smooth her hair and pick up her bag and phone. He watched her step into her shoes and check that she'd got everything and then he watched her cross the room and come around to his side of the bed. She leaned in as if to kiss him, and then turned her head to the side at the last moment to take a drag on the cigarette in his hand. She held his stare as she blew smoke out and laughed. She held his stare for what felt like longer than necessary, and then took a pen out of her bag, wrote a telephone number on the back of the envelope he'd collected from behind the bar and handed it to him and said, 'But I'll call you. OK?'

Chapter Fifteen

He's waiting for her to say something.

He feels the weight of her head on his chest. Her hand lying still on his stomach through his shirt.

He feels the breeze on his face, taking the heat out of the sun as it breathes across him.

He knows that if he opened his eyes the sky would be blue and cloudless.

He knows that if he could see her face she'd be smiling.

He thinks she'd be smiling.

He tries to feel her smile.

She's not said anything. Her fingers have stopped playing with the hairs on his stomach, no longer working their way into him. He wonders if she's still awake.

He pushes his head back into his rolled-up jacket of a pillow and runs his hand over the grass next to him, the tips of it tickling his palm. He strokes her hair with his other hand, smoothing it, feeling the curve of her head, the nape of her neck.

She doesn't respond to the movement of his hand.

He wonders if she's still awake.

He wonders if she heard what he said.

He wonders if she heard him tell her that he thinks he loves her.

He wants to ask her, he wants to be sure, he wants to know what she's thinking, but he doesn't. He waits for her, listening to the sounds around him, a plane above, a dog barking, the voices of other people, other couples, conversations carried on the breeze along with the distant sound of cars running along the bottom of Primrose Hill.

He strokes her hair and waits and feels the sun tightening the skin on his face.

He strokes her hair and waits.

He feels the sun baking his face and then the breeze arrive again to cool it.

He smells the cool of the grass and the sweetness of the air and the deep vanilla caress of her perfume, and then the breeze arrives again to pick them up and take them away.

He feels himself sinking. He feels himself relaxing back into the afternoon, into the grass, into warm, sweet air. He feels himself sinking and relaxing and then he feels her move. He feels the weight of her head shift on his chest, he feels her hair pull between his fingers. He feels her try to make herself comfortable again. He feels her hand move on his stomach and her fingers find their way back into his shirt, winding themselves around the hairs, tighter and tighter and tighter.

He lifts his head to look at her. Her fingers stop. He looks at the back of her head, at his hand tangled in her dirty blond hair. He smooths her hair down again and goes back to stroking it. Her fingers go back to circling and stroking. Alternating between the two. He tries to imagine what she's thinking.

Her fingers mirror her breaths.

He feels her take a deep sigh and he wonders if she heard what he said.

He feels her fingers alternate between circling and stroking, mirroring her breaths and he wonders if she heard him tell her that he thinks he loves her.

He pushes his head back into the rolled-up jacket of a pillow and runs his hand over the grass next to him.

He feels the breeze on his face, taking the heat out of the sun as it breathes across him.

The inside of his eyelids red against the sun, he knows that if he opened his eyes the sky would be blue and cloudless.

He says nothing, listening to the sounds around him, a plane, a dog, conversations, distant cars, the breeze, and then he asks: 'What are you thinking?'

He looks up from the breakfast menu and out of the cafe window for signs of a smartly dressed man with thick white hair and black-framed glasses. Watching out of the window he drinks the last of his coffee and thinks about checking the time on his phone again, but he knows that it's barely been a minute since he last looked and that it doesn't make a difference if it's 08:21 or 08:22. He's been sitting there watching out of the window of the cafe on the corner of the Rue Quincampoix for two hours already, there's no way he could have missed him. He looks at the menu again and thinks about getting something to eat, more for something to do than because he's hungry. He looks at his empty cup and thinks about ordering another coffee, but he doesn't think he can drink any more without having food inside him and, looking at the time on his phone, 08:22, and then at the menu again, he doesn't think he's got the time or appetite even if there was something among the limited *petit déjeuner* selection that appealed to him. What he really wants is a cigarette, but the cafe's busy and he doesn't want to lose his table going outside to smoke. When he first got there he thought about sitting outside so he could smoke freely. Two hours later he's glad he didn't: even with the pavement heaters on he wouldn't have been able to stay out there in the cold for all that time and then he might not have got the table he did with its unobstructed view of the last third of the Rue Quincampoix. He looks up from the breakfast menu and out of the window. He sees a smartly dressed man with thick white hair and black-framed glasses turn out of the end of the Rue Quincampoix and head off in the direction of Les Halles.

He hurriedly finds the money for the three coffees and leaves it on top of the bill on the table. He pulls on his coat and makes his way through the busy cafe and out into the busier street, looking as soon as he's outside for the white hair and black coat moving away along the Rue Rambuteau. When he finds them he walks as fast as he can without running to catch up.

He follows at a discreet distance at first, but fear of losing the smartly dressed man in the crowd as they approach the Métro at Les Halles makes him get closer and closer, to the point where he could almost reach out and touch him. He's just behind his left shoulder as they go down into the station. So close he thinks he can smell his aftershave.

On the platform he stands no more than ten feet away to ensure that they both get on the same car when the Métro arrives. When it does the carriage is full of morning commuters, so he stands by the middle doors for two stops until a seat becomes available directly behind the smartly dressed man with thick white hair, who managed to get a seat the stop before. For some reason he expected them to be heading out to the business district, to the glass office blocks of La Defense. Instead they head south towards Montparnasse on Ligne 4 for nine stops. Watching the back of the smartly dressed man's white hair, the Métro rocking and swaying, his restless night spent dreaming of Sophie and thinking about how he might enlist the help of the man staying in their apartment starts to tell and, despite all the coffee he's drunk at the cafe on the corner of the Rue Quincampoix, he struggles to keep his eyes open and stay awake. The more he tries to focus on the white hair in front of him, the more the motion of the train seems to lull and soothe him to sleep.

At Vavin he comes awake just in time to see the white-haired man get off. He quickly gets to his feet and pushes his way through the carriage, making it out onto the platform as the doors start to close. He picks out the head of thick white hair above those of other passengers making their way up the steps at the end of the platform and hurries to join them, following closely behind up two flights and through the barrier and up another set of steps until they get out onto the street, where once again he drops back to a discreet distance, the wide and relatively empty pavement of the Boulevard du Montparnasse allowing him to maintain the gap between them this time.

They walk in the direction of the Montparnasse Tower. The smartly dressed man walks with unhurried purpose, undistracted by shop windows and his surroundings, focused on where he's going but with time to get there. The gap between them grows slightly as the purpose in the smartly dressed man's stride outpaces the uncertainty of his own. He watches the white hair and black coat, never taking his eyes off them. He watches them move, sensing the increase in distance but comfortable with it all the while the smartly dressed man's still in sight. He follows for two long blocks, watching the smartly dressed man's black coat and white hair hold a centre path on the pavement and then finally veer to the side and enter a nondescript 1970s office building, the only modern building in a typical Haussmann row.

He quickens his pace and arrives at the brown glass of the nondescript office building's reception to see the smartly dressed man with white hair and black-framed glasses disappear behind closing lift doors. He stays watching the lift for a moment, watching the closed doors, watching the numbers above them light up one by one. 1. 2. 3. He watches the numbers, waiting for 4 and 5 to follow in turn. 3 stays lit. Looking through the brown glass he sees a floor directory to the side of the lift. Under *3ème étage* he reads: *Fitzgerald Ellis*.

He reads the words *Fitzgerald Ellis* twice more and is suddenly aware of his heart racing in his chest again and then of a panicked excitement that makes him think he could actually be sick and a dryness in his mouth that tastes coffee-bitter and tired and makes him think that he's not ready yet. He looks through the brown glass and tries to see something, other than the list of companies on the floor directory and the closed lift doors, that might be useful or of interest to him. He sees some pot plants and a couple of boxes and a low reception desk with a middle-aged woman sitting behind it. The receptionist looks up and smiles at him. Instinctively he turns and walks away and at the first break in traffic crosses the six lanes of the Boulevard du Montparnasse as quickly as he can without running.

From the safe distance of the other side of the street he looks back at the office and up at the nondescript 1970s facade and its five storeys, all square concrete and brown glass. He looks up and down the street, up towards the Montparnasse Tower and back down towards the Métro, looking more because it's something to do than because he's hoping to see anything in particular. He looks up and down the street again, taking in the details of the side of the street he's on, the side facing what he now knows to be her office, looking for a cafe or coffee shop or bar. He sees a travel agent's, a dry-cleaner's, a bank, a clothes shop, a couple of restaurants that aren't yet open and what look like either offices or apartment buildings. He looks again, this time along the pavement, trying to find a bench or bus stop or telephone box or newsstand or advertising hoarding, and, not finding any of those, for a doorway or anywhere else he can wait and not be noticed waiting. He turns back to the office, to the nondescript 1970s facade and its five storeys, all square concrete and brown glass, and sees Sophie getting out of the back of a taxi.

She doesn't look up, she doesn't look in his direction, she doesn't see him standing across the road watching, too surprised to hide, too unready to call out or say anything. She's there in front of him for less than a minute, thirty seconds if that. He has only the time it takes her to shut the taxi door, turn, walk a few feet of pavement, open the brown glass door and walk through it, to register everything about her. He sees her face only long enough to know it's her. The hair, the briefcase, the softly determined way her hips sway, confirming the fact that after all these months, he's found her.

He stands across the street, looking at the brown glass of what he now knows for certain is her office, and he feels nothing. He looks at the brown glass of the reception and pictures the lift doors closing and the numbers above them lighting up one by one. 1. 2. 3. He follows the lift's imagined progress, following it with his eyes up the concrete and brown glass of the nondescript 1970s facade, from the ground floor to the first to the second, coming to rest on the third. He imagines the lift doors opening and her stepping out and walking with that soft, determined sway of hers, across the third floor to a corner office or a desk by a window. To a prime position. Somewhere light and airy that matches her status, denotes her importance, that her colleagues are envious of. He imagines her taking off her coat and unbuttoning the grey jacket of her suit. He imagines her hanging her coat on a stand behind her desk and tucking her hair behind her ear as she goes through a pile of post or reads a memo or the front page of the morning's paper. He imagines her going to the kitchen and returning with a cup of coffee or more likely a glass of water. He imagines her setting it down on the desk. He imagines her taking off her grey suit jacket and putting it on a hanger on the stand next to her coat. He imagines her pulling out her chair and looking out of the window before she sits down. He imagines her seeing him standing there, on the other side of the street, looking up at her. Watching. Imagining her every movement. Looking at the windows of the third floor, imagining her looking down at him from behind the brown glass, he feels suddenly exposed and self-conscious, and for the first time he realises how much he likes feeling it.

He looks up and down the street, up towards the Montparnasse Tower and back down towards the previously closed restaurants which are now showing signs of opening. He looks again for somewhere he can sit and wait and not be noticed waiting. He looks at the waiter unstacking tables and chairs and arranging them on the pavement in front of one of the restaurants and thinks that he could do with something to eat, and then he looks back to the concrete and brown glass of the third floor. He looks from window to window. For the first time he's excited by the thought that one of them might be hers. He looks from window to window and feels a lightness that he hasn't felt in months, a calm excitement. He feels the last of the sadness slipping away from him and the space it leaves filling with the warmth of relief. He looks at the third floor and knows that he doesn't have to imagine or hope any more, he knows for certain she's in there.

He looks back at the restaurant starting to open.

* * *

The waiter brings another coffee and clears the plates, the remnants of a three-course brunch and a hunger he hadn't felt since the morning after the night he met Sophie. He smokes a cigarette and drinks his coffee and watches the brown glass of the reception, watching for disturbances in its surface, signs of the doors opening, signs of movement forewarning of her departure. Between smoking and watching and drinking his coffee he pays the bill and thinks about what to do when he does eventually see her again. It's only now, knowing that she is actually in there, on the third floor, close enough to where he's sitting that she could probably see him if she looked out of the window or hear him if he called out her name, that he realises how remote the possibility of ever seeing her again had become to him. Of all the hours he's spent watching and waiting for her, how many of them has he spent actually expecting to see her and how much of it was just for something to do? The doing and the thinking about doing it were the things that made him feel close to her, possibly as close as he feels to her now. He smokes and drinks his coffee and thinks all the things that he's thought before. He doesn't want to scare her. He knows it will be a shock seeing him. He knows that she won't be expecting him to be there, outside her office, in Paris of all places. He knows that whatever her reaction, it won't be the one he would want. But now he thinks them all with the thought that she's in there, on the third floor, that she could come out at any minute and that this could be the only chance he'll get to talk to her. He thinks all the things he's thought before, but this time the conclusion he comes to is that there isn't a best option and that he'll know what to do when he sees her again. It's twelve o'clock before he does.

Distracted by the waiter bringing him his change, he misses her coming out of the doors. He looks up to see her standing on the pavement outside the office, doing up her coat and pulling her hair from down the back of her collar. She finishes arranging herself and turns and starts walking towards him. He watches her walk towards and then past him, six lanes away on the other side of the road, never once looking in his direction, oblivious to the fact that he's there or that she's being watched. The grey morning has given way to a crisp bright winter's afternoon, and to her long dark coat she's added a pair of large dark glasses, glasses which he recognises as ones she bought one day when they were shopping together in London. Glasses he helped her choose. Glasses that he said he liked because they made her look sultry and mysterious, glamorous like a French actress. Even without seeing her eyes, he can tell she's not looking anywhere but straight ahead. There's an urgency to her, a desire to go, an eagerness to be somewhere else, not to be distracted by shop windows and her surroundings, to focus on where she's going and get there. He thinks he might have seen it in her once or twice before, maybe once when he saw her hurry down the road to him.

He watches her pass on the other side of the road, watching her across six lanes of traffic, unaware of him sitting there, not sensing his presence or that she's being watched. He watches her walk further on, watches her until she's walked a safe distance and then he puts his cigarette out in the ashtray, collects together his cigarettes and lighter and change and starts off after her.

Just before the Métro she crosses over to his side of the Boulevard du Montparnasse and turns up a side street. He follows her up the Rue Vavin, run-walking until he's got sight of her again, and then slowing to a walking pace which he senses is still too fast, but which his nervousness at the thought of losing her won't let him slow. He walks up behind her, closer than he should, close enough that he thinks she might feel him, so close that he's surprised when she doesn't seem to. He can hear the heels of her shoes on the pavement and wonders if she can hear his footsteps behind her. He follows behind her, watches her walk, watches her not paying attention to the little restaurants and boutiques that they pass on the shaded side street. He hears the sound of her heels on the pavement and feels her confident stride. He watches her movements, the softly determined way her hips sway from side to side, and for a moment he imagines holding them, his hands coming up around her, from the small of her back, finding her hips and then sliding round and down to the tops of her thighs. He watches her hair and her shoulders and thinks for a moment about kissing them, and a time that he can't quite place when he remembers smelling her skin and her hair. As he follows her he tries to smell the smell of them again, but his memories are overpowered by the smell of restaurants and cooking that brings him back to the Rue Vavin and the sound of her heels on the pavement ahead of him. He watches her walk, he studies her movements, he examines everything about her that he can from this distance and imagines the rest. She's not carrying her briefcase, the briefcase that she had with her earlier, the briefcase that she always has with her. He watches her legs, striding, her ankles turning and straightening to maintain their balance on her heels, and he tries to think if he's ever seen her without her briefcase. He sees her closing the door in Peter's flat, he sees her getting out of a cab, waiting on a bar stool, hurrying down the road to meet him, and always the briefcase is in her hand or at her feet, always within reach, her work never leaving her, her never quite able to let go. He watches her walking and wonders what happened to it.

He follows her to the end of the Rue Vavin, the distance between them less and less until they finally come out of the shaded side street and into the light and openness of the Rue d'Assas with the Jardin du Luxembourg opposite. He stops at the corner and watches her cross the road and walk through an almost hidden gate into the gardens. He watches her disappear from view and he doesn't know what, but something holds him back for a moment. He stands watching the gate from across the street, hoping that she'll reappear, and when she doesn't he's in two minds whether he actually wants to follow her. This isn't where he was expecting her to go. This isn't the lunch meeting or the restaurant. He watches the gate and then he remembers the lack of a briefcase and something about that thought makes him cross the road and go through the gate after her.

He follows the curve of the path from the gate, past a groundsman's lodge and a map of the gardens and the maze of paths around them. He follows the path along under a canopy of lifeless trees and around bare flower beds and bushes, following its curve to the point where he can no longer see the gate behind him nor far enough ahead to know where he's going. He follows the path along and around and as far as he can see, there's no sign of her. He walks along and around and feels a tightness in his chest and a dryness in his mouth and panic in the pit of his stomach where the warm relief of earlier had been. He looks between the trees, trying to see further along the path, to short-circuit the view and catch sight of some future part that she might still be walking along or to see the openness of the formal garden itself where she must be heading. She must be there, she must have come this way, she must be somewhere just up ahead of him, somewhere in the gardens, he knows she must, so he keeps looking but he doesn't see her. He keeps looking, trying to see beyond the lifeless trees, and the more he doesn't see her the more he tries to imagine what the trees and flower beds would look like in the summer, all green and lush and full of colour, anything to take his mind off the fact that she isn't there.

All the cold February afternoons he spent wandering through the Jardin du Luxembourg on his own while she was at work, he spent so many of them imagining the life and beauty and carefully managed elegance he'd find if and when he came back months later, with her. He imagined walking through the gardens, the two of them together, her pulled in close, the softness of the skin of her bare arms touching his, the wide blue sky above them, beauty and greenery all around. He imagined the sunlight streaming through the trees, glinting off the water of the fountain and the pond, her hair blowing in the slight breeze that swirled the sand on the paths, her hair brushing against the side of his face, her turning to him and smiling, lifting her sunglasses and closing her eyes as he leaned in to kiss her. He thinks of the sunglasses, the ones that she's wearing now, the ones she bought one day when they were shopping together in London. The ones he helped her choose.

He stops and looks around at the foliage and path and glimpses of sky, as grey and dismal now as it was on all of those February afternoons. He looks through the trees and can just make out the openness of the formal garden with its balustrades and urns and flower beds and fountain. He moves a step closer and can see the edge of the pond to which the fountain belongs and the benches on the path around one side of it. The benches are all empty, the fountain sending a lonely arc of water into the grey-white November gloom with no one to watch it.

He walks along and around the path and out into the open, watching the fountain loom closer, its solitary splash getting louder. He walks along and around and down the steps, moving around the pond, the benches on the other side coming into view, the fountain's splash now louder than the crunch of the sandy gravel under his feet. He stops and looks across, beyond the fountain's lonely arc, to the benches on the other side. There's a couple kissing on the furthest of them. Locked in a deep embrace. Lost in each other. Oblivious to everything. They're the first people he's seen since coming through the gate and as far as he can see they're the only other people in the gardens with him. He watches them kiss. He watches the way they cling to each other and pull each other close and then he remembers and turns away to look for Sophie. He looks all around him, turning around and around, taking in the edges of the formal garden, the bare trees in the distance, the paths leading into them. He turns another circle and looks again and begins to wonder if she's already left the gardens by another exit, if perhaps she was just passing through on her way to a restaurant after all, if she was just taking the scenic route, and then he wonders if she knew that he was there all the time, if he had got too close and she'd felt him, or if she'd seen him out of the corner of her eye, sitting outside the restaurant, watching, waiting for her. He wonders if coming through the gardens was her way of losing him. He wonders if he has indeed lost her. He wonders if he should give up and go back to her office. He wonders how he could have come so close and still not come close enough.

He stops searching the view and lets his eyes wander from the fountain to the empty benches and the kissing couple. He looks at the paths either side of him, leading in different directions to different exits, and wonders which, if any, she took and which might take him to her, and then with no clue to guide him he decides to go back the way he came. He scans the garden again, just to be sure. He scans the fountain, the couple, the benches. He scans the bare trees, the paths, the fountain, the benches, the couple. He scans the benches and the couple and the bare trees and the urns and the balustrades and the lifeless flower beds and the fountain and the benches and the couple. And then he sees her. As clearly and unmistakably as anything he's ever seen. Sitting on the bench. One half of the kissing couple. Her hands stroking the face of a dark-haired man he's never seen before. Her hands in his hair, digging into it, pulling at it, pulling him closer. Her hands feeling the back of his head, her arms around his neck, her hands, her arms, her lips clinging onto him, pulling him closer and closer, as if feeling his lips against her is the only thing that's ever mattered to her.

He watches from the other side of the fountain. Watches her touch and hold him. Watches her kiss the mouth of this dark-haired man he's never seen before like she knows him, like she's always known him. He watches her and wonders how she can, how she can know anyone like that, anyone other than him. He stands on the path, watches her kiss and stroke his face. He watches her hands. He watches her hands stroke the face of the dark-haired man he's never seen before. He follows her fingers. He takes in the details as they do, or all the details he can from this distance. The light tan of his skin, the suggestion of lines around the eyes, the patches of grey in his dark hair which grazes the collar of his dark overcoat as she pushes her hands through it. He watches through the arc of the fountain, trying to familiarise himself with this man he's never seen before, trying to make him known, less alien, less unexpected, less intrusive and threatening, like that will somehow make the sickness flooding all the way up into him disappear. Even from here, he can see he's well-dressed, successful. Something about the way he's sitting on the bench as she kisses and caresses him is how he imagines a well-dressed, successful man would sit on a bench in Paris to be kissed by Sophie. He's older than her, mid to late forties. He isn't doing anything. He doesn't have to. He has her. All of her. Everything she can give to him she will. She has. She'd give more if she had it. He can tell that, even from here.

He stands on the path, watching through the fountain, and he doesn't care if she sees him or not. He thinks that perhaps part of him hopes that she will, perhaps because he knows she won't. Even from here he can tell that the only things she can see are the lips and the eyes and the hair that the tips of her fingers are so concentrated on. He stands and watches, knowing that she won't look up and find him watching them, watching her kiss and wrap herself into the dark-haired man he's never seen before. Even from here he knows that she isn't aware of anything else, certainly not his presence. So he stays and he watches her kiss and wrap herself around and deeper into the dark-haired man he's never seen before and then after a time, he doesn't know how long, he watches them unwind themselves from each other, stand and walk away hand in hand. They're already out of sight by the time he registers that he's watching an empty bench, that he's the only one watching the fountain, the only one left in the gardens.

Chapter Sixteen

It wasn't even a week before he called her. From the moment she'd given him her number he'd wanted to use it. He hadn't thought that he would, even when he was asking her for it as she was fixing her lipstick in the mirror in the hotel room and adjusting her shirt and skirt as he watched from the bed, when he was reminding her again and again that he didn't have her number, that he had no way of contacting her or knowing that it was her trying to contact him, even as he'd pushed and pushed to the point where she gave in and wrote it on the back of the envelope that she'd left for him at the bar with the room number in it, even then he hadn't thought he'd ever actually use it or want to. Then from the moment after she'd shut the door of the hotel room behind her, sitting up in bed looking at the number on the envelope in his hand, all he wanted to do was call it. To try it. To see if it worked. Before he had it, all he needed was the number itself, to know that he *could* call her whenever he needed to. As soon as he had it, he needed to know that it would work if he ever did. He wasn't sure if he thought it would or wouldn't. He wasn't sure if it was that he didn't trust her, or that he didn't believe it could be that easy, that all he had to do was ask her for it. He didn't know what it was or what he thought would or wouldn't happen when he dialled it. All he knew was that the more he thought about it, the more he needed to know one way or the other. He'd spent almost every minute since looking at the back of the envelope, looking at what might be her number, wondering if it would work, wondering what she would say when she picked up, if she picked up. The rest of the time he'd spent wondering what it was that made him think she wouldn't pick up if she saw it was him calling.

Less than a week after she gave it to him, he was sitting on Peter's terrace smoking, once again looking at the number, only this time he had his phone in his hand and was thinking about what he'd say if she did answer. Hello. It's me. She'd know it was him from his number. How are you? Can you talk? He needed more than that. He needed a reason to call. An excuse. Something to justify going against her parting words, her 'But I'll call you. OK?'

He wanted to tell her that he'd been thinking about that afternoon in the hotel, about the last time he'd seen her, about the fact that something about it seemed like a test but he wasn't quite sure what. He wanted to tell her that he'd been thinking about what she'd said about taking time off and spending it with him, and all the things that she'd said that she wanted them to do together. He wanted to tell her that he wasn't really sure that he believed her, that he wasn't convinced that she meant it. He wanted to tell her that he wanted to take her to the zoo. He didn't know why. The zoo was the one thing that had stuck in his mind. Every time he looked at her number and thought about calling it, every time he thought about that afternoon in the hotel and her fixing her lipstick and straightening her shirt and skirt, he thought about taking her to the zoo. There was something childlike about it, something sweet and vulnerable, something that he had the power to make happen. That and the dirty weekend in Brighton. He kept coming back to that too. Something else he could do for her, a wish he could make happen. He thought about the zoo again, and about all the things that she said she wanted to do. He thought about the zoo and looked at the number on the back of the envelope and then he thought that it probably wouldn't ring and if it did she might not answer and before he had time to think of all the reasons why there was no point calling he had the phone to his ear and it was ringing.

It rang and rang and rang and rang and rang and then he

heard her voice. He would have assumed it was the start of the greeting on her voicemail if it hadn't been for the note of confusion, or maybe discomfort, in her 'Hello.' She was quiet too, almost whispering. He imagined her with her hand cupping her mouth and the phone so as not to be overheard answering.

'It's me.'

'Hi.'

She was polite but uneasy.

'Can you talk?'

There was a hesitation and then, 'Hold on.'

He heard the rustling and scraping of the phone being covered and then the muffled sound of what could have been a door closing and then after another few seconds the rustling and scraping of the phone being uncovered and brought back up to her face and then a 'Hi,' louder than before but still quiet, if less uneasy.

She said 'Hi' again, more relaxed this time, as if trying to reassure him that everything was alright. There was a pause while he waited for her to speak again, to lead the conversation, forgetting for a moment that he had called her, and when she didn't and he remembered, he apologised and said that he knew she had said that she'd call him but he'd wanted to . . . She finished the sentence for him. 'Check that the number worked? What's the matter, don't you trust me? Did you think I'd given you a dud?'

He choked on the smoke he was about to exhale, coughed a couple of times and tried to find some words to get out in his defence, something to cover his embarrassment at being found out, but before he could she laughed and told him that she was joking and that she was glad he'd called, she'd been thinking of him, she was actually about to call him to say that she'd booked the time off that she'd been talking about. Two whole weeks, in a couple of weeks' time. She'd been meaning to call to check that that was OK with him. Was it OK with him?

His eyes wandered around Peter's terrace as he tried to make sense of what she'd said and how that fitted with all of the things that he'd expected her to say. He searched the empty plant pots and garden furniture like he was searching for the thing that would make sense of the difference between this and everything he'd been imagining. Eventually she asked if he was still there because he'd been quiet so long, and when he replied that he was, she asked again, 'Well is it?'

He put his cigarette out in the pot next to his feet and said that it was, that it was perfect, that it would be great, that this was why he was calling, to see if she had been able to get any time off work, and if she had, when and what she wanted to do with it. He said he'd been thinking about all the things they'd talked about, thinking about all the things that they could do together.

'And what conclusion did you come to?'

After another overly long pause while he tried to remember exactly what it was he'd wanted to tell her, other than that he didn't believe that she wanted to take the time off, that he didn't think the number was real and that he felt like he couldn't trust a thing she said and that something about their afternoon in the hotel had felt like a test, he stumbled out the one other thing that he'd thought to say. 'I want to go to the zoo.'

Chapter Seventeen

He wakes up and he's alone.

His eyes suddenly open, suddenly aware.

He looks up at the grey of the ceiling.

He reaches a hand to feel the empty space next to him.

To be sure.

It's still warm.

He blinks and blinks again to see through the sleep. To try to focus.

The room's dark but there, a light coming from somewhere else in the flat filling it with a grey haze. Making the room visible. The ceiling, the light fitting, the grille of the air conditioning, the shelves, the picture frame, the chest of drawers, the wardrobe, all the things that tell him where he is.

He's in his room in Peter's flat. In bed. It's morning.

Almost morning.

The grey haze tells him that it's still dark outside.

The light coming from somewhere else in Peter's flat gives space and shape to his room. Making sides and corners. Picking out things. The bedside table. The lamp on it. The dark block of the clock which tells him it's 06:47. The chair with her coat and briefcase on it.

He hears her in the bathroom. The sound of water. A tap

being turned on and off. And on and off again.

He hears a clink. His toothbrush in the glass. The sound of the tap being turned on and off again.

The bathroom door must be open. The light spilling out through it making its way up the hall and into the bedroom.

He rolls over. To get a better view of the hall. To see her when she comes out of the bathroom.

There's a shadow. And then light. Then a shadow. Then light. Then a shadow and then light and then her walking up the hall. He watches her. He smiles.

He smiles as he watches her softly stride towards him. A dark figure haloed in the light making its way up the hall from the bathroom. A dark outline with swaying hips.

He smiles at her and maybe she smiles back.

She's already dressed. White shirt. Grey skirt. But no shoes.

He can hear her tights against her skirt as she walks into the bedroom and over to the chair.

She balances with a hand on the back of the chair to put on one shoe and then the other.

She adjusts her skirt. She adjusts her shirt.

She puts on her jacket. Adjusts the sleeves. Buttons it.

She takes her coat from the back of the chair, puts it over her arm. Picks up her briefcase.

She checks the chair. Checks she's got everything. She runs her free hand over the front of her jacket to check that she buttoned it.

She takes a couple of steps towards his side of the bed. Tiptoeing. Stealthy strides. So as not to wake him if he's still asleep. As if he's still asleep.

He watches her. His smile mirroring hers. Growing as she gets closer, as she moves her briefcase to the other hand, tucks her hair behind her ear, as she leans in.

He closes his eyes. Feels the warmth of her as she leans over him. Leans in to him. He feels the warmth of her breath on his lips. He feels her lips smile as they touch his. He feels their smile *widen as he kisses back. He feels a murmur of approval. He feels her pull away. He opens his eyes.*

Her lips smile wide and she says: 'Go back to sleep.'

She tucks her hair behind her ear again, leans in, kisses his lips and repeats the command: 'Sleep.'

He closes his eyes. Closes them tight. Tighter. Tighter. Laughing sleepily. Letting her know that he's doing as he's told. He keeps his eyes closed. Waiting for his reward. To feel the warmth of her over him. To feel her breath on his lips. To feel her lips widen into a smile. He keeps his eyes closed. Tight. Tighter.

He opens his eyes and hears the door to Peter's flat close.

The hall in darkness. The bathroom light turned out.

He wakes up and he's alone.

His eyes suddenly open, suddenly aware.

He looks up at the grey of the ceiling.

He reaches a hand to feel the empty space next to him. To be sure.

It's still warm.

He blinks and blinks again to see through the sleep. To try to focus.

The room's dark but there, a light coming from somewhere else in the flat filling it with a grey haze. Making the room visible. The ceiling, the light fitting, the grille of the air conditioning, the shelves, the pictures, all the things that tell him where he is.

He's in his room in Peter's flat. In bed. It's morning.

Almost morning.

The grey haze tells him that it's still dark outside.

The light coming from somewhere else in Peter's flat gives space and shape to his room. Making sides and corners. Picking out things. The bedside table. The lamp on it. The dark block of the clock which tells him it's 06:30. The chair with her coat and briefcase on.

He hears her in the bathroom. The sound of water. A tap being turned on and off. And on and off again.

He wakes up and he's alone.

    His eyes suddenly open, suddenly aware.

    He reaches a hand to feel the empty space next to him. To be sure.

    It's

He wakes up and he's alone.

    His eyes suddenly open, suddenly aware.

    The bedroom and hall in darkness. The bathroom light turned out.

He waits until they've come to a stop and the doors have opened before looking over his shoulder into the next carriage to check that she's still there, to make sure that this isn't where they're going. It isn't. She's still there. Still sitting in the aisle seat in the middle section of the carriage. Still dressed for a night out. Still reading the paper. Still looking completely at home.

    He wonders how much further they can be going. The station sign says Saint-Lazare. He looks at the map and counts the stops from Montparnasse where they got on. Nine. Nine times he's looked over his shoulder and seen her sitting in an aisle seat in the middle section of the carriage, dressed for a night out, reading a paper like someone who gets the Métro every day.

    The doors close and the train whirrs and the platform starts to move until it blurs and slides into darkness again. He looks at the map and then at the other passengers in his carriage. People heading home from work, people going to work, people going out for the evening. He looks along the crowded carriage, at the tops of the heads of people reading books, reading magazines and papers, people asleep. He looks at them in the hard synthetic light, all pushed together, a dark mass of heavy coats and scarves, forced into too-small spaces, not talking to each other, not looking at each other, trying not to be aware of anyone around them, each in their too-small world in their too-small space made smaller by the added bulk of bags and shopping and other people's coats. He looks at his fellow passengers and he wants to look back over his shoulder again to check that it really is her in the next carriage. He looks at the people pushed unhappily together, all dirty and tired in the hard yellow light and he can't believe that Sophie is there as one of them in the next carriage, reading the paper.

When he saw her heading down into the Métro at Montparnasse he wondered if he'd made a mistake, if in trying not to be noticed he'd lost sight of the real Sophie and was now following someone else. She made her way to the platform with the ease of someone who knew where they were going, not looking at signs, not phased at having to negotiate the flow of commuters. In all the time they were in Paris together she'd never once suggested that they take the Métro. Waiting on the platform at Montparnasse he'd wondered how far she was going. Too far to walk but not far enough to warrant a taxi, he decided.

Pulling into Trinité he gives up trying to make sense of it. Ten stops. The Sophie he knows would have taken a taxi. The doors open and he looks over his shoulder. She's still there. Still reading the paper. Not even looking up to see where they are. The Sophie he knows would have taken a taxi and would probably be wherever she's going by now. The doors close, the train whirrs and the platform starts to move until it blurs into darkness again.

He went straight to her office in the morning. He was there at seven. Waiting. When she still hadn't shown at eleven he went and sat outside the restaurant on the other side of the road and ordered a breakfast that he didn't eat. He drank two coffees, smoked cigarettes and tried to think of all the places she might be. When he couldn't think of any he tried to think of all the things he could do to try and find her if she never came back to the office again. When he couldn't think of any he decided to wait a while longer and ordered another coffee.

He saw her get out of a taxi about an hour later. She was in the office for half an hour, no more. At just gone three he paid the bill and followed her, from the safety of the other side of the road, along the Boulevard du Montparnasse, past the Vavin Métro entrance and up the Boulevard Raspail to the Mercure Hotel, where she went inside. He waited on the other side of the street for her, watching, wondering if this was her hotel or maybe the scene of one of her afternoon assignations, wondering if she'd come home for the night or if this was her 'screwing in the afternoon'. He watched the comings and goings, guests arriving and departing, businessmen and women checking in and out of a mid-priced business hotel. He watched the lights coming on in the hotel reception and in the rooms as it started to get dark, and he decided, with a mix of relief and excitement, that this wasn't a hotel of Sophie's fantasies, it was a hotel booked by a PA and paid for on expenses. He waited for an hour, maybe an hour and a half, the afternoon turning to early evening and getting colder as it got darker. When she came out she was still wearing the long dark coat, but everything else about her had changed. Her hair and make-up, her shoes, her tights, the black dress where the grey skirt of her suit should have been, all said that she was going out for the evening and that it wasn't for business purposes. Still on the other side of the street, he followed her back up to the Boulevard du Montparnasse, back past the Vavin Métro entrance, back past the nondescript glass and concrete facade of her office, all the way to Montparnasse Tower and down into the Métro.

Notre-Dame-de-Lorette. She's still there. Still reading her paper.

Saint-Georges. She's still there, though for the first time he sees her look up from her paper to see which station they're at.

Pigalle. The doors open and he looks over his shoulder. Someone else is reading the paper in her seat. He pushes his way towards the doors, trying to see out onto the platform, trying to see if she definitely got off, trying to see which way she might have gone. On the platform he looks but can't find her. The train whirrs and starts to move next to him. He follows the flow of people towards the exit. He looks at the backs of the heads of the people in front of him. He looks for her dark blond hair. He looks for her dark coat among all the other dark coats making their way up the steps.

He follows the office workers on their way to after-work drinks and the tourists on their way to see the Moulin Rouge, he follows them through the barriers and up the steps onto the street.

It's raining now. He looks up and down the street. None of it looks familiar to him. He looks for her but sees him first, the dark-haired man from the Jardin du Luxembourg. He sees him standing on the corner outside a restaurant. He sees him smile and open his arms wide and he sees Sophie walk into them to be swept up into an embrace. He sees them kiss. He sees them hug. He sees them pull apart and him take her hand and turn towards the restaurant. The dark-haired man from the Jardin du Luxembourg opens the door to the restaurant for her; she smiles, thanks him.

The rain turns to a light drizzle. Cold and saturating. Cars splash past him sheltering at a covered bus stop across the road from the restaurant. He can see them. Sitting at a table by the window. Their faces, their smiles, their eyes lit by candlelight. He can see them smile and laugh as they read the menu. He can see them smile and laugh as the waiter takes their order. He can see them lost in the moment, unable to take their eyes off each other, like they were once. Their eyes fixed on each other. Their eyes never straying. If they did, if either of them looked out of the window, looked across the road, through the rain to the bus stop, they would see him, cold and wet and unable to take his eyes off them. He watches them, unblinking, willing one or both of them to look his way, to meet his eyes, to see him, to feel him watching them. He watches them smile and laugh and longs to intrude, to have one or both of them notice, to make them feel his presence. He watches them talk and eat and drink and smile and laugh and look at each other in that way, watches them flirt with each other, and tries to think of ways he could make them focus on him for a moment, ways he could get their attention.

The restaurant looks warm and inviting. A glowing cliché of a Parisian bistro, made all the more touching and romantic by the lights and neon signs reflecting in the puddles collected between the cobbles in the street. He wants to go but he can't. He wants to leave them. To find somewhere warm and inviting of his own. He wants to walk across the street and take a seat at the table next to theirs. He wants to see her face, to see her reaction to him, cold and wet and dejected and replaced, and he wants to know what she would say and how she would explain him to the man who has replaced him. He wants to look into her eyes and see if there's any care left there for him. To see if she even recognises him, the him he is now.

They have a starter and a main. They skip dessert and go straight to coffee. Just as they used to. They finish the last of the wine and then the dark-haired man from the Jardin du Luxembourg pays the bill, helps her on with her coat, kisses her, smiles, says something that makes her laugh and leads her back to the door of the restaurant, which he holds open for her. She smiles, thanks him.

Outside on the street, the dark-haired man from the Jardin du Luxembourg helps her pull her hair from down the back of the collar of her coat. He turns up the collar of his own dark overcoat, puts on gloves and offers her his arm. She takes it, looping her arm through his and pulling herself tightly into him, the top of her head against his chin. He watches them start to walk off together, arm in arm, and he can feel the softness of her hair against his skin, the firmness of her as she pulls herself into him, he watches them walk away from the restaurant and he thinks he can smell her hair mingled with the sweetness of her perfume. He closes his eyes, he wants to savour the thought, the feeling, the memory that's so vivid that he can't quite place. He draws in a deep breath to take in every molecule of that smell. He breathes deep and hard and all he can smell is the damp of the rain.

He follows them. They cross the Place Pigalle and walk down another cobbled side street. They walk arm in arm, her pulling into him. As tight as she can. He follows them, getting closer and closer. He follows them at a distance that he knows isn't discreet and he doesn't care. He follows directly behind them. On the same side of the street. In their footsteps. So close he thinks he can almost hear pieces of their conversation, the edges of it, the sound of their voices at least, her voice saying what would be words if she wasn't pulled so tightly into him that only the occasional syllable can escape the two of them.

They turn right, into another narrow side street, like so many of the side streets he's walked down in Paris. They walk at a steady pace, faster because of the rain. They cross to the other side of the street, and he follows them past doorways which look more familiar to him, past shuttered shops whose graffitied fronts he thinks he recognises. Before they stop, before he mistakes his sense of recognition for déjà vu, he realises he's been there before and immediately knows exactly where he is.

He stops before they do and crosses back to the other side of the street and finds a doorway to step into and watch from. From the safety of the other side of the street he sees them stop in front of an anonymous doorway with no sign above it, just a black door and a brass plaque on the black wall next to it. He watches Sophie reach for what he knows is a buzzer above the plaque, the plaque which he knows bears only the word *Privé*. He watches her press the buzzer, watches them wait, watches them huddle together as the rain gets harder. He watches them pull tighter into each other. He watches them watching the black door. He hears the door buzz. He sees Sophie move her arm from around his and take his hand instead. He sees Sophie push at the door and lead him through it. He watches the door close behind them.

Chapter Eighteen

On the Monday and Tuesday of Sophie's first week off they went shopping. She said they could start in the West End, do Selfridges, Bond Street, Regent Street, get him sorted with all the basics and then they could spend a day East, in Brick Lane and Hoxton, looking for more interesting bits and pieces. He suggested the King's Road too. She said no, not the King's Road. She told him that she hated the King's Road. She hated all of Chelsea and Knightsbridge for that matter.

They went to Selfridges. She bought him shirts and trousers and shoes, smart and casual, along with a few of what she termed household essentials, including a new coffee machine and Egyptian cotton bedding, which was crisper and whiter than anything he had ever imagined sleeping in. He helped her pick out a pair of sunglasses which he told her made her look glamorous, like a French actress, but which she refused to let him pay for. She took him to Bond Street and bought him a wallet from Asprey's and a keyring from Tiffany's. He told her she didn't have to pay for everything, that he had plenty of Peter's money left and that he thought Peter would approve of the style in which she could help him spend it; he'd certainly approve of it being lavished in Asprey and Tiffany more than the meagre existence it was currently going on. She said she wouldn't hear of it. She said that this was the first time she'd taken off work in ages, that she was normally too busy earning money to ever have the time to spend it, and that he should stop protesting and let her enjoy her moment.

The next day they went East. She stayed over at Peter's flat and in the morning picked out an outfit for him from the previous day's purchases: denim shirt, slim-cut flat-fronted black trousers and black Chelsea boots. She said that he'd have to get used to dressing for different places and occasions, now that he had more than one option. With anyone else, with Audrey, he would have snapped back something bitter and mean at a comment like that, but she was having so much fun, she was clearly so happy to have someone to look after, to take care of, to think about, even if it was just about what to wear to go shopping with the hipsters in East London, that it never occurred to him to take offence. He didn't care what she bought or what he looked like in it, she was so excited, so enjoying him, so enjoying them. She did attempt to get him to try a hat in Spitalfields Market, at which he told her there was a line and hats were well and truly on the other side of it, yet it was half-hearted resistance. A small amount of pride mounting an even smaller defence against being made over too much into someone else. As it was, she confessed over a lunch of overpriced burgers and underseasoned fries that she wasn't particularly a fan of hats on men either. She thought only a particular type of man could get away with them, usually the less attractive kind, a man looking to distract from his face or cast a shadow over cruel eyes. She told him he was far too beautiful and kind to need one.

They spent the majority of the third day in bed, leaving it only briefly to bathe together in Peter's rolltop bath and then make a brunch of toast and eggs and coffee from his new machine, all of which they took back to bed. At one point he had suggested that they could go to the zoo, now that he had an appropriate wardrobe. She had shaken her head and said that today she wanted to make the most of the bedding she'd bought him.

The fourth day they went to the zoo. It was the Thursday of Sophie's first week off. The hottest day of the year so far, according to the news. The hottest day of the hottest June for more than a decade. Beautifully sunny, unseasonably warm, but still not hot enough for the little summer dress she wore. Another purchase that he helped her pick out that she wouldn't let him pay for. A flimsy little dress that the sun made see-through and the rain seemed to dissolve when they were caught in a sudden downpour in Little Venice. He'd taken her to see the houseboats on the canal on the way to the zoo. She said she'd never seen them. He told her that she'd love them and she did. From the little bridge at Warwick Avenue they stood and looked at the boats with their brightly coloured panels and colourful masses of geraniums spilling out of pots and jugs. She said that she'd like to live on one. Could he imagine it? The peace and quiet, the escape, the solitude, the wonderful soothing of being rocked to sleep at night by the gentle sway of the water. It was then that the heavens suddenly opened, pitting the calm surface of the canal with big fat raindrops of the kind that only ever fall in summer. The gentle patter was soon a violent assault that sent them running for the shelter of the awning of a nearby coffee shop. There they stood shivering in the warmth of the mid-morning sun, watching the rain pour down off the edge of the awning, him with his arms around her, feeling the cold wetness of her little summer dress and the softness of her skin underneath it; her pulling his arms around her, shivering, trying to get warm.

The rain lasted only minutes and by the time they'd walked to the zoo the sun had all but dried out the streets and pavements and her little summer dress. The zoo was nothing like he remembered or she had feared. The lions and tigers and giraffes were all still resident, only the elephants and rhinos had been relocated and she said that much as she liked an elephant, she could live without seeing one.

They watched the gorillas lazing in the sun and the penguins diving to the depths of their new pool, the one that replaced the art deco pool from his memories of school trips to the zoo. In fact all of the zoo, apart from the jutting mesh roof of the aviary and the towers of the giraffe house had changed. The stark walled enclosures were replaced by naturalistic settings which mimicked the great plains of Africa or the jungles of Sumatra. They walked hand in hand from Asia to Africa to America, from the Antarctic to the Outback, from day to night, watching monkeys chase each other and hippos cool off, seeing porcupines parade their sharp spines and kangaroos bounce effortlessly by. They stopped to have lunch in the cafe and then watched the pelicans have theirs, catching fish in their long beaks as it was thrown to them by the shovelful.

The whole time they were there Sophie didn't once stop smiling. He'd never seen anyone happier. She kept asking him if he was having a good time, and all he could manage in reply was a broad grin at how cute she was, how beautiful she was, how lovable she was in that moment, in the sunglasses and little summer dress that he'd helped her choose, smiling the happiest of smiles, a smile that shut everything else out and made only that space and that moment matter. The smile that people have in mind when they imagine never having a care in the world. He laughed and said that he didn't have to ask if she was having a good time, if she was happy, to which she went shy and blushed and the smile got bigger. She was the one who suggested going to sit on Primrose Hill.

The thick heat of the afternoon which had built up in the zoo was whisked away by the breeze at the spot where they finally collapsed, halfway up the hill. They'd started to race each other up, her getting a head start, shouting back that she'd see him at the top, him almost catching her before they both ran out of steam and dropped to the grass. Below the most amazing view of London was laid out before them, the BT Tower, Centre Point, the jutting aviary of the zoo and the tightly packed greenery and acres of open space of Regent's Park, the Eye in the distance, yet neither of them moved to look at it. Lying on the grass, Sophie next to him, his fingers sliding between the blades of cool grass, he was enjoying the breath of the breeze across his face too much to commit to the effort needed to sit up. Minutes passed and then Sophie's head was on his chest and her hand was stroking his stomach through his shirt, her fingers finding the skin between the buttons, playing with the hairs that covered it. After a time she asked him what he was thinking.

He didn't answer straight away, at first pretending not to

have heard and then assuring her as unconvincingly as he could manage that he wasn't thinking anything. He felt a sharp pull at the hairs on his stomach, her response to his teasing refusal to share. Another minute passed. The breath of the breeze, the weight of her head on his chest, her hand on the skin and hairs of his stomach, the tickle of the grass on his palm as he ran his hand over it, he was thinking how perfect all of it was, how happy he was in this moment and how saying so would never be enough to make her feel how he was feeling, his only hope of her understanding being that she was feeling it too. He felt her fingers tighten, ready to tug at the hairs again. He felt her smile and felt the movement of her mouth as she asked, again, what he was thinking.

He smiled a smile that he knew she couldn't see and thought it all again, how perfect it was, how happy he was, how soothed he was by the breeze and how totally in love he was with her. Another tug at the hairs and a demand of 'Tell me,' followed by a repeat of the question 'What are you thinking?' and he finally relented. 'That I think I love you.'

Another minute passed.

She didn't say anything.

She didn't have to.

He was sure he could feel her smile.

He was certain, as certain as he'd ever been about anything, that she was feeling the same as him. He sensed it in her, in the lightness of her body against his, in the shallowness of her breathing and the way her fingers had stopped playing with the hairs on his stomach and were now still and weightless against his skin. He could feel her contentment, how happy she was in that moment. He could feel her smile and he knew that she understood. That she felt it too. The longer she went without saying anything, the longer he waited, the more certain he was that he could feel her smile widen, her contentment turning to mischief. Now it was her turn to tease.

He waited. He let the breeze soothe him, let the grass tickle the palm of his hand, let her have her moment. He waited and then when he felt she would probably burst if he didn't ask her, he returned her question.

178

'What are you thinking?'

She didn't say anything.

She didn't have to.

He felt her tense as soon as he went to speak and hold her breath so as not to give anything away.

He played along. He asked again.

'What are you thinking?'

Still she didn't say anything, so he jabbed her gently in the ticklish spot at her waist and added a 'Tell me,' followed by a repeat of the question: 'What are you thinking?'

At once he felt her head move and heard her say, 'That I'm cold and I should have brought a jacket.'

With that she sat up, pulled his rolled-up jacket from under his head, put it over her shoulders and said, 'And that I'm hungry. Let's go and get something to eat.'

He smiled, propped himself up on one arm and, undeterred by her evasiveness, tried again: 'Tell me what you're thinking first.'

'That I'm hungry and we should find somewhere to eat.'

The next morning he woke to find her already dressed and collecting together her things into the overnight bag she'd brought with her. He asked what she was doing, what time it was, where she was going. She told him to go back to sleep, that she needed to go home to pick up some other bits and pieces, that she would be back soon enough. Still half asleep, he couldn't think quickly enough to pick holes in anything she'd said. He asked when she would be back, she said soon and told him again to go back to sleep. As she got to the end of the hall, as she opened Peter's front door, she looked back and gave him a half-smile and quietly said she'd call him, soon.

When he woke up properly on the morning of the fifth day of Sophie's two weeks off, he wasn't sure if he'd imagined their earlier conversation or her promise to call him, soon, or what that might actually mean. All he knew was that her side of the crisp white sheets was cold and she was nowhere to be found in Peter's flat.

He didn't hear the phone in the hall ring while he was in the shower. When he came out of the bathroom and heard the answering machine bleep, his insides stiffened to quickly shut the door to the wave of sadness that he knew the message would bring, but not quickly enough. He listened. It was Sophie. She said that she was really sorry to run out on him like that, she'd realised that she hadn't brought enough clothes and toiletries with her and had gone home to pick up a few things and when she got home she'd found messages on her home phone from the office asking her to call, there'd been some kind of emergency and they'd been trying to get hold of her and they needed her to come in right away, apparently they'd also been leaving messages on her mobile, which she'd left at home precisely because she didn't want to be disturbed by work, but now she'd got the message she couldn't help herself and she'd called and it was indeed an emergency and she was going to have to go in and would probably have to work all weekend and definitely all next week, so they'd have to take a rain check on their second week off together, she was sorry, she hoped he'd understand, she'd call him, soon, there was no point him calling her as she'd be too busy to pick up, she was sorry. She hung up. The machine beeped to signify the end of the message.

He picked up the phone and called her back.

Dripping all over Peter's hall, holding a towel around his waist, he stood and listened to her phone ring in his ear, then go to voicemail as promised.

Chapter Nineteen

She's laughing.

> *Running for cover from the rain, his jacket over her head.*
> *Splashing through puddles.*
> *Her dress almost see-through. Sticking to her skin.*
> *He waits and watches her. Running to him. His jacket over her head. Running for his outstretched hand. Running to catch up. Laughing as she loses her sandal again. Hopping back to reclaim it.*
> *He waits and watches. Rain running down the back of his head, down his neck, trickling down between his shoulders, down to the small of his back. Rain running down his forehead. To his eyes. To his mouth. Rain running along his outstretched arm.*
> *He waits and watches her running and laughing. He watches the tips of his fingers, waiting to feel the touch of hers. He watches her, her outline, her hips and her breasts, made clear and naked, her little summer dress barely there.*
> *He holds out a hand to her, waiting for her to catch up.*
> *He hears her laugh and splash.*
> *He sees the outline of her underwear. The white of her knickers.*
> *He feels the grab of her fingers and turns to run with her for the shelter of the awning of the coffee shop.*

She's laughing.

Shaking her hands and arms.

Shaking the rain off her. Pulling her wet dress away from her skin.

Her little summer dress. Wet and clinging.

She's shivering.

Wet hair stuck to the side of her face. Drips dripping from the ends of it. Beads of water running down her neck to her chest. Rolling between her breasts. Drips dripping onto her arms and rolling down their tanned and goosebumped skin.

She's shivering and laughing.

Soaked through but happy. Her little summer dress clinging to every bump. Every curve. The cold of it against her skin making her shudder. Making her teeth chatter. Making her laugh hard enough to be heard above the sound of the rain on the awning. Almost as loud as the water cascading off it and down the pavement to Little Venice.

He reaches out to her.

Pulls her close.

Pulls her backwards into him.

He pulls her wet hair back. Smooths and squeezes it, wrings what he can from the ends and places it over her shoulder. He leans in to kiss the back of her neck, to smell her damp hair, to watch drips from the end of it fall and roll down between her goosebumped breasts.

He runs his hands down her arms then slips them under and round her waist. Pulling her back. Pulling her in. Pulling her close until he can feel her shiver through him.

He pulls her in tighter. Smelling her hair and her neck. Feeling the cold wetness of her dress on his arms and the warmth of her coming through it.

He holds her tight and feels her shiver.

He kisses the top of her ear and breathes into her.

She laughs.

A small, contented laugh. Full of happiness.

He feels her relax into him.
He feels her shiver ease.

He watches the windows of the hotel. His eyes wandering over its seven storeys. Drifting from one balcony to the next. Travelling left and down and back and right and up and forward in no particular pattern, looking for signs and clues, shivers of the opaque white curtains, hints that she's behind them, proof that she's in there with him.

He lets his eyes search for her of their own accord because he can't bring himself to direct them. He doesn't want to find her there. He wants to concentrate on the ground-floor restaurant in the hope of finding her lunching with a client or colleague, a reasonable explanation for why she should have led him to a hotel on the Avenue de l'Opéra at midday. But it's no good. His eyes have already registered all of the beautiful details of the grand facade of the Hôtel Édouard VII: the elegantly carved stonework, the deep red of the awnings above each of the floor-to-ceiling windows, the ornate ironwork of the balconies, the overflowing greenery of the window boxes attached to them, details which tell him that this is definitely a hotel of Sophie's fantasies.

The noise of the traffic of the Avenue de l'Opéra makes him think she could have taken a quieter room, something at the back of the hotel, facing a courtyard, overlooking the tables and chairs and potted plants and managed hush of a restaurant or breakfast-room terrace. He tries to focus on the possibility, to concentrate on how pointless it would make his watching of the windows overlooking the Avenue de l'Opéra. He extends the thought to how ridiculous the whole thing is, his waiting and watching, hoping to catch a glimpse of something he doesn't want to see but somehow can't resist looking for. He tries to make an argument for giving up and going home, or at least abandoning his post for now and starting again tomorrow: if she has taken a room at the rear of the hotel he'll see nothing where he is, and when she leaves and he follows her back to her office or to a restaurant or to her hotel, he'll know no more and feel no closer to her than he does now watching from the distance of the other side of the Avenue de l'Opéra.

He allows himself to be distracted by the movement of people passing by on the pavement. He feels the pull of them, wonders where they're going, what they've got waiting for them, where they have to be. He feels the attraction of their movement and wishes he could join them, wishes he could just pick one to follow and see where they lead him. He tries to imagine that it is actually a possibility, that it's what he really wants, that he might even do it. But his eyes are already scanning the hotel's windows again, more intently now, this time directed by him and by his need to find something to keep him there just a little while longer.

He goes from window to window, thinking he should go, searching for a reason to stay. He studies each in turn, looking, assessing and moving on, moving in order now from one to the next, no longer passive, an active, focused, methodical participant. He starts dividing windows into groups of five, running from one to five and back again, looking for signs of change, before moving on to the next five and the next five and the next five. The more focused and methodical he becomes in his work, the calmer and happier he is. He feels the sadness expand in him – not rising up from the bottom of his stomach to the top of his throat and making it hard to take anything but the most shallow of breaths as it usually does, rather growing fuller and round, filling him, filling the empty space where everything else used to be. It's not the same as the feeling of contentment or wellbeing, but it's a close substitute. He likes it. This feeling of active sorrow. It's not helpless. It has the same effect that he imagines anger or bitterness might have if he was the kind of person to feel them – which as far as he can remember, even when Peter died and she left him, he never has been.

He moves along the groups of five, window by window, studying each for the exact same amount of time. After the fifth window he returns to the fourth and then the third and then the second and then the first and then back to the fifth, comparing and contrasting each with its previous self, looking for changes, for things that are out of place or different. After travelling back and forth through each set two or three times he moves on to the next, and then the next, and then up or down a row depending on which floor he was on last.

Back and forth along each of the seven floors of the Hôtel Édouard VII he searches, and then, to be sure, up and down in columns, first single file, then in stacks of groups of five. In the interests of thoroughness and to give him something to do, he repeats and repeats the exercise, working in different variations on the theme as they occur to him, gradually getting more and more hypnotised by the counting and checking off of windows which all look the same. Gradually being consumed by the act and forgetting what it is he's looking for. So much so that he almost doesn't see it. He's not actually sure that he did. Something on the fourth floor. Fourth window from the left. Or the fifth. He can't be certain. He looks back, watches for a moment and sees nothing in either. Nothing different to all the other times he's looked at them. Just the opaque white curtains, hanging motionless, with no signs of movement behind them.

He goes back to the beginning of the row and re-examines each window in turn, coming to rest on the third and fourth windows from the left, which for some reason he imagines are attached to the same room. He watches both windows at once, trying not to focus on either, trying not to look too hard for fear of seeing what's not there, or missing something important. He watches, not focusing, barely breathing, unaware of anyone or anything around him. The sound of the Avenue de l'Opéra fades. The people, the cars, the buses, the scooters and bikes, the taxis, everything other than those two windows and their opaque white curtains ceases to register. And then he sees it. Whatever it is. A man. A woman. Someone. Possibly. Movement he can sense more than see. He watches for another long minute and then sees it again, only this time he feels sure it's a man, and at the same time certain, for whatever reason, that the person before was a woman; that there are two people, a couple.

The opaque white curtain moves, as if on the breeze or through the touch of someone passing it. He watches, fixated, and sees it again, this time it's a woman, he's sure he can see the silhouette or shadow of a woman, and the certainty that the outline he thinks he can make out is that of a woman makes him think that she must be either naked or in no more than underwear, or why would he think her to be so distinctly feminine. His eyes don't move from the curtains of the two windows. He doesn't blink for fear of missing something that could confirm or disprove everything he's thinking: that it's her and him, in there together. He senses the other figure, the man, taller, maybe with dark hair, move past both windows and then nothing. No movement. No figures, real or imagined, seen or sensed, move past the windows again. The white opaque curtains hang still. He knows for certain that there's nothing further to see because his eyes stay locked to the spot, trying to see or imagine what's behind the curtains of the two windows on the fourth floor.

He's so intent on the windows of the fourth floor that he almost doesn't see her leave. Something, a sixth sense when it comes to her, calls his attention to the street below to see her standing on the pavement, doing up her coat, pulling her hair from down the back of her collar. He recognises it immediately, that look, the composure, the togetherness. She looks exactly as she did when she arrived, not a hair out of place, not even slightly ruffled, her suit, her coat, professional, perfect, exactly as they should be, exactly as they always were every time she left him in bed in a hotel.

She stands in front of the hotel doors for a minute or more, almost directly opposite him, looking up and down the Avenue de l'Opéra, looking for something in particular, not seeing him. She doesn't look in his direction and he doesn't worry that she might, convinced as he is of her inability to see him now. He watches her from across the Avenue de l'Opéra. At first he thinks she might be looking for a taxi, then after several free taxis pass without her moving to hail them, he wonders if she might be looking for someone.

He watches her look at her watch and then back up and down the Avenue de l'Opéra. She looks at her watch again and he thinks she must be expecting someone to meet her there, in front of the hotel, and then he watches her open her briefcase and take out her phone and answer it.

He watches her face light up. He watches her smile a wide, pleased and welcoming smile. He wonders who it is that's lucky enough to have that effect on her. He wonders if it's him, if maybe they weren't in the hotel together after all, if he's been letting his imagination run away with him again, maybe it really was an innocent lunch meeting. He watches her smile and wonders what her smile would be like if he was calling her. Her wide, pleased smile softens into something more attentive as she listens and takes in what the person on the other end is saying. He thinks that maybe it's the person she's expecting to meet, perhaps they're calling to say they've been delayed, perhaps they're telling her that they're going to have to cancel or reschedule. She smiles. She laughs. She laughs again and smiles and turns and starts walking off in the direction of the Métro.

He stays where he is on the other side of the Avenue de l'Opéra, letting her get a little ahead of him before following. He waits and watches her walk, still on the phone, her head rolling back and to the side in a way that he knows means she's laughing. He watches the back of her head, he watches her laughing at whatever the person on the phone is saying and then he turns back to the hotel and the fourth floor to have one last look before moving off after her. The curtains behind the third and fourth windows from the left are still and untouched. There's no movement. No sign of anyone behind them. No sense of anyone there.

He moves to look away, to find her again on the street, and then something, a sixth sense about the situation or a movement almost too slight to perceive, causes his eyes to flick back up to the windows of the fourth floor. To the third window from the left. The glass of the floor-to-ceiling door catches the light as it opens and the dark-haired man from the Jardin du Luxembourg steps out onto the balcony and lights a cigarette. He takes a long drag and exhales into the cold air, tipping his head back, watching his breath and smoke disappear into the grey afternoon. His shirt is untucked from his trousers, the buttons at the top and bottom undone. He takes another drag on the cigarette, exhales more frozen breath and smoke, and, as if suddenly feeling the cold, puts the cigarette back between his lips and buttons his shirt to the neck and tucks the bottom of it into his trousers. He leans into the room and retrieves his suit jacket from behind the curtain. He puts it on and then takes the cigarette from his mouth with one hand and runs the other back through his dark hair, brushing the front of it from his face.

He watches the dark-haired man from the Jardin du Luxembourg from the other side of the Avenue de l'Opéra almost excitedly, transfixed, unable to look away. It feels like the first time the two of them have really been alone together, the first chance they've had to really get to know each other or at least for him to properly take in the details and understand who he is. He watches the dark-haired man from the Jardin du Luxembourg smoking, watching him take drag after drag on his cigarette and repeatedly brush the front of his hair back from his face as he leans on the balcony, watching him survey the long sweep of the Avenue de l'Opéra, seeing all the people below yet somehow unaware of the man watching him from the other side of the street.

He watches the dark-haired man as much in admiration as jealousy, noting the handsome features and athletic frame of a successful middle-aged man who's looked after himself. More than that, there's a sense about him of a measured calm, an assuredness that even from a distance is attractive. He watches him take one last drag on his cigarette and thinks he can see the attraction, not just of him, but of being him and being with him. He watches his ease, his relaxed manner, and understands why she would choose to replace him with him.

He watches the dark-haired man from the Jardin du Luxembourg stub out his cigarette on the ironwork of the balcony and then bury the evidence in the window box attached to it, and he knows that if he were her, of the two of them, he would probably make the same choice she has. He watches him run his hand through his dark hair once more and then turn and disappear back behind the opaque white curtain, and for the first time since being aware of his existence, he feels that the man with the dark hair and the handsome features and athletic frame of a successful middle-aged man who's looked after himself whom he'd never seen before he saw him in the Jardin du Luxembourg isn't really competition for Sophie's affections. He already has them. Completely.

He feels the sadness expand and make itself more comfortable inside him, soothing away any last lingering knots of anger as he watches the window and the motionless curtain behind it, hoping to catch one last glimpse of the man who has come to take his place, a man he's not convinced he'll ever be. Then he remembers the reason he's standing there and turns back to the Avenue de l'Opéra and the direction of the Métro and realises that she's nowhere to be seen.

He strains to see, to look over and past all the people who must be hiding her, all the pedestrians and cars and buses between him and the other side of the Avenue de l'Opéra, the advertising hoardings and newspaper kiosks and traffic lights between him and the entrance to the Métro which must somehow be obscuring his view or at least his view of her. He starts walking, his eyes fixed on the other side of the wide road, concentrating on the people four lanes of traffic away, repeatedly knocking into those passing next to him. He feels the sadness shift and curdle inside him, churned and pushed aside by a tight knot of panic which gets tighter with each faltering step. The knot tightens and his steps quicken and, still searching the other side of the road and finding it hard to breathe, he breaks into a run, an upright, below-the-knees run, propelled and constricted by the panic of having lost her.

A chased man running from an invisible spectre, he collides with everyone who doesn't step aside quick enough, the constant assault of shoulders and French swear words not distracting his attention from the distant pavement and the lack of her on it. He looks back and across the two blocks between where he was and the entrance to the Métro he's running towards. Seeing all the same people, with the only additions and subtractions coming from and at the Métro, he reaches the already comforting conclusion that if she's not on the pavement above, she must be on the platform below, waiting for a train. His eyes retrace the steps he imagines her to have taken, to be sure. He quickens to a full-stride run as the thought that the Métro is the only place left for her to be, the only place she could have disappeared so completely into, becomes a self-certified fact. He abandons the pavement opposite for his own, focusing on where he's going, the platform with Sophie waiting on it now his goal.

At the end of the next block he waits as patiently as he can for the green man of the pedestrian crossing to see him across the Avenue de l'Opéra's four busy lanes of traffic. His eyes flit between the lights and the Métro entrance opposite as he imagines her standing on the platform, waiting. Buses and delivery vans pass by, intermittently obscuring his view of the entrance, as he imagines the Métro slowly pulling into the platform. As the buses and vans form a steady stream, completely blocking his view of the lights and the entrance, he imagines the doors opening and then closing behind her, the train jolting and taking her away from him, all before he can make it across the road and down the steps.

The stream of buses and vans comes to an end and his view across the Avenue de l'Opéra is restored. He looks first to the entrance of the Métro, almost to check that it's still there, and then to the woman staring at him from the other side of the Avenue de l'Opéra, frozen mid-action, her purse in one hand and an open briefcase and a sandwich bag from the Paul's boulangerie behind her in the other. For a moment something about her feels familiar. There's a jolt of recognition which makes him study the long dark coat and the grey suit skirt, the dirty blond hair and the look of sick panic on her face. It's the expression he doesn't recognise. The fear and vulnerability in it are so intense and distorting, they make him think that maybe he doesn't know her after all. Then they too feel suddenly familiar. He realises a moment too late that he's seen that sick, panicked look once before, in the reception of Sophie's office on the one occasion he surprised her by meeting her from work. By the time he's brought this Sophie to mind, she's already running down the steps into the Métro.

He makes it down onto the platform to find her waiting impatiently halfway along it, her gaze flicking between the departure screen and the stairs and the blackness of the tunnel. Though anxiously scanning commuters as they descend and file along, she doesn't see him either on the stairs or the platform. He knows this from the sudden jolt of shock that he feels through her when he says her name and touches her arm from behind and from the horror he sees in her eyes when she turns to look at him.

At first she's so frozen to the spot that she doesn't try to move or pull away. Then the shock transforms itself into a fury, a quiet yet determined anger with which she yanks her arm free of his hand.

'Leave me alone.'

The words lash out at him despite being kept under her breath to avoid a scene.

'I'm warning you. Stay away from me.'

'I'm sorry, I didn't mean to scare you. I just need to talk to you.'

'Didn't mean to scare me?'

'No. I'm sorry.'

'Didn't mean to scare me? What are you even doing here? How long have you been in Paris? How long have you been following me? You are following me, I mean, I have got that right? Right?'

He doesn't say anything.

'How did you even know I was here, in Paris? How did you find me?'

He can feel her eyes searching his face, but he can't raise his own to meet them.

'What are you doing here? How many times do I have to tell you? When will you get it?'

'I came here to explain. To put things right between us.'

'Put things right? Are you actually deranged?' Her voice rises to a whispered shout. 'You think that this is how you go about making things better? By stalking me? It was bad enough when you were calling all the time. Now you're actually following me, to another country. And what, you've been following me all around Paris, watching me go about my business, business that has nothing whatsoever to do with you, skulking in doorways to see where I'm going and what I'm doing and who I'm doing it with? You're mad. You need help. Get the message. I'm not interested. It's too late. If you really cared about us you wouldn't have done what you did. But you did and now it's too late. Whatever you've got to say, I'm not interested. I wasn't interested before and now, now I definitely don't want to know.'

'Who is he?'

This time it's her who doesn't say anything. He watches her eyes harden and her mouth hesitate as if searching for an answer.

'Who is he?'

'None of your business. That's who he is. Now fuck off.'

'Did you bring him to Paris like you did me, or is he the reason you came here?'

'You're the reason I came here.'

He looks in her eyes and sees hatred and a loathing which her glare burns into him, and for an instant all he wants to do is hurt her.

'Is it serious or another one of your fleeting amusements? Like I was.'

He watches the loathing give way to confusion. 'What's Audrey been saying?'

'How long until you get bored with him?'

The Métro pulls into the platform.

'Just stay away from me.'

She turns to watch the Métro cars pass and slow. As they come to a stop she goes to move towards the nearest door of the nearest carriage. He reaches out and grabs her arm, tightening his grip on it as soon as he feels the sleeve of her coat. Instinctively she tries to continue towards the open carriage door which the surrounding commuters file into. Her forward motion and his tightened grip combine to create the effect of him yanking her back and spinning her around, a sudden jolt which instinctively has her yell, 'Let go of me,' at the top of her voice. The scene that she had tried to avoid but which his grabbing and her yelling have instantly created cause a passenger already on the Métro, a tall black businessman, to shout '*Monsieur*' and step back onto the platform. With one stride the tall black businessman is at her side with a large firm hand on his offending wrist, pulling it free of her arm, commanding him to '*Arrêt, arrêt, arrêt.*'

Her arm free, Sophie runs to the carriage like she's running for her life, the tall black businessman following as soon as she's safely on board. The drama over, and with all the other passengers staring out at the lone madman on the platform, eyeing him with horror and disgust, the doors close and the Métro starts to pull away.

Chapter Twenty

He sat in the reception, on the low sofa facing the three canvases of modern art, and looked again at the piece of paper in his hand. He looked without reading, knowing the details by heart already, but still feeling the need to check them off, the dates, the times, the Brighton address, the Brighton telephone number, the charge for the double room with sea view, his credit card, as if to confirm that they were there and that he'd really done it. Satisfied that they were, he refolded the booking confirmation and returned it to the inside pocket of the suit she'd bought for him, and went back to waiting for her – an overwhelming sense of contentment making him relax into his seat, the knowledge that he was about to do something good, about to surprise her with something he knew would make her happy, bringing a smile to his face.

He watched the steady stream of workers file through the security barriers, eager to put another day at the office behind them, wishing colleagues a good night, occasionally coming over to hug and kiss someone waiting with him on the low sofas. The comforting sound of heels and voices reverberating around the marble and glass of the reception filled his head and shifted his thoughts from how long he'd been sitting there and whether she might be in the next lift, to what her reaction would be when he told her that he had a surprise for her, that she'd been working too hard and he was going to take her away from it all, that he'd booked it, exactly as she'd said, Brighton, a sea view, chip fat and vinegar in the air. Having lost one of their two weeks together to work, the least she deserved was a dirty weekend in Brighton, he heard himself say. And there was more, he'd booked a table for tonight at one of her favourite restaurants, Quaglino's, he would tell her, although there was no mention of the sneak peek at her work diary which had told him just how much of a favourite it was, and in his imagined version of events she wouldn't think to ask how he knew to choose it. Then finally his thoughts drifted to her finding him there, in reception, unexpected and unannounced, waiting patiently to meet her from work, and what her reaction might be to being surprised that way. To that and everything else he only imagined happiness and excitement, equal to the happiness and excitement he'd been feeling ever since he'd decided to surprise her with dinner at her favourite restaurant and the news that he'd booked her fantasy weekend away. He didn't think about the one previous occasion he'd met her from work, when he'd suggested waiting in reception and she'd asked if he could wait in the coffee shop across the road instead, explaining that she couldn't guarantee she'd be out on time and it would be better for him, more comfortable, to get a coffee and wait for her there. He didn't think about it because it didn't occur to him that there was anything to think about.

It was only that morning that he'd decided that a surprise was what she needed. He hadn't seen her since she'd cut short her holiday for work that couldn't wait, and in the three weeks that had passed he'd only spoken to her once on the phone, when, after a week's worth of voicemails, she'd finally called him back, but then only to say that she was sorry, she was still busy and that she'd call him to talk properly when she could. He hadn't been surprised that it had taken so long for her to reply to his messages. The first few that he'd left had been blunt and to the point, angry and more than a touch sarcastic. He'd been looking at things solely from his point of view, saying that he felt hurt and rejected and couldn't see how else he was meant to feel, or how else she wanted him to feel given that she'd chosen work over him, left while he was asleep like she was ditching a one-night stand and, one brief answerphone message aside, she hadn't even tried to explain or apologise. After a couple more messages along similar lines, he told her that he was sorry, he'd got over himself and would stop behaving like a child, and he understood that work was important to her, more than important to her, and she was committed to it, and he loved that about her, and it actually made him love her more, and he was sorry, he was fine with it, if she could call when she could, he'd love to hear from her. He left another saying that he hoped she wasn't working too hard and that he'd love to see her, and then another saying that he just wanted to hear the sound of her voice, and then one more saying he was sorry for leaving all of these messages, she must think him a spoiled child or something and that he wouldn't call again, that he'd wait to hear from her. It was after that message that she called. He was at home, on Peter's terrace smoking, when his mobile rang. He didn't even look to see who it was, he was so sure it was her. He answered with a Hi how are you? She replied, with a Fine, but I can't really talk, I just wanted you to know that I'm sorry I walked out on you, sorry I haven't been in touch, I don't think you sound like a spoiled child and I'll call you to talk properly as soon as I can. He told her again that he loved her. She told him that she had to go.

For the next couple of days he was contented by a new sense of connection to her, feeling that they were closer than ever in a strange way, now that he had been able to act like an idiot and not scare her off. Then as he started a third week of not seeing her, he started to think about how hard she worked, how busy she always seemed to be, and the tone of her voice in their last conversation took on a tired and anxious lilt as he replayed the memory of it over and over. He started to feel an unease about her voice and what he was reading into it: that she had taken on more than she could cope with, that things might be starting to come apart for her, that she needed someone or something to rescue her, or at least something to look forward to. That's when he thought of Brighton, and the chip fat and vinegar and sea air.

As the number of office workers filing through the security barriers began to dwindle, so too did his attention to them, the activity of the reception fading to vague colours and occasional movement, the centre of his focus blurring to a happy daze of contentment. The sense of someone standing next to him and the sound of a familiar voice asking what he was doing there woke him out of it.

He looked up at the person next to him, not surprised to see her but thrown by the discomfort, almost panic in her face.

She asked again what he was doing there and then made a small but to him discernible effort to affect a smile, managing only half of one with no conviction or pleasure in it.

'That's not happiness to see me, is it?' he said, looking up at her.

The sides of her smile pulled wider, with extra effort or enthusiasm, he couldn't tell which.

'Try surprise,' she replied, her mouth relaxing and softening into something more welcoming.

Sensing that he may well have misread surprise as hostility, he stood and said, 'Surprised in a good way, I hope?' and leaned in to kiss her, but she pulled away, making it into a two-cheeked continental kiss of polite acquaintances, apologising as she did so, very quietly, saying: 'Not here, it's not professional.'

By the time they got to the restaurant she seemed to have adjusted to the unexpected turn her evening had taken. Her moments of distance on the way there he took for preoccupation with work, or at least that's what she told him they were and he saw no reason to doubt her. Eventually she seemed to come back to him and leave whatever else she was thinking about to one side long enough for him to believe that, while she was clearly distracted, she was pleased to see him.

They arrived early, a full hour before their reservation. Considerately, he thought, he had allowed time for them to go back to hers so she could change before dinner, a suggestion she quickly batted away with 'I'm starving, let's just eat.' When he'd told her he'd booked a table at Quaglino's, she'd barely reacted. She made no mention of the fact that it was one of her favourite restaurants, she didn't even acknowledge that she'd been there before; on the contrary, her only comment, that she'd heard good things about it, implied the opposite. When they walked in he looked for signs of recognition, first from the maître d' as he showed them to the bar, and then from the bar staff who furnished them with wine and a selection of nuts, olives and miniature breadsticks to sustain them for what the maître d' apologetically confirmed would almost certainly be an hour's wait for their table. As the maître d' smiled and promised to do everything he could to make it less, he thought he caught a flicker of something which could have been an acknowledgement of having welcomed Sophie before, or could just as easily have been the familiar way he went about making all of his customers feel like welcome regulars. In Sophie he saw nothing to suggest that it was anything more, and if it was, the flatness of her smile discouraged the maître d' from pursuing it.

A drink in and their conversation was again as easy and relaxed as usual, if a little vague when it came to the work that had been keeping her away from him. All she would offer was that there was a lot of it, that it was complicated and she was grateful to have a night off from it. She smiled and raised her glass and said, 'Seriously, thank you,' and having clinked and sipped, she added, 'and I'm sorry about earlier, at the office. I was surprised and stressed and didn't mean to seem ungrateful. I am grateful, really. It's just that I've had a lot going on and . . . well, you know how it is.'

He nodded and said that he did. He put his glass down on the bar and took her hands in his. He repeated that he knew how it was, which was why he thought she deserved a night away from it. 'And speaking of getting away from it,' he said, 'I've got something else, another surprise.' Her eyes widened and her familiar mischievous grin returned a playfulness to her lips and her face which had been missing all evening. 'Really?' she said, trying to read his face. 'Will I like it?'

'Definitely.'

'It wasn't expensive, was it, you know I don't want you spending money on me, you know you don't have to do that, don't you?' She eyed him with suspicion, ready to both reprimand and thank him for going against her instructions.

'It's all relative, but if it was, hopefully it will be worth it.'

'Intriguing.' She edged forward on her seat and leaned in to him. 'Tell me.'

Her phone started vibrating on the bar.

Before he'd registered the source of the buzzing, she'd pulled her hands from his and was reaching to pick it up. He couldn't see the caller ID, but as soon as she did the tension and discomfort he'd been so surprised to find in her face earlier returned and she was on her feet, moving away from him. 'I'm sorry. I've got to take this.' She was halfway down the steps to the front door before he saw her say hello.

She was still on the phone, smoking and pacing up and down outside the restaurant, when he came to find her to tell her that their table was ready. She'd been gone ten minutes or more, and when the maître d' had come to say he had a table for them, he'd been grateful for the excuse to go and find her.

'I know, I'm sorry. I can't get out of it,' he heard her say as he stepped out from the comfortably controlled climate of the restaurant into the evening's dense summer air. 'Not right now, no. I will. As soon as I can.' She punctuated the sentence with drags on her cigarette and exhalations that were at least in part for the benefit of the person listening. 'No, I know, I know I did. I know, and I will, as soon as I can. I'm sorry. I know, but it's work.' Her face knotted into a scowl, tinged perhaps with guilt or frustration, or maybe even embarrassment. 'I can't just leave. I can't. Not now. But I will, as soon as I can. Yes. Tonight.' She passed an arm's length from him, oblivious to him standing in the doorway of the restaurant, and then turned and paced away from him again, agreeing, smoking and reassuring the person she was speaking to that she would, as soon as she could, definitely, she promised. As she turned to pace back again she looked up and saw him watching her. She stopped and stared at him, as if waiting for an explanation for an intrusion by a stranger or office junior, compelling him to speak and not just stand there. Mindful of the phone to her ear, he mouthed that the table was ready. She replied to the phone that she was sorry, she was going to have to go, she was needed elsewhere.

'Sorry about that,' she said while smiling thanks to the waiter as he handed her a menu.

'Problems?'

'Not that I want to talk about . . .'

'Nothing that I can help with, then?'

'No.'

The waiter poured water and asked if he could get them anything else to drink. She ordered a bottle of wine, told him that they would have the crab followed by the duck and handed her menu back to him. The waiter hesitated and looked to him for confirmation that this was indeed what he wanted.

'God, I'm sorry, is that alright?' she asked, acknowledging the exchange of looks between him and the waiter. 'It's just I'm starving. You like duck, don't you?'

He nodded, said that he did and, unsure whether to be amused or embarrassed, handed his menu back to the waiter, who without missing a beat smiled and settled the matter with a reassuring 'An excellent choice.'

The waiter did a slight bow as he left them and once he was out of earshot she turned back to him and asked, 'So where were we?'

'I don't remember.'

The childish, wounded note in his reply made him both wince and feel even more hurt at her having allowed her phone call to interrupt his big moment. Despite himself, he could feel the all too often indulged, if unwelcome, self-sabotaging juvenile inside readying itself to make the rest of the evening as difficult as possible in the name of getting her back for having left him sitting at the bar on his own for ten minutes when he was trying to do something nice for her. He wanted to pick up where they'd left off, as she'd invited him to, but his 'I don't remember' had already started the process of forcing her to drag it out of him, a humiliating and miserable dance of apology on her part and petulance on his, which would ruin any chance of his surprise being the joyous gift he'd had planned.

'Yes you do.' She leaned into him and dropped her voice to a warm breath, more suggestion than whisper. 'You were about to tell me about the surprise you've got for me.'

'Was I?'

'Yes. You were.'

'It doesn't matter now. I'll tell you later.'

'No. Tell me now. I want to know. You can't leave me guessing like that.'

'I can't tell you now, it's been built up too much.'

'Please. I promise I won't look disappointed.'

'If I'd been able to finish telling you earlier, you wouldn't have to promise anything. You'd have loved it. Simple as that.'

'Then I'll love it now.'

'It's not . . . Just, let's leave it.'

'I'm sorry about the call, really I am. I had to take it. But it was terrible timing. It ruined your surprise and I'm sorry. It could have been worse though. My phone could have rung just after you'd told me what it was, and that really would have crashed the moment.'

He didn't say anything, he just stayed focused on the knife that he'd been toying with throughout the exchange.

'Look,' she said, turning her phone face up and holding the power button until it switched off. 'There. Now you can tell me without fear of interruption.'

'I can't. Please, just leave it.'

'You can.' She leaned in as close as she could without moving her chair, and dropped her voice to a breath that was so suggestive he could almost feel it stroke the side of his face. 'And I won't leave it.' He felt her hand on his thigh. She squeezed it, slid her hand an inch higher and squeezed it again, and then an inch higher and squeezed and said, 'So you might as well tell me.'

'I've booked a weekend away, for the two of us, in Brighton, week after next.'

He felt her hand on his thigh loosen and pull away. She sat up, slowly righting herself. He looked at her face for signs, good or bad, clues to whether she'd heard what he'd said and what she thought about it. There was nothing. Her expression was composed, not blank, reserving the right to express whatever conclusion she came to once she'd finished absorbing what he'd said and computing what it meant. Finally she said, 'Oh.' And then, 'I wasn't expecting that.'

Her expression was still non-committal. He felt the juvenile inside readying the hurt and bitter outburst he'd been building up to ever since she'd left him sitting at the bar, and was for once grateful to be interrupted, this time by the waiter returning with their crab salads.

She welcomed the arrival of their starters with an enthusiasm too immediate and profound to be believed. Her expression went from blank to effusive and the 'That looks lovely' that went with it was offered with such excitement that even the waiter seemed to think he'd missed something. The brightness of the smile she beamed to them both told him that her mind was still weighing the implications of a dirty weekend in Brighton and trying to find the correct facial response. What he couldn't tell was whether her difficulty lay in being overwhelmed by his perceptive thoughtfulness and incredible generosity, or in hating the idea full stop. He couldn't imagine for a minute why she would hate the idea, but something in her reaction, or panicked lack of one, made him think it the more likely option. He watched her focus her attention on the waiter and decided that if she couldn't give him the response he was looking for, then at least he could provoke her into giving the one the destructive child inside wanted to hear.

'See, I told you it was too late,' he said as the waiter withdrew wishing them *bon appétit*. 'I shouldn't have told you. I should have waited for another time. Now you've got to pretend to like it, which makes me sure that you probably don't.'

'No,' she said with a deploring assurance, while focusing intently on the fork she prodded her crab meat with. 'It's not that. I love it. It's so . . . sweet. So thoughtful.'

'I wasn't really looking for sweet or thoughtful. I was hoping more for exciting, thrilling, debauched, outrageous, that maybe you'd be so thrilled and excited by the thought of me making your fantasy dirty weekend a reality that there might at least have been more of what your hand on my thigh was hinting at just before I wowed you with my big surprise and made you recoil in disgust.'

'I didn't recoil. You're being overdramatic and childish.'

'Well how should I be, given your reaction?'

'What reaction?'

'Exactly. What reaction? You were hardly jumping for joy, or anything else for that matter.'

'It's not as easy as that.'

'What isn't?'

'I can't just go away for a weekend.'

'What? Why the hell not?'

'It's complicated.'

'What is?'

'I have commitments. I have things I have to consider, to work out.'

'Like what?'

'Work things. I'm sorry, look, I'm not saying no, and I'm not saying I don't want to, I'm just saying I don't know, I need to look at where I am with things, check that I can make it, that I can get away, from work.'

'It's the weekend. I don't understand.'

'I know, and I probably *can* come and if I *can* I know it will be absolutely amazing and we'll have just the best, filthiest time anyone's ever had on a dirty weekend, but I need to check that I can get away. Things are crazy for me at the moment, honestly, you don't know the half of it and I don't want you to, because I don't want to talk about it with you, I want to escape from it to you. But I have commitments, I have responsibilities, I have people who need me to be here.'

'Well I'm sorry. I was just trying to do something nice, trying to do exactly what you're saying and get you away from it all. If I'd known it was going to blow up in my face like this, trust me, I wouldn't have gone to the effort.'

'Don't say that. I love that you did. It's just that you need to ask me first. To check with me that I can make it, otherwise we'll both be disappointed.'

'And where's the surprise in that?'

'Well, it's better than the surprise being me saying I can't make it. I'm sorry. Leave it with me. I'll see what I can do. I promise I'll do everything I can to make it. And thank you, it was very sweet. Now eat your salad, this crab is amazing. Good call on coming here. That was a lovely surprise. Thank you.'

The rest of the meal passed in a hard-to-read haze of polite enthusiasm, for the food, for the wine, for each other, which made it impossible for him to tell if she was looking to avoid more awkwardness or merely trying to compensate for earlier and find the right tone for a happy rest of their evening. He hated it. He, like her, smiled at the right moments and made all the appropriate gestures and noises, when really all he wanted was to reach across the table to her, to touch her hands, her arms, her face, and ask what was going on with her, with them, now, this evening and beyond, to ask if there even was a them. He wanted to. Instead he went along with the saddening lightness of the conversation, sitting close enough to reach out and touch her face, yet feeling like to do so would be to overstep a mark which he had never previously known existed.

For once he hadn't felt the sadness reaching up to pull him under, he'd found himself submerged and drowning in an instant, letting go of his anger at being interrupted by her phone call and falling to the loneliest of distant places as soon as her hand had slipped from his thigh. Now he was smiling and treading water because he was too afraid to grab onto her. Their waiter, perceptive to the last, sensed either the sadness or the lack of anything else between them and made himself as scarce as his role would allow, depositing and clearing courses with only his own polite smile for conversation. She accepted the dessert menus when they were offered, and once the waiter and his polite smile had communicated that he'd be back in a few minutes and bowed away again, she asked if he wanted anything else to eat, 'Or . . .'

'Or what?'

'Or . . . I don't know.' She looked confused by the snap of

his interruption. 'Did you have something in mind?'

He wanted to say that he had, yet he waited, unsure if it was the right thing, or in any way appropriate. He could feel the expectation as she waited for him to reply, and he matched it with his own frustration at his inability to find an order or tone for what he wanted to say. In his ears he could hear only breathy, playful suggestion, an amorous boudoir murmur which now made him wince with embarrassment as it repeated the words and incoherent phrases. He thought of saying nothing at all, or of telling her that he had nothing more in mind than she probably did, or that he would look at the dessert menu if she was having something, and when all of those felt as unappealing as going back to the eggshells that they seemed to have spent most of the evening walking on, he resigned himself to the fact that he'd broken the tepid atmosphere, so he might as well just come out and say it, and trust that straight talking and sincerity would be enough to lift the mood and bring her back to him.

'I don't want anything else to eat. I don't want coffee. Let's pay the bill and go . . . back to my place, back to Peter's. Let's start this evening again. Let's put all of this behind us and . . .' He stopped and watched her eyes and the playful smile that he knew so well as it broke out across her face, spreading from her lips to her cheeks, bringing her eyes to life. 'What do you think?'

'I think I'd like nothing more,' she said, her smile melting away the sadness within him as quickly as it had come. She reached out for him and stroked the side of his face, her eyes focused on his, glinting in the candlelight. 'I'd absolutely love to. But I've got an early start in the morning. I really need to go home and get a good night's sleep for once. Another time.'

The waiter returned to the table and, sensing something in the atmosphere had changed, beamed hopefully in her direction and asked with renewed conviction: 'Can I get you anything else, Madame?'

'Just the bill please.'

Chapter Twenty-One

He gets off the Métro at Vavin and runs along the platform and up the steps, not caring what he looks like or what his fellow commuters might think. Her office is the only place he can think of. It's the first and only place he can imagine her going to.

He runs up the steps and into the street, and then runs as hard and as fast as he can along the Boulevard du Montparnasse, hard and fast enough to look as if he's actually giving chase. He runs in the direction of the Montparnasse Tower, his eyes scanning the typical Haussmann blocks, following them into the distance, searching for the only modern building, for the nondescript 1970s facade and its five storeys of square concrete and brown glass. His eyes run ahead of him, bouncing between the shop fronts and doorways and the pavement, searching for signs of her building or of her and finding neither.

He runs along the Boulevard du Montparnasse, the Montparnasse Tower steadily looming ahead of him, the seemingly unbroken run of ornate Parisian architecture stretching all the way from him to it. He runs as hard and as fast as he can, hard and fast enough to almost miss the nondescript facade of her building when he runs past it.

He comes to a stop just beyond the line of sight of the reception, outside a florist's that in all of his hours of watching for her he'd never noticed was there. He has to take a moment to catch his breath. He hasn't run since school, and with his heart racing in his chest and the lack of oxygen burning his lungs, he feels sweat breaking out on his temples as they throb with a pulse that makes his eyes lose focus and his head swim. He tries to catch his breath and steady himself. He tries to take deep lungfuls of air, but all he gets is the sweet perfume of the flowers which makes him feel like he's suffocating. He looks up at the deep greens and wintry reds of the flowers, at the rows of whites and buckets of pinks, and at the man standing in the doorway watching him pant and struggle for air. He looks at the man watching him, perhaps the florist, perhaps wondering who the man bent double in front of his shop is running from, and he feels the need to move, even though he doesn't feel in any fit state to. He straightens himself up and turns back to the brown glass of the reception.

The middle-aged woman behind the reception desk looks up and smiles an instinctive smile, the one she always smiles when the opening of the brown glass door or the sense of someone approaching causes her to look up from whatever it is that she does when not directing visitors or asking them to sign in. She smiles her broad and welcoming smile, but there's a flicker in it when her eyes make contact with him. Although only a momentary dimming of intensity, it's enough to tell him that something about his appearance has made her uncomfortable. He's sweating, and if he had to guess he'd say his face was either crimson or deathly white, either one a worrying accompaniment to his laboured breathing and the distress he knows to be in his eyes. The middle-aged woman doesn't actually stop smiling, and she manages to return her smile to full brightness before he's within speaking distance, but he knows before she says anything that she doesn't want him there.

She stretches her smile to show that she means it and then asks: '*Est-ce que je peux aider?*'

He smiles an equally awkward and doubtful smile, apologises in broken French for his poor Français and then struggles to find somewhere to start.

'You speak English?' she asks with what to him appears to

be genuine hope and encouragement.

He tells her that he does. She smiles and repeats her question: 'How can I help?'

He tells her that he's looking for someone. She asks for their name. He tells her he's looking for a Ms Carlson. She smiles, nods, says: 'One moment please,' and turns to the screen in front of her. He watches her type C-A-R-L-S-O-N, noting each careful keystroke, checking her spelling as she types. She looks at the screen. He watches her hands, watches them hover above the keys as she looks at the screen in front of her, watches them hover above the keys wondering what to do next. After a short moment she turns to look for something under the counter of the reception desk and then hands a pen and a pad of paper up to him. 'Could you write the name, please?'

He takes the pen and writes 'Ms Carlson' on the pad, thinking that even though he watched her type 'Carlson' correctly, she may still have made an unseen mistake. He hands the pad and pen back to the middle-aged woman behind the reception desk, whose smile is now dimmer and less convincing than before, and then as she reaches to receive it he changes his mind and takes the pad and pen back and writes 'Ms Sophie Carlson' under the 'Ms Carlson' he'd already printed on the page. He hands the pad and pen back to the now confused middle-aged woman behind the reception desk, who then smiles and nods a nod of understanding before trying both options, C-A-R-L-S-O-N—S and S-O-P-H-I-E—C, to be certain.

She looks at her screen only briefly, it having confirmed what she clearly already suspected, and then she turns to him and apologises. '*Je suis désolée monsieur*,' she says before remembering herself, 'I'm sorry, *monsieur*, there is no Ms Carlson here.'

She smiles and hands back the piece of paper as if to confirm that their business is concluded.

'There must be some mistake.'

'No, *monsieur*. There is no Ms Carlson here.'

'Yes, there is. I've seen her. Here. I've seen her come through that door,' he points to the brown glass of the door behind him and then motions towards the lift, 'and I've seen her get into the lift there.'

'Perhaps she was visiting, *monsieur*, for a meeting?'

He looks from the lift to the floor directory next to it.

'She works on the third floor, for Fitzgerald Ellis.'

Her smile fixed and resolute, the middle-aged woman behind the reception desk assures him that she has checked, and there is no Ms Carlson on her computer. If she worked in the building, even for a couple of days, there would be a record of Ms Carlson on her computer. 'I'm sorry, *monsieur*,' she adds by way of closing, 'she, Ms Carlson, does not work here.'

He looks at her, fixing on her eyes, which he can see are already starting to waver in their conviction, and he implores her to look again, to try something else, to help him, to please, please, please, help him. He tells her that she doesn't understand, that he has to find her, that he knows she's here, that he doesn't understand why she can't find her on her computer, but she has to be there, she has to look, she has to try again, she has to help him.

He speaks more quickly than the middle-aged woman behind the reception desk can comprehend, although the panic which replaces her practised smile confirms that she understands the desperation in his voice and she doesn't like it. She in turn replies with agitated rapid-fire instructions which his French isn't good enough to decipher. Only the word '*sécurité*' seems to reach his ear unscrambled and, accompanied by her lifting of the receiver of the phone in front of her and repeating '*sécurité*' and adding '*à la réception*', makes him turn back to the brown glass of the reception door.

The smartly dressed man behind the hotel reception desk shakes his head. 'No, I'm sorry, sir, I don't have a Ms Carlson registered.' He continues to look at the screen of his computer for another couple of seconds, as if to prove to the dishevelled and perhaps slightly distressed man on the other side of the counter that he's thorough and professional, and then he looks up, adding, 'Maybe she's staying at one of our other hotels, we do have several in Paris.'

'No, it's this one. I know it's definitely this one.'

He stops short of saying exactly how he knows that it's this Mercure Hotel, of explaining to the smartly dressed man behind the hotel reception desk that he's followed her there, from her office on the Boulevard du Montparnasse, past the Vavin Métro entrance and up the Boulevard Raspail, and watched her enter the hotel through the reception door behind him. He looks at the back of the computer while the smartly dressed man behind the hotel reception desk looks at him.

'There must be some mistake. Can you check again, please?'

'I'm sorry, sir, but I'm quite certain, there's no one by that name registered at the hotel. If it would help I can perhaps check with our other hotels, maybe there's some confusion and she's actually . . .'

'No. It's here. I've seen her . . . She's tall, blond hair, below the shoulder, darker blond, dirty blond, not bright blond, not white blond, slight wave in it, long dark coat, grey suit, always in a grey suit, with a white shirt, slim, professional, businesswoman, always carrying a briefcase, always has a briefcase, works for a company called Fitzgerald Ellis, a law firm, they're probably paying the bill.'

'Oh, yes, the briefcase. The lady with the briefcase. Yes, she's been staying with us for some time.' The smartly dressed man behind the hotel reception desk turns back to his screen and types and scrolls and types and then frowns and turns back to him. 'But she wasn't staying under the name Carlson.'

He waits for more and when no more is offered he fixes on the face smiling at him from behind the hotel reception desk and asks: 'What do you mean?'

'She wasn't staying under the name Carlson.'

'What name was she staying under?'

'Oh, I'm sorry, sir, I can't tell you that.'

He watches the smile of the smartly dressed man behind the hotel reception desk as it happily informs him that there's nothing more to say and unless he has any further questions their business is concluded. He watches the smile, waiting for a flicker or a dip, for signs of wavering or dimming, and as the length of time when no words pass between them grows longer, he looks for signs of embarrassment or discomfort. He finds none.

'I see. Can you call her room for me?'

'I'm sorry, sir. She's already checked out.'

'When?'

The smartly dressed man behind the hotel reception desk checks his screen and returns with his fixed smile. 'About thirty minutes ago.'

'No, there must be a mistake. I saw her thirty minutes ago. She was on Avenue . . . there must be a mistake.'

He checks his screen again. 'Yes. She settled her bill over the telephone by credit card.' He looks back and adds, 'It happens quite a lot, you know, a sudden change of plans.' His smile briefly offers a gossipy disapproval, as if the dubious nature of such behaviour needs no further explanation, before returning to its professional default.

'What about her things? Her clothes, her luggage? She'll have to come and pick them up.'

'Ah, no, she asked us to forward them for her. Again, it happens a lot, last-minute flight, no time to come back to the hotel, people have to go straight from the office to the airport and we forward their belongings and luggage. It is all part of the service.'

'Where did she ask you to forward them? Do you have an address for her that I could have?'

'Ah, no. I am sorry. I cannot give out that information, I have already said too much I think.' The faint laugh and good-humoured apology in his voice imply a mutual understanding that this is the obvious and only possible response to a request that they both know to be unreasonable, and which, as such, should not be repeated.

'Please. I wouldn't ask if it wasn't important. You have to help me. I have to see her, or speak to her, maybe you've got a number I could have, if not an address then a telephone number, a mobile or office number, or an email maybe. You must have an email for her. Some way of contacting her. So I can tell her. So I can let her know. She doesn't have to know where I got it. Please, just an email address. I promise I won't tell her that you gave it to me. I could have got it anywhere. Come on, please. Just her email address.'

The smartly dressed man behind the hotel reception desk has stopped listening. He shakes his head and holds his hands up to the man now making a scene on the other side of the counter to signify as much and to communicate that he cannot entertain such things.

'Please. Please. Just an email. What harm can it do?'

'I'm sorry, sir.'

'You'll probably only send junk to it anyway.'

'I'm sorry, sir. Now if you will excuse me.' He turns back to his screen, the smiling default now replaced by deaf concentration.

He watches the smartly dressed man behind the hotel reception desk as he thoroughly and professionally ignores him and then, swallowing the one last plea still caught in his throat, he turns to walk away. He feels the desperate determination begin to drain away and the sadness flood his insides in its place. He feels the weight of it, pulling him down, smothering him. He walks towards the door, almost hoping to be pulled under before he gets there.

'London.'

The voice of the smartly dressed man behind the hotel reception desk is quiet but enough to stop him and the sadness halfway across the reception.

He turns back to the reception desk to see him leaning slightly forward on the counter top.

'She asked us to forward her luggage and belongings to an address in London. I can't say any more than that, *monsieur*. I'm sorry. I hope it helps.'

Chapter Twenty-Two

He called Audrey as soon as Sophie finished telling him that she wasn't coming to Brighton and put the phone down. She was his first thought. He didn't know why. He didn't know what he expected her to say or what he wanted her to do. There wasn't anything she *could* do. Sophie wasn't coming, that was that. But still, his first thought was Audrey.

It was just after seven on the Friday evening. He'd been about to leave to meet her at Victoria to get the train to take them to Brighton for the dirty weekend that she'd told him twice that week she couldn't wait for. He was standing in the hall when she called, putting on his coat, his overnight bag on the floor next to him. He knew before he answered who it was, before he'd even seen the *Unknown Number* caller ID, he knew it was her and he knew what she was going to say. She blamed work, said she couldn't get away, reassured him that she'd done all she could, that she'd left it to the last minute to call, to be sure. As he stood with his coat on and his overnight bag on the floor next to him, he wondered if there wasn't an element of cruelty in the way she always left him to the last minute, always left him waiting, wondering, never giving him time to make other plans or alternative arrangements for himself or for them. As her phone hung up, his first thought was to call Audrey.

Audrey answered, as she always did. Audrey, always there,

always dependable. At first, though, she misunderstood the purpose of the call. He told her what had happened, about Brighton and Sophie waiting until the very last possible minute to let him down. He told her how she'd apologised, saying that she was sorry, that she'd done all she could, and how this time he didn't believe any of it. Audrey reacted angrily, saying that she didn't want to hear it, that she was sick of hearing about Sophie, sick of having to listen to him go on about how wonderful she was and then having him on the phone days later bleating about how he couldn't get hold of her, that she hadn't given him her number, that she wouldn't return his calls. She said she didn't really see the point of listening to it. It was always the same and days later it was always all forgotten. Suddenly she was back to being amazing company and understanding him like no one else ever had. She didn't want to hear it any more. She couldn't hear it any more. She said that Sophie would never make him happy, that she didn't know how to, that this, her dumping on him again, was proof, and that he should take note and come to his senses, but as usual he probably wouldn't, and he certainly wouldn't listen to her. He never did. Why would he? It wasn't like she was the only person who actually gave a shit about him or anything. Without giving him time enough to speak let alone correct her, she said that she was sorry, but she didn't really see what she could do and if she was honest, she'd had enough of being both a go-between and his shoulder to cry on. When she finally stopped, he told her that he didn't want her to do anything. 'I just wanted to hear you, that's all,' he said. 'That's probably why I always come to you. Talking to you, hearing your voice, it always makes everything feel better. But you're right, I shouldn't rely on you like that. I shouldn't burden you. I never bring you anything but my problems, and that's not fair. So I'm sorry. I'll speak to you soon. Have a good night, and again, sorry.' And with that he hung up.

He was out on Peter's terrace, smoking and not drinking the glass of wine he'd poured himself, when the buzzer went. He didn't react at first. The buzzer rarely buzzed and never when he wasn't expecting it to, so he assumed it was the buzzer from one of the neighbouring flats where, like him, they were making the most of the summer evening with their terrace doors and windows open. It was on the third buzz that he rested his cigarette on a flower pot and went inside to investigate. At the fifth buzz he put his eye to the peephole of the front door and saw a black bob and a trench coat on the other side. He smiled as Audrey looked furtively left and right and then buzzed again. 'I know you're in there,' she shouted quietly, leaning in to the door. 'For God's sake let me in. People are going to think I'm some kind of nutter.'

He opened the door and smiled at her impatient scowl.

'Sorry, I wasn't expecting company. I certainly wasn't expecting you.'

He opened the door wide and walked off down the hall towards Peter's miniature kitchen, leaving her to close the door behind her.

'I'm full of surprises,' she said, following him to the kitchen, her tone perhaps a little more sardonic than she intended.

'Do you want a glass of wine?' He opened the fridge door and retrieved the bottle of white wine that he'd opened and poured himself a glass of but not drunk yet. He showed her the bottle as she hovered in the kitchen doorway, wrapped up tight in her little trench coat, positively teetering on her un-Audrey-like heels. 'It's very good apparently. Sophie chose it. Bought me a load of it because she couldn't stand the stuff I used to offer her. I can't tell the difference myself. Want some?'

'Fuck that shit,' she said, pulling a bottle from behind her back and holding it aloft like she was sixteen and had just got away with buying it. 'I brought tequila!'

Without saying anything he dropped the nearly full bottle of wine into the recycling bin, got two shot glasses out of the cupboard and followed her into the living room, where she'd already taken off her little trench coat and chucked it on the back of Peter's sofa. She was wearing the same figure-hugging black dress and the same thin black tights as she had last time they'd been out together, the night he met the other Audrey, the Audrey with the shapely legs and delicate ankles and suggestive intonation. The sultry, strong

Audrey who'd wanted him to notice her. She was wearing the same heels and the same make-up and trying for the same focused and efficient femininity but was too wired on nervous excitement to pull it off. The party that the tequila promised was evidently more to her taste than the evening of low lights and smouldering that her eyeliner and the rest of her make-up had been applied for.

He put the shot glasses on Peter's coffee table as she broke the seal on the bottle.

'I haven't got any limes, but I can do salt.'

Audrey filled the two shot glasses.

'Fuck salt.'

She clinked glasses with him and threw the shot back. He did the same, watching her as she winced, shuddered, blinked her eyes wide and said, 'I love tequila.'

She poured herself another shot and waited for him to wince and shudder and offer her his glass.

'I'm not disturbing anything, am I?'

'No. I was just on the terrace smoking, not drinking a glass of apparently very good wine, thinking about the incredible evening of sleazy sex I wasn't having.'

'Sounds great. Let's do it.'

'Do what?'

'Let's go smoke.'

'You don't smoke.'

'I do when I'm drinking tequila.'

With that she downed her second shot, winced, shuddered, inelegantly got to her feet and headed to the patio door, grabbing the bottle of tequila as she went. He followed her out onto the terrace and sat next to her on the bench seat, where she was already helping herself to his cigarettes and fumbling with his lighter. He took the lighter from her, sparked it for her and then lit his own cigarette.

'I used to love it out here,' she said, exhaling sweet tequila smoke into the still evening. 'I always loved coming out here in the summer. Long evenings. You and me talking shit. Peter playing his records. Let's put some music on.'

She was in the living room, flicking through Peter's vinyl,

cigarette still hanging from her mouth, before he had a chance to respond or protest. He watched her through the living room's opaque white curtains, watched her kneeling on the floor, at home in the warm glow of Peter's various table lamps, pulling out records and putting them to one side and finally slipping one out of its sleeve and putting it on Peter's turntable. A series of slow and quiet piano arpeggios came through the curtains and then gave way to the main double bass motif. She turned it up and came dancing through the curtain as the band reached full swing and Miles Davis's 'So What' wafted out around her. She bounced her hips to the ride cymbal as she came towards him, taking the cigarette from her mouth and knocking the ash off the end as the trumpet kicked in on the track that Peter played late at night on all the best nights, the one record in his collection that couldn't help but be associated with drinking and smoking and laughing and talking until the small hours.

She shimmied and hip-bounced her way over to him and he handed her another shot, which she downed and held aloft as she shimmied in front of him some more. She held the empty glass out to him and took another drag on her cigarette as he refilled it.

'You shouldn't smoke in the flat.'

He didn't know why he said it. He wasn't even sure if he cared if she smoked in the flat or not, and said it more in the style of looking out for a co-conspirator than as an admonishment.

'Why not?'

'I don't like people smoking in the flat.'

'Fuck it. Peter didn't like people smoking in the flat. You'll smoke anywhere. Smoke in the flat if you want to.'

'I don't.'

'Why not? It must be the only place you don't.'

'It doesn't seem right.'

'Fuck. You're weird. More tequila I think.'

She waited for him to fill his glass and then downed hers, wincing, shuddering and dropping down on the bench seat next to him.

'Let's redecorate.'

'What? Now?'

'No, not now. Now we're drinking tequila.' She took another cigarette out of the packet and tried to light it with the end of the last. 'And we're smoking cigarettes,' she said, taking the still unlit cigarette out of her mouth to do so. He took it from her hand, lit it and put it in her mouth. 'No, when we've finished drinking tequila and smoking cigarettes and maybe slept for a couple of days, we should redecorate. Make Peter's *casa* your *casa*.'

'*Su casa*.'

'Or *mi casa* in your case. You know what I mean.'

'I do. I do. But fuck it. I might just go and live somewhere else instead.'

'What? Are you completely mad? I mean, I know you're . . . I know you're a little unstable.'

'True.'

'But you can't leave this,' she waved her arm in the vague direction of the terrace. 'And all of that,' she waved her arm again, this time in the direction of the ornamental lake, the Barbican Centre and the rest of the dark, light-studded concrete blocks. 'I mean, get a grip on yourself, this place is amazing.'

'I was thinking about going to Paris for a while.'

'Seriously? You'd swap this amazing flat for some poky, probably damp hole in the wall in Paris? Are you out of your mind? You'd swap this amazing flat . . . ?'

'Peter's amazing flat.'

'Fuck it. I said. We'll decorate.'

'And that will be enough?'

'It'll be a start.'

He poured her another shot, she offered him a drag on her cigarette. He leaned in towards the cigarette in her hand. He felt the soft warm breath on the side of his face and the tension as she tried to control it, to not make it too obvious. He felt an intense wave of happiness rise from the depths of him, rising through his chest and his shoulders and making his head go light and dizzy as he turned instead to kiss her. He felt the plump softness of her lips, at first unresponsive and then kissing back deep, long, tender kisses. Her kisses were softer and more tender than he thought they would be.

He knew for certain then that he had thought about this moment. He didn't remember where or when he'd imagined it, but it had familiarity and differences enough for him to know that he must have done, and while he didn't remember the specifics of what he'd imagined, the reality was so much better.

It wasn't like it was with Sophie. It wasn't tense and aggressive. It wasn't snatched or dangerous. There was passion and intensity, yet with it came care and quiet and a willingness to luxuriate in the moment, to savour taste and touch, to experience and remember everything like they both knew it was a one-time act, never to be repeated.

When he woke up in the morning she was gone. He felt the space next to him and when he found it to be empty and cold he looked over the side of the bed to the floor where he knew their clothes had been. His were still there. Hers, the little black dress, her thin black tights, her red bra, the strap of which he had a vague memory of being hypnotised by when she was bouncing her hips to Miles Davis, and the black knickers which didn't make a set, were all gone. Scooped up in a hurry. Thrown on while he slept. He looked at the bedside table, hoping for confirmation that she'd been there, that he hadn't imagined it, but there was no note.

He got up and wandered to the kitchen and the living room, looking for a message, for a sign, for a piece of paper with a kiss or for proof of the events that had taken them from the bench seat on Peter's terrace to the bedroom, via the sofa, the dining table, the kitchen and the hall. The terrace door was shut. Her little trench coat was gone from the back of Peter's sofa. The shot glasses were clean and in the cupboard along with his wine glass. There were no notes or messages waiting for him next to the kettle or on the fridge or in the fridge, he checked and double-checked them all. If it wasn't for the empty tequila bottle in the recycling and the lipsticked cigarette ends in the flower pots out on the terrace, he would have been sure that he'd imagined the whole thing. He looked by the phone in the hall to be sure that she hadn't left him a note there, and then he checked the answering machine to see if maybe she'd called from work to leave him a message apologising for running out on him, and then he remembered it was Saturday.

He looked at the front door and then the phone and then up the hall to the bathroom. He went to the bathroom, for the briefest of moments hoping to find her there, adjusting her black dress and her hair, hoping that she would look up and see him and smile at him and ask what he wanted to do for breakfast. He opened the door of Peter's bathroom and turned the light on, to be sure. He stood in the doorway, looking at the clean untouched sink, at the empty bin and the neatly arranged towels, looking for the slightest sign of her, and when he found none he felt the sadness twist and turn and start to rise up again inside him.

Chapter Twenty-Three

He can feel the pulse of the anonymous Parisian house music.

The low bass.

The hypnotic tisk tisk tisk tisk.

He can feel it getting louder.

He can feel it getting louder and the girl on the platform losing herself in it.

He watches the girl on the platform.

He watches her bare arms and legs. He watches her bare feet. He watches her head with its sharp bob of black hair as it rolls on her shoulders. Slowly.

He watches her swaying.

Swaying to the low pulse building around her. Swaying in half time to the tisk tisk tisk tisk. Swaying slowly at first, and then deeper and wider, her head rolling on her shoulders, changing direction with each beat, leaning further back and further forward with every bar, the sharp points of her black bob brushing her cheek, touching the edges of her mouth.

He watches her feeling the pulse of the anonymous Parisian house music, feeling the same low bass he is, the same tisk tisk tisk tisk.

He watches her getting lost in it.

Being freed by it.

He watches her being alone under her white light in the darkness.

He watches her white skin, made whiter by the light, and he wants to touch it.

He feels Sophie's hand tighten on his thigh.

He watches the girl on the platform and tries not to be distracted by the red table lamps behind her, by their on/off on/off, by the sense of waitresses in white dresses moving between them in the dark.

He feels Sophie's hand start to move. Slowly.

Back and forth.

In time to the music.

Kneading. Higher and higher. In time to the sways of the girl on the platform.

He watches the girl on the platform.

He watches her white skin against the black of her slip and the red of her bra straps. He watches a strap slip off her shoulder as she moves. He watches her not notice.

He watches her and feels a sense of recognition. That she's familiar. That he knows her. That he could reach out and touch her if he wanted to. That she'd let him.

He feels Sophie's hand move higher on his thigh. He feels the warmth of her breath on the side of his face. On his neck. On his ear. Her breathing. Slow and deliberate. Breathing him into her and her onto him.

Holding him in.

One. Two. Three.

Letting him go with a shudder.

He watches the girl on the platform. Her eyes closed and her head back. Swaying and swaying and swaying and swaying, lost in the dark, alone under her white light, unaware of anyone else in the room, willing him to touch her, letting him know that it's alright. That he can.

He feels his lips kiss her shoulder. He feels the back of his hand brush against her thigh. His fingertips stroking their way to the inside. Between. Circling the soft skin. Feeling its warmth.

Drawing patterns. Drawing a shudder from her.

He feels her knee. He feels her thigh on his. He feels her start to climb onto him, pushing him back into the booth, pulling herself up into him. Closer. So close there's nothing between them.

He hears her open her mouth to say something, to breathe a suggestion into his ear, and then he hears a telephone start to ring.

Ring.

Ring.

He sees the red light of the table lamp and the white of the waitress's dress as she holds the tray with the telephone out to him.

'It's for you, sir.'

He wakes up to his phone ringing. At least he thinks he's awake. He can hear the regular repeat of something trying to rouse him from his sleep, but his eyes won't open. It's as if they don't want him to leave, as if they want him to stay where he is, in the dark, with her and the girl on the platform. It's as if they too want to know who is on the telephone ringing in his dream. For a second he thinks he can actually hear it, the ring ring of the phone on the waitress's silver tray. His eyes closed, he can still see her, leaning forward, in her white dress with its top and bottom poppers undone, showing just enough to control his attention as she leans forward and says it's for him. His eyes fighting to stay closed, he wants to ask her who it is and how they know he's there, in the dark, in a club in Paris. He watches her chest straining another popper as she leans and breathes and he listens for the sound that woke him, for the ring ring of the phone on the silver tray, and then he hears the noise of his phone vibrating up against the clock on the bedside table.

The buzz of his phone on the bedside table replaces the ring of the phone on the waitress's silver tray and with it the waitress herself fades into the blackness of his eyelids and he knows he must be awake because he's aware of thinking that he will never see her again. His eyes still refusing to open, he reaches towards the long insistent buzz, his fingers searching the bedside table, finding the clock and then the moving form of the phone vibrating up against it.

For a second he thinks it's her calling him, trying to reach him from the dream, and then he thinks how unlikely that is and with that thought realises that he's no longer asleep enough to believe in such possibilities. He feels the phone against his fingertips and is suddenly aware of the urgency in its vibration. His fingers find their way around it just enough to pick it up and carry it in an exaggerated arc to where his head lies heavy on his pillow.

His eyes still closed, he brings it to his ear and answers without saying anything.

A female voice he recognises says, 'Hello?'

It's Audrey. As asleep as he almost is, he knows it's Audrey. The tone and meaning of the hello itself fail to register with the active and awake part of his brain for another full second; the raised intonation making it more question than greeting, checking if anyone is actually there, or whether she's about to find herself talking to his voicemail. When she doesn't she repeats the question.

'Hello?'

He opens his eyes to the darkness, a darkness tinged with light, with brightness spilling in around the edges, the outside coming in.

He says hello. At least he thinks he says it out loud. This time *her* lack of response makes him wonder if there's anyone there.

He looks at the clock on the bedside table.

It says 11:59.

He watches it.

Waits.

One. Two. Three. Trying to decide if it's morning or night. Four. Five. Six. Seven.

12:00.

Finally he hears her breath against the mouthpiece and her voice asking him where he is.

He lifts his head from the pillow to check that he is where he knows he should be, even though he has no memory of how he got there. The room's dark but there. He can make out vague shapes, the brightness spilling around the edges of the blind, filling the room with an empty grey haze, picking out the shelves, the picture frame, the chest of drawers, the wardrobe, the chair in the corner, the grille of the air conditioning, the light fitting, the ceiling of his room in Peter's flat.

He tells her that he's at Peter's.

He hears the relief in her voice before he hears the words themselves.

She says, 'You're back. Good.'

He lifts his head again from the pillow and looks about the room, to be sure. He has no memory of getting back from Paris the night before. He has no memory of what he did after he left her hotel, after the smartly dressed man behind the hotel reception desk told him that she'd checked out and asked for her things to be forwarded to an address in London. He doesn't remember going back to his hotel and packing, or how he got to the Gare du Nord or anything about the Eurostar or getting back to Peter's flat. He looks at the barely-there outline of the chair in the corner with his clothes hung neatly over the back of it and then at the window and the edges of cold white light straining to flood the darkness. He doesn't remember coming in, or closing the blind or undressing or getting into bed. But the evidence is irrefutable, he must have done, he must, as Audrey said, be back, although he doesn't feel it. Most of him is still there in the dark, in a club in Paris. He looks again at the chair in the corner and sees that his bag is still there, on the floor next to it, either waiting to be unpacked or ready and waiting for him to depart again in search of her. In the grey dark of morning in his room in Peter's flat, he can't be sure of which.

He says, 'Yes.'

She says, 'We need to talk.'

She says, 'I've spoken to Sophie.'

He hears her hesitate and then she says, 'Can we meet?'

She's already waiting for him in the cafe on the corner of Winsley Street when he gets there. He sees her through the window, sitting in the last booth, nursing a cup of tea, looking thoughtfully into it. He thinks he can hear her rehearsing her speech from here, talking into her tea, telling it that she's worried about him, that she was shocked but not surprised when she got Sophie's call telling her what had happened, that he'd been in Paris, following her, watching her, stalking her. He can almost hear her hesitate before saying it, stalking her, and then adding, quickly if not reassuringly, that it was Sophie's word, not hers. He watches her looking at the stained white mug in front of her and he can hear the words being lined up and rearranged as she tries to find a way to tell him what she thinks without him reacting. He can feel her thoughts and the eggshells she's preparing to walk on, and he feels suddenly angry and then sad and then angry again. That it's come to this. That she, Audrey, his oldest friend, his only friend, doesn't know how to talk to him. That she's scared even to try.

He watches her watch her tea, and she looks so sad, and he knows that he's made her this way, that it's him, and Sophie, but mostly him who's put her in this position, that they are the reason she's mournful and sad, talking to her tea in a Soho cafe, dreading seeing him.

He doesn't want to see this Audrey. He watches her through the window and wishes that he was about to see the other Audrey, the fun, loving, kind, nearly carefree Audrey who would stay up all night with him and Peter, who would drink them under the table and then suggest shots, who'd sit for hours poring over Peter's vinyl collection and then pull out some jazz or soul or blues masterpiece that even Peter had forgotten he owned and then play it loud and with an ecstasy on her face that said there was nothing better, nothing more important, nothing more worth doing right at that moment. He wishes he was about to see the Audrey who always made him feel that this was the best moment, and that wherever she was was the best place to enjoy it. The Audrey who was an expert at finding all the simple pleasures that everyone else missed in favour of fashion or money or appearances, who knew the secret to finding the happiness in everything was to let it find you. He wishes he was going to see the Audrey whose face lit up every time she saw him, not the Audrey he can see now, tense, almost fearful at the prospect of his arrival. He wishes he could walk in and change the subject. Tell her not to worry, that he's over it, that he'll stop, that he's done with Sophie and all the excitement and joy and escape and relief and happiness that he found by letting her into his life. He wishes he could tell her not to look so worried, that things will be better, any moment now. He wishes he could make it easy for her, and looking at her though the window of the cafe on the corner of Winsley Street, watching her preparing to be strong and stand her ground and say all of the things she knows she's got to, he thinks that maybe he should, to make her feel better, to lift the burden if nothing else. Then he remembers her part in all of it. He remembers her intervention, her actions which, through carelessness or determination, caused her to come between him and Sophie. He remembers that she is the reason he and Sophie aren't together. That she is why Sophie left him and ran away to Paris, why she replaced him with an older, smarter, more sophisticated, more worldly and wise and distinguished and successful man that he will never be. A man he will never be able to compete with. And when he remembers all of this, he knows that he can't. He can't forgive, and no matter how much he wants to, he knows that he won't be able to make this or any of it easier for her.

He opens the door and steps into a scene of post-lunch calm. The cafe's empty except for a workman at the table by the window and an old man slowly chipping away at a generous portion of shepherd's pie at a table under the back wall's exhaustive four-panel menu. The radio and the man behind the counter scraping the hotplate are the only sounds. It's a quiet place for a serious conversation, picked by Audrey not because of its location or the fact that at this time they won't be listened to or hurried along, but because of its memories and the comfort they offer. He lets the door close behind him and instantly feels the familiarity of the place, of the tables and bolted-down chairs, the exhaustive four-panel menu on the back wall with its columns of fried breakfasts and rolls and hot dinners, the smell of fried onions and bacon. It's all as reassuring as he, and no doubt she, had hoped.

He doesn't look at her as he slides into the booth, he can't bring himself to. He wasn't going to come, but his need to know what Sophie had said and the fact that she suggested the cafe made it seem somehow more manageable. The cafe, where they used to go for lunch back when he would come into the office for meetings or was doing shifts to cover holidays, is as close to neutral ground as they were ever likely to find.

He doesn't look at her as he settles himself, clumsily taking off his coat, dragging it from under and behind him, folding it and laying it on the torn vinyl of the seat next to him. He doesn't look at her as he tries to make himself comfortable and find somewhere for his hands on the chipped Formica of the table, or as he takes in the salt and pepper pots, the squeezy red and brown sauce bottles, the sugar, the table's faded and scratched yellow pattern, the water marks on the white mug between her hands. When he's run out of things to look at, he can still feel her eyes on him. He can feel her eyes watching his as they avoid her. He can feel her eyes watching his, searching for clues as to how this might go.

She looked up and smiled as he came in, an unsure smile, aiming for pleased to see him but too strained to be believed. He broke eye contact as soon as she made it. He can feel that she didn't. He can feel that her eyes are still on him, still there like the strained smile which he knows will only make things harder.

'I'll get you a tea,' she says after a pause.

He senses her movement as she signals to the man behind the counter that another tea is required, then a second later he hears her add, 'Can you make that two?' and then to him, 'I must have let mine get cold.'

The man from behind the counter puts the two fresh teas on the table between them and removes her cold one. Audrey whispers a quiet sorry-to-be-a-nuisance 'Thank you'.

He watches the man walk back to his counter and then, still unable to look at her, he says:

'What did she tell you?'

Audrey looks down at her tea, drags it by the handle towards her and puts her hands around it for comfort, only to immediately pull them away again.

'It's hot.'

She shifts in her seat, and, at a loss for what to do now with her hands, puts them under her thighs.

Still looking at the tea, not at him, she says:

'She said that you followed her to Paris. That you followed her around Paris.'

She pulls her hands from under her thighs and puts them back on the table.

'She said that you waited outside her office and a hotel. That you followed her to meetings. That you stalked her.' She lets the weight of the last accusation hang in the air, long enough to suggest that she can see the logic of the assumption, before looking up and adding, 'Her word, not mine.'

There's a long, uncomfortable pause. He watches the old man still chipping away at his shepherd's pie. She watches the mug of tea in front of her, her hands edging ever closer to closing around it again.

'You've got to stop this,' she says taking the mug in her hands. 'It's no good. It won't change anything. It won't work.'

'Is that what she told you to tell me?'

'No. It's me telling you the truth. It won't.'

'What else did she say?'

'That I was to tell you that if you don't stop she'll go to the police.'

'What for?'

She looks up from her tea and fixes him with a look too incredulous to be anything other than genuine shock.

'Are you serious?'

The snap and volume of her reply forces him to meet her stare for the first time since he got there. Sensing that perhaps her reaction was a touch violent and loud, she leans in and drops her voice to an insistent whisper.

'You followed her to Paris. You followed her around Paris. You confronted her in the street and then physically grabbed her and tried to stop her getting on the Métro.'

'I didn't do that.'

'At the very least she's probably got grounds for a claim of some kind of harassment. At worst she could probably have you locked up as a stalker.'

'This is no good. I need to talk to her.'

'Are you not getting this?'

'I need to talk to her.'

'She doesn't want to talk to you.'

'I need to hear her say it.'

'What? What happened in Paris, the way she reacted, that wasn't enough?'

'What do you know about how she reacted?'

'She told me. She said she made it clear that she didn't want you there, that she didn't want to see you, that she didn't want to talk to you.'

'I need to explain. If she understood, she wouldn't be talking about the police.'

'Understood what?'

'About what happened. About us. That it was a mistake.'

'It won't make a difference. It's too late.'

He feels the thrust of whatever he was about to say by way of a counter-argument dry in his mouth and the energy with which he was about to say it suddenly dissipate. Her 'It's too late,' is the first thing he's recognised as a possible truth. Quieter, feeling almost resigned, he says:

'Who is he?'

'Who?'

'The man in Paris.'

'How should I know?'

He looks up, directly into her eyes, holding her stare.

'She didn't tell you about him?'

He looks for signs of hesitation or pretence.

'No. Why would she?'

He sees nothing. No hint of a lie nor flicker of deceit. He senses a possible reprieve, a slight glimmer of hope restored.

'Then it might not be serious. There might still be a chance. I need to talk to her. You've got to tell me where she is.'

'I can't believe you. I tried to tell you. That this is what she does. But you wouldn't listen, you're still not listening.'

He watches her eyes watching his, trying to understand or at least find a way of getting through to him. She says:

'I tried to warn you.'

'You tried to warn me off.'

'Because I didn't want you getting hurt.'

'Because you were jealous.'

'Not true.'

'You're still jealous.'

'Not true.'

'You are. You did everything you could to come between us. This is all your fault. You practically told her about us. You made sure she knew.'

'That's not true.'

'You don't care about me. If you did you'd tell me where she is.'

'So she can hurt you some more? So you can make a fool of yourself?'

'You'd rather protect her than help me.'

'Not true.'

'You'd rather protect yourself.'

'How so?'

'You'd rather let her think that you and I meant something.'

'Not true.'

'You don't want me to talk to her because you don't want me to tell her the truth.'

'Which is?'

'That what happened between us was nothing. Less than nothing.'

'You don't mean that.'

'That it was a mistake. A bad mistake. The worst mistake I've ever made.'

'You don't mean that.'

'You see. It's true. You don't want me to tell her that I was angry and upset and that you were there and it was just . . .'

'You getting your own back?'

'Something like that.'

'Fine,' she says, tears already rolling down her face. 'Fine,' she says, rummaging through her bag, pulling out a pen and a notebook and scribbling something in the back of it. 'Tell her what you like,' she says, tearing the page out of the notebook and pushing it in front of him. 'Give her my love when you see her.'

She grabs her bag and her coat and slides out of the booth, tears running mascara down her cheeks, some already finding their way to the faded and scratched yellow pattern of the table.

She gets to her feet, pulls on her coat and turns to leave, and then, remembering something else, leans in close to him, so close to his face that he can feel the heat of hers and hear the anger and wetness in her mouth.

'One thing though,' she says, sniffing back tears and replacing them with a cold, spitting meanness, 'when you find out what she's really like, when you find out that I was right, that I was telling you the truth, or most of it, all along, don't say I didn't warn you. And don't you dare come crying to me about it.'

Chapter Twenty-Four

He spent the rest of the Saturday after the Friday that he slept with Audrey wondering what to do about it. He felt her quiet departure had been to save them both from awkwardness, to make it easier, or maybe because she thought it the right thing to do. Maybe that's what she thought he wanted, for her to go, so it would be like it never happened; for the first few minutes after waking up and finding her gone, he wondered if it actually had. Perhaps that's what *she* wanted, to pretend that they hadn't. He wondered if she'd woken full of regret and didn't want him to see, or if she just couldn't deal with it, didn't know how to. He imagined her waking before him, rolling over and seeing him asleep. He imagined her quietly slipping out of the bed, gently sliding one foot from under the covers and onto the floor, and then the other. He imagined her gathering up her clothes, piece by piece, all the while watching him sleep, holding her breath when he moved or stirred. He imagined her seeing her opportunity to save them both the discomfort of not knowing how to be with each other, or what came next. He closed his eyes and imagined her closing the door behind her, quietly. Maybe that was what she wanted, to leave it all where it was and say no more about it. Maybe.

Selflessness or regret, whatever her reason for leaving as she had, he wished she hadn't. After wandering from room to room looking for signs of her and finding none bar a couple of cigarette butts and the empty tequila bottle in the recycling, he felt disappointed, not relieved, and at the edge of his disappointment he felt the sadness stirring and stretching, readying itself, impatiently waiting its turn.

For the next hour or so the hope lingered that she would return, that she'd popped out to buy them breakfast and was planning to surprise him in bed with it, and then as time dragged too far on for breakfast to be a realistic possibility, he began to tell himself that she'd gone home for a change of clothes and would be back at any minute. When she wasn't, he thought about calling to tell her that he wished she was there, that he hadn't wanted her to leave, that he wished she would come back, but then the other possibility, that this was the way she wanted it, began to seem ever more likely and so he decided that the only sensible thing to do was to put Audrey out of his mind altogether.

For the rest of the day Peter's flat seemed to have even less life in it than usual. He found himself restless, trying to busy himself, telling himself that he was trying to busy himself to pass the time, yet knowing that it was to stop him thinking about her. He tried to watch a film and when he couldn't concentrate on what was happening on screen he thought about reading a book or entertaining himself with the internet and when he couldn't be bothered to do either of those he thought about just lying on Peter's sofa and doing and thinking about nothing. Instead he decided on music. He leafed though Peter's vinyl and after finding nothing that he wanted to listen to, he played what was already on the turntable. Miles Davis's 'So What' wafted out of the speakers but it was flat and lifeless. In the listless afternoon light of Peter's living room the magic that the night before had been in every piano chord and every bounce of every beat was gone. He played no more than a minute of it and then had to turn it off.

He went outside and sat on Peter's terrace to smoke a cigarette and found himself looking at her lipstick marks on the cigarette butts in the flower pot. If it had been a conscious thought he might have stopped it. As it was, it was just there. He didn't have

234

to close his eyes to taste the tequila or hear her laughing. He didn't have to concentrate to see her shimmy and hip-bounce her way over to him. He didn't have to think about her to feel her absence. Everywhere he looked she was missing. The living room, the open patio door, the bench seat next to him, the kitchen, the bedroom, wherever he thought of, there was nowhere in Peter's flat that he could go that he wouldn't find her missing. For a moment he thought that he might actually have been thinking it on purpose, that he was trying to imagine that he was somehow missing her because she was all he had, all he could have, and as his only option he was trying to make himself feel something for her. Then he realised that the only *her* he'd thought of all day was Audrey. From the moment he'd opened his eyes and found her gone, when he'd thought of *her*, he'd been thinking of Audrey, not Sophie. Sophie hadn't once come into his thoughts all day. The anger of the day before, at being stood up, at having his carefully made plan dismissed as unimportant and missable, had all been forgotten, overtaken by the life that Audrey and her bottle of tequila had brought to Peter's flat. Replaced by the colour that Audrey had brought to what should have been a dismal summer evening spent alone drowning his sorrows. And then he realised that every thought he'd had since waking up and finding her gone, every single simple thought, what to eat, what to watch, what to listen to, whether to have tea or coffee, had been followed by the thought of her. He hadn't had to try. There was no need to convince himself that he was missing her. The emptiness of Peter's flat had done that for him.

He sat alone on the bench seat on Peter's terrace and he tried as hard as he could to think of nothing for a moment. To have blank thoughts. To have the space to not think. To have peace and quiet and nothing, just for the time it took to take and let go a deep, slow breath, and as he let go that breath he saw her throwing back the tequila and wincing and shaking her head, he saw her throw her head back and bounce her hips to the music that a moment before he'd had to turn off, which was now playing loud and vibrant in his head. He felt the music waft over him, he felt her lips and their softness and the tenderness with which they kissed him back. He

saw the little black dress and her hips shimmying in it, the thin black
tights and her shapely thighs and ankles beneath them, her black
knickers and red bra which didn't make a set, that stood out in stark
contrast against the ghostly white of her skin that glowed almost
luminescent in the blue dark of his bedroom in Peter's flat. He felt
the touch again of her lips as they went from passive to positive,
kissing him. He felt the softness of her pale white skin as he traced it
up and along the inside of her thighs, the tips of his fingers gently
sinking into the soft fleshiness of them, circling, tracing. He felt the
softness of her luminescent skin against his cheeks, he felt the
smoothness and the warmth and sweetness as he kissed it, and then
he felt again the disappointment, at having found her gone, at her
clothes not being on the floor by the bed, at not finding a note giving
any clue as to her thoughts about what had happened between them,
at the lack of her presence and the emptiness it left behind, at her
not being there, next to him, on the bench seat on Peter's terrace.

He finished his cigarette and thought again about calling
her and this time his hesitation was less about whether or not it was
the right thing to do, and more about the unfamiliar and unexpected
nervousness and excitement that he felt at the thought of hearing
her answer and say 'Hello'. Never before had the thought of calling
Audrey made him excited, and certainly never nervous. Audrey was
Audrey. What was there about Audrey to be excited or nervous
about? Yet he felt it, deep inside, pushing the disappointment and
the waiting sadness back into their dark corners. He felt the knots of
his excitement and nervousness tighten and with them his chest
tense and flutter as he decided that he was actually going to do it.

He took his phone out of his pocket and as he went to his
recent calls and saw her name something in his heart quickened, so
much so that he wanted to laugh, he felt like an adolescent about to
call a girl for the first time, only this wasn't the pretty girl in class
who he fancied, this was Audrey, the best friend who for all he knew
he may well have been in love with the whole of his life and just
never stopped to realise it. He looked at her name, his thumb
hovering above it, and then as if trusting the outcome to fate he
blinked his eyes closed, touched his thumb to the screen and

brought his phone to his ear. As her phone began to ring, he opened his eyes and instantly became aware of the pounding of his heart and the sound of Peter's buzzer. Audrey's phone ringing in his ear, he went inside. Peter's buzzer buzzed again, a long insistent buzz, the same long insistent buzz that Audrey had buzzed the night before. As he walked down the hall to Peter's front door and the buzzer buzzed another long insistent buzz, he suddenly pictured Audrey on the other side, impatient and uncomfortable, in her little trench coat and heels, worried that the neighbours might be watching and that he might leave her out there all night. As Audrey's phone rang in his ear he tried to hear it ring on the other side of Peter's front door, between the sound of the buzzer and his feet and heart hurrying him down the hall. At the fifth buzz, with Audrey's phone still ringing in his ear, he put his eye to the peephole ready to see a black bob and trench coat, ready to smile and hang up. He saw the trench coat and smiled, and then he registered an unexpected panic at the fact that the furtive figure looking left and right and buzzing again was Sophie. It took another buzz before he'd sufficiently reoriented himself to open the door, touching the screen to end the call as Audrey answered and said, 'Hello, I was just wondering if you'd call.'

'Thank God for that,' she said as he opened the door wide, allowing her to step inside. 'I thought you were going to leave me out there all night.'

He didn't say anything as he took another step back, allowing her to come properly into the hall and the front door to close behind her.

'Which would have been awkward,' she said, following him as he backed further into the hall, stopping two steps after he did so she was close enough for him to feel her breath against his face as she leaned into his ear and said, 'Because I'm not wearing anything under my coat.'

With that she let her little trench coat fall to the floor and leaned in to his ear again 'I felt so bad about last night, about letting you down. I wanted to make it up to you. Will you let me make it up to you?'

Her breath on his ear made him close his eyes despite

himself and a shudder of weakness pass all the way through him. His eyes closed, he turned his mouth to her ear and said, 'That depends.'

He heard her lips part into a smile.

'On?'

'On whether you really understand just how pissed off and upset I was.'

'I can imagine.'

'I really don't think you can.'

'Let me try. Let me try to show you that I understand and let me try to make it up to you.' Her hand left the side of his face, where the backs of her fingers had been gently stroking his cheek, and slowly travelled down his chest, to his stomach, to his waist, carrying on down. 'What would you say was adequate compensation?' Her hand stopped at the top of his thigh and took hold of his hand. Her lips almost brushing his ear, she said, 'How about we start with an exchange? One dirty weekend away,' she pulled his hand from his thigh and slid it up her own, sliding it higher and higher, 'for one very, very, very,' she eased his fingers home, 'very dirty evening at home?' She squeezed his hand between her thighs, pulled herself closer into him and said, 'And the best thing is, you don't have to do anything. It's only fair.' She eased a sigh into him. 'I let you down, so I should do all the work.'

Before she could explain more, they were grabbing handfuls of each other, pulling and tugging and forcing themselves against each other, forcing each other against the wall of Peter's hall, not tentatively trying to find a way into each other as he and Audrey had, not finding excitement in the slightest touch of skin, but pawing each other roughly, angrily, a mixture of lust and resentment and relief at being able to hurt each other, at least that was how it felt to him. He pulled at her hair and kissed her shoulder hard enough to feel it against his teeth. The fingers of the hand between her thighs he dug deep into her, as hard and spitefully as he could. She responded in kind, gouging the back of his shoulders through his shirt, scratching into the back of his neck and his head, pulling him deeper into her, letting out deeper and deeper sighs the angrier they got with each other.

He woke up the next morning to find her in a deep, contented sleep next to him. He rolled over to look at her properly, to savour her happily dreaming smile, and then he quietly slipped out of bed, sliding one foot then the other from under the covers and onto the floor. He gathered his clothes from the floor by the bed and dressed and went down the hall to the kitchen to make breakfast. Wanting to surprise her, he worked as quietly as he could, making toast and coffee with exaggerated caution and taking extra care when opening the fridge so as not to disturb the bottles in the door. He poured two glasses of orange juice, got spoons, knives and serviettes out of the gently opened drawer and added them to the tray with the toast, coffee, butter and jam, arranging everything as artfully as his excitement would allow.

'I was looking under the bed for one of my shoes.' He looked up to find her standing in the kitchen doorway, her little trench coat tied tight at the waist, her shoes in one hand. 'And I found these.'

With her other hand she held out a red bra and a piece of notepaper.

She stood motionless for a moment, the bra and notepaper hanging in mid-air between them, her eyes glazed over but fixed on him, making him feel all of the hurt and anger that she was too hurt and angry to express, and then she calmly put the bra and notepaper on the kitchen counter and said, 'I'll leave these here.'

Without looking at him again, she put her shoes on and turned to leave. She paused in the hall, her back to him still, and said, 'Don't call me again.'

As the front door closed a sudden and final emptiness swept in to fill Peter's flat. He looked at the bra and notepaper and at the tray with the still-warm toast and steaming coffee and tried to process the events of the last minute that had turned a morning full of possibilities into nothing. He took a couple of steps along Peter's miniature kitchen to the bra and the piece of notepaper. He picked up the bra. Red and instantly familiar, the mere touch of it made him sick with regret and panic, the kind that only comes with knowing that it's too late to fix whatever's broken. With his other hand he laid flat the folded notepaper and read:

Thanks for last night. I have no regrets, hope you don't either.

If you want more of the same, call me.
Audrey xxx

Chapter Twenty-Five

A tourist boat passes beneath them.

> *Its engines reverberating under the bridge.*
>
> *Its floodlights illuminating the left bank as it emerges.*
>
> *Throwing shadows of trees against the buildings.*
>
> *Turning everything yellow. Leaving the darkness blacker*

behind it.

> *He hears the sound of the water churning in its wake and*

feels cold.

> *He pulls his scarf and collar tighter.*
>
> *He pulls her closer to him.*
>
> *She moves to resettle herself. To nestle deeper into his*

coat.

> *Her arms tighten around his.*
>
> *Her head pushes further onto his shoulder, deeper into his*

neck and scarf.

> *He can feel her through his coat. Pressing into him.*

Holding on tight. He can feel her contentment growing deeper with
every deep breath and sigh. He can feel it in the weight of her head
on his shoulder. In the way she wraps herself deeper and tighter
around his arm. In the stillness in the dark around them.

> *There's no one else on the bridge. It's just the two of them.*

Sitting. Being together. Watching nothing in particular. Letting the cold night wash over them. *The glow of the Eiffel Tower. The lights of the bridges and buildings reflecting in the water. The night, making everything magical.*

Making everything unreal.

He tries to take it in.

To memorise all the faraway details.

The Musée d'Orsay. The glass roof of the Grand Palais. The sights of Paris shining gold in the distant dark.

He tries to absorb the darkness.

To focus on all the little lights lost in it.

He tries to savour the feeling of being alone on an island in the middle of the Seine. Of being adrift from it all. He tries to savour the view of Paris and the feeling of being lost to it.

He closes his eyes.

He can still see everything. The Musée d'Orsay. The Grand Palais. The lights of the bridges and buildings reflecting in the water. The glow of the Eiffel Tower.

He can still feel it. The distance between them and everything out in the darkness.

He keeps his eyes closed.

He can hear it.

He listens to the sound of the late-night Paris traffic on the quai. He listens to her sighs. To the sound of the water lapping against the bridge beneath them. He hears the distant sound of a scooter pulling away from traffic lights and of tyres on cobbles. He feels her move again next to him, as if the scooter or the tyres have woken her from a deep sleep.

He waits for her to settle again.

He listens for her sigh. He waits to feel her contentment.

Then he kisses her hair and asks her again if she'd like an apartment on the Rue du Bac. One with a secret courtyard. And two perfect children. And a wardrobe where everything in it is meant to be worn with pearls.

He hears her smile and say, 'Sounds lovely.'

He kisses her hair again and opens his eyes.

The Eiffel Tower's gone. Its lights turned off.

He wakes up in the driver's seat of Peter's car. The car Peter used to drive in London, a little blue BMW, which, though perhaps not as pretty as the little white Mercedes he had in the South of France, was equally old and loved. It's dark now. The stereo's still playing the Rolling Stones compilation Peter left in it, which means he can't have been asleep long, but long enough for afternoon to turn to evening and the street lights to reach their full glow.

He pushes himself up in the seat and tries to make himself awake. He tries to focus on where he is and why he's there. 'Under My Thumb' struggles to be heard above the whirr and rattle of the little BMW's ancient heater, which is doing nothing to clear the car's steamed-up windows. His view of her house, of her windows, of her door, or at least the windows and door of the house Audrey gave him the address for, the windows and door he was watching before he fell asleep, is now obscured by a layer of condensation coloured orange by the street lights.

He stretches to wipe a hole in the windscreen with his hand and wipes the window of the driver's door with the sleeve of his coat. He looks through the wet glass to the black-and-white-tiled steps leading up to the black front door. He looks at the windows, now illuminated with a warm and welcoming glow, three floors of them. He looks at the railings and what he can see of the basement windows, also now glowing and warm. He looks back to the front door and the porch at the top of the steps. A large porch for a large house. A porch with columns either side and a canopy and a hanging lamp illuminating it. He looks at the front door, its deep gloss gleaming in the light of the hanging lamp, and he tries to imagine her walking through it.

He looks up to the top floor of the house, to the three small windows, then down to the large bay windows, one above the other, of the two floors below. He looks at the large bay window next to the front door. Even though the angle of his view prevents him from seeing in, he knows that if he could he would find the opulent interior of a wealthy family home that he can't imagine her living in. He looks to the other similarly grand yet less well lit houses in the terrace and back to the bright porch of the address Audrey gave him and can't believe that there isn't some mistake. She is not the type of person who would live in a house like this. He can't equate this serious house and the established lifestyle it represents with Sophie, or at least not with the Sophie he knows.

He checks again the address on the page from Audrey's notebook. He checks the name of the square against the name on the Royal Borough of Kensington and Chelsea street sign on the railings of the house on the corner. He checks the door number against that painted on the porch's right-hand column. He looks at the page of the notebook again and wonders if maybe Audrey was mistaken, if she was in some way confused or in her moment of upset she had written the address down wrong. He looks back at the number on the column to the right of the front door and wonders if she might have given him the wrong address on purpose, if this was her still protecting Sophie or keeping her out of his reach.

'Miss You' starts to play. He watches a well-dressed couple turn into the square and walk towards him on the opposite pavement. He watches the couple, him the older side of middle-aged, her several years younger, and notes their smart evening dress as they pass under the street lights walking towards him. He watches them walk to the black-and-white-tiled steps and up them to the front door. He watches them ring the bell. He watches them wait for the door to be answered as Mick Jagger laments his lack of sleep and waiting by the phone for the woman who's been haunting his dreams to call.

The door opens. Sophie greets the couple, opening the door wide, inviting them in, kissing both in turn as they enter, closing the door behind them. She's there for only a couple of seconds. Not long enough for him to fully absorb her, not long enough for him to make out any of the details let alone take them in, but long enough for him to see her differently, to know that this is her home and that she does belong here, at least this Sophie does.

He watches the door for several minutes, unable to look away in case it should open again and she should be there. He waits, hopeful and disappointed, still not awake enough to make sense of the little of her he did see or to understand what it might mean, knowing only that this is where Sophie lives and that that was not the Sophie he knows.

A taxi turns into the square and pulls up in front of the house. The first notes of 'Gimme Shelter' fill the inside of the little blue BMW, rising above the sound of the heater as a couple get out. He pays the driver, she waits at the bottom of the steps. Her long coat gives little away about what she's wearing, but her hair says that she is not dressed for a casual evening with friends. The Stones are in full effect by the time they get to the top of the steps and press the bell. The three of them wait for the door to open. Mick wails that something indecipherable is just a shot away and the front door opens. This time he's ready for her. Ready to see her smile and her eyes grow wide with a sociable excitement that he's never seen before. Ready to see her hug and kiss with businesslike enthusiasm that he doesn't recognise or believe. This time he sees that she too is dressed for an evening of polite conversation and good manners. She's wearing a black pencil dress which although not familiar suits her, with her hair up in a neat Princess Grace bun which doesn't. He wonders if they're clients or work colleagues, if this is personal or professional entertainment.

This isn't the real Sophie. Seeing her there like that, he's sure that the Sophie he knows is the real Sophie. This hostess isn't her. He thinks about ringing the bell and her opening the door and wonders if he'll see the real Sophie then. He wonders if he'll recognise her when she sees it's him. If the real Sophie will slip out or if she'll hold it all together with a calm hostess Sophie politeness. He wonders what she'll say. He wonders what he'll see in her eyes and whether it will match what comes out of her mouth.

He watches hostess Sophie broaden her polite smile and laugh and welcome the couple into the hall. He watches her guide them through the front door, nodding and gesturing towards something as she closes it behind them. He watches the closed front door. He tries to picture the scene behind it. Hostess Sophie offering to take their coats, thanking them for the bottle they brought with them, saying that she'll put it in the fridge, that they'll have it later,

245

lying that she's heard good things about it, that she's looking forward to trying it, telling them who's already there, that they're in the living room, that they should go through, she'll hang the coats up and put the wine in the fridge and be right with them. He imagines the real Sophie discarding the bottle on the worktop in the kitchen and opening the fridge to get another bottle of the wine she once bought him. He imagines hostess Sophie taking it through to fill the glasses of her guests, who tell her how wonderful it is, and then her telling them that it's her favourite and she buys it by the case and she'll give them a bottle to take home if they like, she's got plenty.

He watches the closed front door and listens to the choir of 'You Can't Always Get What You Want' and imagines the laughter and smiles in the room behind the large bay window that the angle of his view through the damp windows of Peter's little blue BMW prevents him from seeing into. He imagines the couple he's just seen arrive talking to the couple he saw arrive before them, and he wonders how many more couples there are to come. Then he decides that this is better than anything he'd hoped for. He was hoping to find her alone, so they could talk, so they wouldn't be disturbed, so he could tell her all the things he had to say without them being overheard or made to feel uncomfortable. He was hoping that finding him on her doorstep, knocking on the front door of her home, would force her to listen to him. That the fact that he'd found her and there was nowhere else for her to disappear to would leave her no choice but to ask him in and allow him to apologise and try to put things right. Or at the very least she'd have to explain why she'd reacted the way she had and the real reason why she didn't want to see him any more, if only to make him give up and leave her alone. For a moment after the front door closed behind the first couple, his heart had sunk and beneath the wave of adrenaline brought on by seeing her he'd detected the movement of the sadness starting to stir. The disappointment of finding her home but not alone seemed to put her so far beyond his reach that it made an impossibility of the thought of ever being near her again. He thought about leaving. But then when he watched hostess Sophie greet the second couple, when he saw her polite smile and cordial hugs and kisses, he felt the sadness melt and fade again. As he pictures the opulent interior beyond the bay window and hears the sound of civilised dinner-party conversation, he decides that this could be the perfect opportunity to get the real Sophie's full attention.

He watches the closed front door and listens to Mick sing about seeing her today at the reception with a glass of wine in her hand and he knows that if he wants to get through to the real Sophie, if he wants her to listen to him, he needs hostess Sophie to want to avoid a scene. He watches the front door and the square for another few minutes. He waits to see if anyone else arrives, to give latecomers time to negotiate traffic or find their way. He waits long enough to be sure that he and the real Sophie won't be interrupted. He waits until he's as sure as he can be that no one else is coming and then he gets out of Peter's little blue BMW, shuts the door, locks it and turns and walks towards her front door. Once he's moving he doesn't stop. He doesn't give himself time to think or change his mind. He walks across the road and up the steps and rings the doorbell like an invited guest, pressing it without a pause for breath for fear that he might think better of it and have to creep back down the steps. He hears the bell ring. A short, clear, electric ring. He hears the hammer on the bell and thinks he feels his heart stop. He hears the hammer of the bell and then nothing. He waits and listens to nothing and then waits and listens some more, his eyes closing as he tries to steady his breath, as he tries to hear his heartbeat or at least the sound of movement behind the door. He waits and he listens and he hears nothing and then the click of the lock and maybe laughter over classical music and then he opens his eyes to see the door open wide and the smiling face of the man from the Jardin du Luxembourg, who says in a quietly welcoming voice: 'Hello.'

He looks at the older, wiser features of the man from the Jardin du Luxembourg. He looks at his lightly tanned skin and the lines around his eyes. He looks at the firm line of his jaw and his dark hair. He looks at the patches of grey that he could only just make out from the other side of the Avenue de l'Opéra. He looks at his worn but attractive face, even more assured and handsome close up, and he can read all of the charm and success and ease that at a distance he'd only guessed at. The man from the Jardin du Luxembourg's older, wiser features break into a questioning smile, to which he adds: 'Can I help you?'

Without thinking he hears himself say Sophie's name and then after too long a pause he hears himself ask if she's there, if she's available, to talk to, that is. The man from the Jardin du Luxembourg's questioning smile drops to just questioning, but a voice behind tells him as calmly as if it were true that it's alright, it's work, she won't be a moment, and then asks if he can keep an eye on things and get another bottle of wine.

He watches hostess Sophie hand the man from the Jardin du Luxembourg an empty bottle of her favourite wine, the one she once bought for him, and he sees her smile a smile he doesn't recognise as the man from the Jardin du Luxembourg nods, then nods goodbye to Sophie's awkward work colleague and heads off to the kitchen. Still smiling, hostess Sophie watches him go and when he's no longer in earshot she steps outside and pulls the front door closed behind her. The smile he doesn't recognise turns to a thin grimace and a bitter look that he hasn't been able to forget since he saw it last on the platform of the Paris Métro.

'What the hell do you want?'

Again her words lash out at him despite being kept discreetly under her breath.

'To talk.'

'Here? Now? In the middle of the bloody night?'

'I tried to talk to you before but you wouldn't let . . .'

She cuts him short, her voice raised to a whispered shout of someone who's heard enough.

'Haven't you got the message yet? Whatever it is, I'm not interested. Certainly not here. Not now.'

'Well when?'

'Why can't you just leave it alone? Why can't you just leave me alone?'

He watches her searching his face and he watches the anger and shock and energy drain from her, leaving only tiredness and exasperation. He sees all the spitefulness and hate she threw at him in Paris go with it, leaving before him the soft and vulnerable Sophie he knew when they first went there together, the tender Sophie only he knows, the girl behind the grey suit and the smart shoes and briefcase. The real Sophie. This Sophie he recognises. The Sophie he knew and loved. The Sophie who loved him back.

The sound of laughter comes through the crack in the door.

She looks behind her and then back to him, her face now sad and imploring. Her face is so sad, she seems so vulnerable, that he wants to comfort her, to stroke her hair like he used to, to show her that he still cares and that the last thing he wants to do is make her unhappy. He feels her desperation. Her helplessness. He reaches a hand out to her, to touch her hair, and for a moment she lets him, until the sound of conversation and laughter from inside makes her pull away.

'I can't do this. Not here. Not now. I've got guests. I've got to get back inside.'

'I need to see you. Properly. Please.'

'I can't.'

'Please.'

'Why?'

'I need to.'

'No you don't.'

'Please. Just once. And then I'll leave you alone if you want me to.'

He watches her searching his face and he watches the kindness and sadness and care break her.

'Tomorrow. I'll meet you tomorrow.'

'I don't believe you.'

She looks at him with such sadness that he knows that no matter how much she protests otherwise, no matter how angry and resentful she may claim to be, he can see in the sadness in her eyes, that she still cares for him. He can see that she still cares for him and that she doesn't want it to be like this any more than he does. She looks sad and tearful and moves her hands in a way that suggests she wants to touch his and then thinks better of it.

'No, I will. Really. I promise.'

'Where?'

'The cafe on the corner of Winsley Street. I'll meet you there after lunch. Three o'clock. I promise I'll come, I'll be there, but you've got to go now. Please.'

Chapter Twenty-Six

He looks through the window of the cafe on the corner of Winsley Street. It's empty except for a workman reading a newspaper at a table by the window and the man behind the counter scraping the hotplate. She's not there. He checks the time on the clock above the counter, looks up Winsley Street and left and right along Eastcastle Street, looking to see if he can see her coming, not really expecting to. He checks the time on the clock above the counter and the tables under the back wall's four-panel menu and the booths along the left-hand side, to be sure.

     He looks through the window of the cafe on the corner of Winsley Street and feels neither angry nor stupid, because he didn't really believe that she'd come. He knew when she said that she'd meet him there that she would have promised and said anything to get rid of him, to get him off her doorstep and save herself from the discomfort or embarrassment of having him there. On his way there from Peter's flat he'd already resigned himself to the fact that she wouldn't be there and was half expecting to find Audrey waiting for him, sitting in the last booth, nursing a cup of tea, looking thoughtfully into it, rehearsing all the things Sophie had told her to say. Then he'd remembered the last time he saw Audrey, the last time he'd been to the cafe on the corner of Winsley Street, and the way she'd been and the way they'd left things, and he decided that he was probably the last person she would be willing to mollify or console, or, at the very least, that she was done with acting as his and Sophie's go-between.

He looks left and right along Eastcastle Street and back up Winsley Street again. He knows that she's not coming and that he should go, if not back to Peter's flat, then to anywhere where he won't sit watching the door and the clock for hours, hoping to be proved wrong. Nonetheless, he opens the door and goes in, knowing that to be sure that she didn't come, that she wasn't delayed, caught up in a meeting she couldn't get out of, on a conference call that overran, stuck in traffic or in a tunnel by a signal failure on the tube, to be certain that she didn't arrive minutes after he left, he knows he'll need to wait, all afternoon if he has to, to be sure.

The man behind the counter doesn't look up as he comes in and the door closes behind him. He waits at the counter for the man behind it to notice him, to take his order of a tea and ask him if that's all, as he always does. He waits by the counter, watching the man on the other side of it scraping bits of egg and grease and onion from the hotplate, pulling the scrapings into the hotplate's gutter, working at tough spots with his scraper, oblivious to everything other than the state of his cooking equipment. The radio plays interchangeable decade-old pop hits at low volume in the background, and after the second or third he's almost as engrossed by the scraping as the man behind the counter is.

They both hear the door open behind him, the man behind the counter looking up for the first time, surprised by the new customer at the counter, smiling past him to Sophie shutting the door behind her. He wipes his hands on his apron. 'What can I get you?'

'Two teas please.'

'Is that all?'

'Yes. Thanks.'

The man behind the counter pours two teas from the pot, adds milk and tops them up with hot water as Sophie slides into the last booth. She's back in her usual uniform, grey skirt, grey jacket, white blouse. He watches her lay her coat and briefcase next to her and pull her hair from her collar and straighten her jacket. He watches her and sees an awkwardness that he doesn't think he's ever seen before. Her eyes and lips are drawn thin with discomfort, as if she's trying her best not to give anything away, not to be vulnerable, not to look embarrassed.

'Two teas. That's one forty please.'

He hands over the one forty and takes the two stained and chipped mugs over to the booth and sets them down on the faded Formica. She looks at the tea, then briefly at him to smile and say 'Thank you,' like someone accepting the kindness of a stranger and trying not to look in need of it. She looks down at the mug in front of her and pulls it towards her, wrapping her hands around it for comfort, only to immediately pull them away again.

'It's hot.'

The smallness of her laugh, the nervousness of the rest of her, seem pitiful next to the thought of hostess Sophie from last night. Watching her in her black evening dress and Princess Grace bun, with her practised politeness and gracious smile, and watching her in front of him now, seeing her discomfort, realising that she doesn't quite know where to put herself or where to start, he realises that for the first time things are on his terms and he's not sure he likes it. Strength and confidence, control, not contrition, are what he needs from Sophie. He knows that he should be amazed that she turned up, relieved, grateful even. Instead he's disappointed that this is the Sophie who came. Part of him wants to reach across the table and shake her, to grab her by the arm and drag her off to a hotel for the rest of the afternoon, if only to make her the Sophie that he knows he wants. He watches her avoiding eye contact, like someone who's been caught in a lie, and part of him longs for the bitter anger of Paris, for the indignation and horror, for anything other than this.

'I didn't think you'd come.'

'Don't say that.'

'It's true.'

'I promised I would.'

She looks at her tea and then at him.

'But I only came so I could explain. So I could put an end to this.'

He shakes his head.

'I need to explain about Audrey.'

'No, I do. And I need you to listen.' She looks at him. She looks him in the eye and says, 'I want you to let me say what I need to say and not interrupt and not say anything until I've finished.'

He doesn't say anything. He doesn't respond or react. He holds her stare until she breaks it to look down at her tea, the awkwardness and embarrassment returning to her face just before she does. He waits and watches her suffer under the weight of his attention, not knowing what to do with it now she's got it, not knowing where to start. He waits and listens as she starts to explain. He listens as she says she's sorry about last night, that she's sorry about everything, that she never meant it to be like this, that she never meant it to go that far, that things got out of hand, that she didn't know how to stop them, that there was a point where she didn't want to stop them. He listens as she says that she really did like him, that she liked him a lot, and that she enjoyed being with him and that he'd made her life so much better those first few months, that she hadn't had that much fun in years and that things had been going so well, and that they had been having so much fun together and she'd sensed, right from the start of it, right from the very first night at the magazine's Christmas party, she'd sensed that each of them was exactly what the other was looking for, what right at that moment they were looking for. He listens as she says that he changed her life, that she'd been so alone, so adrift, cut off from everything except work, which itself was suffocating her. And then she met him and everything changed. She had fun back in her life, she had something to look forward to. He listens as she tells him that she'd always looked forward to seeing him, to being with him. He was her secret, her escape, her way out of her life, her work, herself, he was perfect. He listens as she says that what they had was perfect.

He interrupts her. He says that they can be perfect again. She shakes her head and he says that they can make it like it was,

Audrey meant nothing to him, sleeping with her meant nothing, he did it because he was angry, because she'd let him down one too many times, that he'd done it to hurt her, that he didn't love Audrey, he loved her.

He sees her eyes welling up and goes to put his hands on hers, stopping short as she pulls back from him. She looks at him. She looks him in the eye and smiles and says, 'That's the problem. I don't love you. I never loved you. That's the point.'

He hears her say that they were perfect when they were just a bit of fun, when she thought that was what they both wanted, but then he started to get too close, he started clinging, and then he told her that he loved her and she knew it was over. He hears her say that she tried to put distance between them, tried to break it off gradually, tried to make them grow apart, but he wouldn't let go and in some way she probably didn't want him to because every time she pushed him away he would try to reach out to her and she kept letting him. Until he started turning up at her office and trying to organise her life for her. He hears her say that she knew then that that could never work and she had to end it once and for all.

He interrupts her again. He tells her that he doesn't understand. They were good together, why couldn't she just go with it? If she liked him so much, if they had such a good time together, why wouldn't she want to be with him?

He sees her hurt at having to repeat the most painful part of what she's been trying to tell him. 'Because I don't love you. Because I never loved you. Because I couldn't love you.'

He hears her say that she can see now that they weren't what each other needed at all. That she'd needed a distraction, something to fill in the gaps, something to save her from the loneliness that came from being left on her own for months on end, whereas he wanted to love someone, to become part of someone else, and she could never allow that to happen.

He watches her face. He sees the hurt and desperation and feels the significance if not the meaning of what she's trying to tell him. He thinks about what she's said and about what she's trying to say and asks: 'Who is he?'

She looks at him. She looks him in the eye and says: 'My husband.'

He knew what she was going to say before she said it. In a way he knew the moment he first saw him in the Jardin du Luxembourg, when he first saw them together. He knew from the way they looked at each other, from the way they touched, from the way she clung to him, that this was more than a passing amusement like he had been. He knew that what he saw between them was love, not entertainment. He knew that this was the kind of man she would be able to fall in love with and devote a lifetime to and that he was just something that happened along the way. He knew, yet hearing her say it is something else. He doesn't respond or react. He doesn't know how to. He doesn't think or feel anything. Even the sadness has deserted him, the one thing he could depend on.

He feels her eyes searching his face, looking for a reaction. He can feel her trying to judge if he's broken or about to explode and cause the ugliest of scenes. He feels the tension in her, her growing anxiety, her need for someone to speak. He hears her start to talk again. He hears her say that she's sorry. He hears her say that she never wanted to hurt either of them, him or her husband. He hears her say that she loves her husband, that they've been together for twelve years, that she met him at a party a year after she graduated. It was her first serious relationship, he swept her off her feet and they fell madly in love and got married six months later. Although he's not really there, not really listening any more, he can hear the smile in her voice and the affection and care as she tells him that she loves her husband very much, that she's never stopped loving him since the day they met. Although he's not interested, he can hear the change in her voice, the sadness, perhaps pain, when she tells him that while she loves her husband very much, things aren't always that simple. He hears her say that he works hard and is away a lot on business, that he's away often and often for long periods, months at a time sometimes. She tells him that there are times when she doesn't see him for two, maybe three months and that every time he goes away, the time apart and the loneliness feel harder. And then she met him. One night at an office Christmas party she met someone who instantly took her out of herself, made her forget, someone so fun and easy to be with that the loneliness which sometimes used to well up inside her, to the point where she felt like she couldn't breathe any more, suddenly disappeared. She went from drowning to alive in a night. He did that. He did that for her and she was so grateful. She could never express to him what that meant. She says she's not going to lie, there had been others, Audrey probably told him as much or strongly hinted, but none like him, none who really took her out of herself and gave her another life, one outside of being a workaholic going home to a very large, very empty house while her husband was on the other side of the world. He had. He was different. He was the fun and the escape that she had needed. And then she realised it was all getting too serious, that he was getting too serious. She wondered if she'd led him on, if he'd misunderstood, and by the point that she realised that she probably had, she couldn't find a way to tell him about her life and her husband.

He hears her say that she didn't want to hurt him. That she tried not seeing him, tried putting distance between them, hoping that he'd lose interest or forget her or find someone else. She tried to make a clean break of it, to not hurt him, to not cause a scene, and when that didn't work, she turned to Audrey. She tells him not to blame Audrey. She says he must know that Audrey's in love with him. She says she's not sure how much Audrey admits it to herself, but she can see it in the way she looks at him, she can hear it in the way she talks about him. And then there's what she's willing to do for him, to protect him, to save him from getting hurt.

He hears her say that she's known all along how Audrey feels about him and that it was obvious from the start that Audrey wasn't happy with them seeing each other. She thought at first it was jealousy, then she realised that Audrey knew him better than she did, that she understood what he needed and that she knew that she, Sophie, married Sophie, lonely and looking for a distraction Sophie, couldn't give it to him and would only end up hurting him. He hears her say that Audrey knows him better than anyone, and that she really does care about him, no matter what he might think. He hears

257

her say again that he mustn't blame Audrey, that it was her idea, not Audrey's, that she asked Audrey for help and she knew that she would do it because she loves him and wants to be with him and didn't want him to be hurt any more than he had been. He hears her say that she told Audrey that she'd tried to end it with him, that she'd tried to put distance between them and that it hadn't worked, that they kept pulling each other back together, that he wouldn't let go. She told her that they needed a proper end, something that was final, something unambiguous and irreparable that they couldn't get over. He hears her say that it was her idea that Audrey sleep with him. That Audrey had been reluctant at first, more than reluctant, she'd point-blank refused the first, second, third time of asking, and then she seemed to have a sudden change of heart, the day they were supposed to go to Brighton. A couple of hours after she'd asked again for Audrey's help and Audrey had again refused, she'd got a call from Audrey saying she'd spoken to him, that something he'd said had changed her mind, that she'd do it. He hears her say that she told Audrey all she had to do was sleep with him and leave some evidence for her to find and that would be that. He hears her say that she thought it was for the best for all of them, a clean break which might actually bring him and Audrey closer together.

He hears her say that if she'd known that he was going to take it out on Audrey, or that he was going to come after her like that, she wouldn't have suggested it. He hears her say that she wishes now she'd been honest with him, that she'd told him the truth as soon as he started getting more serious, that she should have told him she was married as soon as he said he loved her, that with hindsight she can see that that would have been the best way to a clean break, that that would have saved them all a lot of pain and upset. He hears her say that she never wanted to hurt him or Audrey. That she never wanted to come between them. He hears her say that she never dreamed that he would take things the way he had.

He looks at the cold mug of tea in front of him. He hears the thin beats coming from the radio and the distant sound of Sophie still talking, still telling him that she didn't mean to hurt him, still saying that she wishes she'd done things differently, still telling him that he shouldn't take it out on Audrey, and he realises that he's heard enough, perhaps too much. He stands up and hears her ask him where he's going. He puts his coat on and hears her asking what he's going to do. He feels her worried eyes looking up at him, searching his face for clues. He hears panic in her voice as she says: 'Please don't do anything stupid, don't bring more people into this.'

He looks at her. He looks her in the eye and says: 'Your husband?'

'Please don't say anything.'

'Doesn't he deserve to know?'

'Not like this.'

'No. Maybe not. That's your business anyway.'

'Where are you going then?'

He walks to the door without answering. He hears the thin beats coming from the radio and the distant sound of Sophie telling him again not to take it out on Audrey, telling him, 'She only did it because she loves you.'

Chapter Twenty-Seven

He stands on the step outside Audrey's flat, pushing on the buzzer, leaning in to the speaker, listening, straining to hear her voice. He looks at the speaker, waiting for it to say something. He looks at the street door, waiting for it to open. He looks at the first-floor windows and then at the buzzer again, wondering how long to wait before pushing it again. He pushes the first-floor buzzer again, holding it down, leaning into the speaker, listening to it buzz.

He hears a click, a heavy breath and a voice, Audrey's voice, saying: 'Hello?'

Hearing her voice takes him by surprise, as if he wasn't expecting her to answer, as if he thought she would know why he was there and would want to avoid him.

He hears another heavy breath and Audrey's voice again saying: 'Hello?'

He looks up to the first floor, looking to see if he can see her, to see if he can see her looking at him, and then he says: 'It's me. Let me in.'

Audrey's waiting for him with her door open when he gets to the first-floor landing. He pushes past her into the flat without saying anything.

'No, please, come in. Make yourself at home.'

She closes the door and follows him through to the living

room.

'I was about to get in the bath,' she says, pulling the kimono-style dressing gown she's wearing tight around her. 'But as you're here now I might make tea instead. Would you like one?'

'She's married. Why didn't you tell me she was married?'

She doesn't react, she doesn't say anything or show any signs that she's about to, she just looks at him.

He watches her not saying anything, not reacting, not looking like she's about to, and he knows that she's been waiting for him to turn up at her door like this. He watches her eyes glaze over and her face empty of all signs of anything and he knows that she's thinking that it was only a matter of time before he came to blame her for everything. He looks at the blankness of her, of her face, of her eyes, of the way her shoulders and arms have eased themselves into resignation and he knows that she's already preparing to take whatever abuse he's about to throw at her, with no thought of giving him the answers that he's come for.

'Well, say something.'

'What do you want me to say?'

'Why you didn't tell me she was married.'

Audrey lets out a heavy sigh, allowing her own sadness to fill her face and her eyes and the rest of her. She pulls her kimono-style dressing gown tighter still and says: 'If you're going to have a go at me, do you mind if I go and get dressed first?'

'Why didn't you tell me?'

'I tried to.'

'Not very hard.'

'I did.'

'Not hard enough, clearly.'

'I tried to warn you.' She sits down on the sofa and folds her arms tight across her chest. 'I tried to tell you that this is what she does, when she gets bored. I tried to tell you.'

'You should have tried harder.'

She looks up at him, the sadness in her face now bitter, angry.

'I did everything I could to discourage you, to stop you

261

getting involved.'

'Everything except tell the truth.'

'It was too late for that. I could see it the moment you saw her. The truth was the last thing you wanted to hear. It's always the same with her. This is what she does. This is what happens.' She looks around the coffee table in front of her for a cigarette and having found one in a packet under a magazine turns back to him. 'Men only have to set eyes on her and they're falling all over themselves and blind to the obvious fact that she's not serious about any of them. You're all just a distraction for her. Something to pass the time. Would you have listened if I'd told you? Would you have believed me?' She puts the cigarette in her mouth and lights it. 'Or would you just have pushed me away, called me jealous, which in point of fact is pretty much what you did, and ignored everything you didn't want to hear about her, which would have been most of it?' She puts the match in an ashtray and tucks one side of her bobbed black hair behind her ear. 'I didn't want you to get hurt, but I didn't want to lose you either. I tried to make you see it for yourself. I told you this is what she does. But be honest, by that point, if I'd told you she was married, would it have made a difference?'

'Of course it would.'

'Really? Assuming that you'd believed me that is, which you probably wouldn't have done because I was jealous and bitter and angry, though God knows at what, being passed over by you? Please.' She tucks the other side of her hair behind the other ear. 'No. You were so smitten with her that you'd probably have convinced yourself that she was about to leave her husband for you, which she isn't, before you get any ideas. She never will. She loves him, she just gets bored when he's away, so she uses that ferocious charm of hers and those lovely legs to get her something to keep her occupied. Only this time she ended up with a stalker.' She pauses only long enough to take a drag on her cigarette and exhale. 'What was with you anyway, why couldn't you just deal with it when she didn't want anything more to do with you? Why did the pair of you have to drag me into it?'

He watches her watch the end of her cigarette as she

rounds the ash off it in the ashtray. He senses that it's his turn to speak, but it's come at a point in the conversation where he has nothing to add, the length and ferocity of her contribution having been far more than he was expecting. Instead he watches her and the end of the cigarette and wonders how it is that it's him who's ended up being held to account.

She takes another drag on the cigarette, and with them both still watching the end of it, she laughs and says, 'The tragic thing is, you don't know anything about her. Or you didn't. The Sophie you were so smitten with doesn't even exist. All that crap about you knowing the real her, knowing what she wants, what she needs . . . you didn't even know her name.' She turns a spiteful look to him as she says it and holds his gaze. 'That's why you could never find her. Carlson's her maiden name. She only ever uses it when she . . .' She trails off and looks back to her cigarette and the ashtray. 'That's how I knew, when she introduced herself at the party, when she gave Carlson as her name, I knew then that she'd already decided you were going to be her next distraction, and I knew from the way that you were looking at her that it wasn't going to end well.'

'And yet you didn't say anything.'

'What could I say?'

'You could have told me that she was married. You could have told me not to get involved. You could have told me that this is what she does. You didn't have to wait.'

'I didn't exactly have the chance. The pair of you disappeared off together and then I didn't see you again until New Year, and when you didn't mention her then I thought I might have been wrong, that maybe it *was* just a one-off.' She looks up at him, her expression matching the defensiveness in her voice. 'I didn't know for certain that you were seeing each other until you got back from your jaunt to Paris, and I couldn't exactly say anything then, could I? Not after you'd spent a magical month in the city of love and wouldn't shut up about how happy you were and how grateful you were to me for introducing the two of you.' She looks at him until she can't and turns her attention back to her cigarette. 'I have tried to tell you. When you thought she was playing hard to get. After you split up. When you started back on this whole trying to find her madness, I told you to forget about her, that she wasn't worth what she was doing to you, but by then you were too fucked up to think straight, never mind take the news that she was married. And even when you weren't, I only had to hint that she might not be perfect life-partner material for you to jump down my throat and call me jealous. So what was I supposed to say?'

He doesn't answer and she doesn't push him to. Neither of them says anything for a minute. He watches her watching the smoke gracefully snake up in front of her and then he watches her stub out the rest of the half-smoked cigarette in the ashtray.

'You didn't even know her name,' she says with a bitter laugh that's the only thing holding back tears. 'You didn't know anything about her. You liked the idea of her. You were in love with who you thought she was, and that Sophie, the one you imagined, she doesn't exist. *You* made her up. I mean, what did she actually tell you about herself? How much of the Sophie you knew did you get from her and how much was what you wanted her to be? You were as happy to go along with it as she was to let you, so don't come round here and start blaming me for it. You didn't want to know who she really was any more than you would have wanted me to tell you that she was married.' Still moving ash around the ashtray with the long-extinguished butt, she says: 'Why couldn't you just have gone for someone who actually really cares about you?'

'Someone like you, you mean?'

'Yes. Someone like me.'

She looks up at him, tears closer now than at any point before. 'And what's so wrong with that? I care about you. I really care about you, not that you ever notice. But everything I have or haven't done has been because I didn't want you to get hurt.'

'So that's why you fucked me for Sophie, is it? Because you care about me? Is that what you do to someone you care about? Sleep with them as a favour to someone else, to help that someone else get out of a relationship they don't want to be in? Really?'

He watches her face and the horror working its way across it and he knows that she didn't think Sophie would have told him that. He watches what colour there is in her bleached white cheeks fade away and he knows that now she too is feeling the shock and disappointment of someone's betrayal.

He hears her say that she knows what he's thinking, that she did it for Sophie, but she didn't, she did it for him. He hears himself call her a liar. He hears himself say that she did it for herself and he hears her snap back: 'And what if I did?'

He sees a tear start to roll down her cheek and he hears her say that she did it because she loves him. He watches her wipe the tear away and hears himself say that she did it because she was jealous.

He hears himself say that she was jealous of him and Sophie and when he hears her protest, he hears himself say that if not of him and Sophie, then certainly of Sophie. He hears himself say that just because what she's saying about him and Sophie is true, it doesn't mean that she wasn't jealous. He hears himself say that whatever he and Sophie did or didn't have, she was jealous of it. He hears himself tell her that she's jealous of everyone when it comes to him, she was jealous of Sophie, she was jealous of Peter, she calls herself a friend but really she's only ever acted in her own self-interest. He hears himself tell her that that's why she's so angry now, because she's jealous and bitter and she knows that he doesn't love her and that she'll never have him. He hears himself tell her that she doesn't know what it means to be a friend, not a real friend, that she smothers him, suffocates him, and that just because he and Sophie are done doesn't mean there's hope for them. He sees her wipe away another tear. He sees her try to hide the third and the fourth. He hears himself tell her that the only reason he came here today was to tell her that he understands why she did what she did, the real reason why she did what she did, and that what she did was unforgivable. He sees her wipe away more tears and light another cigarette. He hears himself tell her that after what she did, and with all her bitterness and jealousy, he doesn't think he can stand to be around her, that he can hardly look at her and when he does all he sees is bitterness and jealousy. He watches her take a drag on her cigarette and exhale. He watches the shake of her hand as she puts the cigarette in the ashtray and wipes her eyes. He watches her get up from the sofa without bothering to pull her kimono-style dressing gown tight around her again, and he watches her walk out of the living room to the front door and open it. He sees her not looking at him and hears her shouting at him to get out.

Out on the landing, her door closed behind him, he stands for a moment, not sure where to go or what to do now. He waits at the top of the stairs, looking down them, and feels the need to talk, to get all of the things inside his head out in the open even though he's not sure what any of them are, to release the pressure of the noise and frustration, to unravel the confusion before it unravels him. He stands on the landing and wonders who he can talk to now. He waits at the top of the stairs, looking down them, not wanting to be alone, yet for once not relishing the company of strangers. He waits and listens to the white noise building in his head and his ears, feeling the sadness stretching and yawning in the lowest parts of him. He waits and hears the sound of crying coming from the other side of Audrey's door. He hears her cry, hard and inconsolable. He hears the breathless anguish, and he knows that she too feels suddenly lost and alone and out of reach of anyone who would care. He hears the pain of her sobs, the deep, empty hurt of them, and he wishes he could take it all away. He wishes he could walk in and change the subject. Tell her not to worry, that he's over it, that he'll stop, that he's done with Sophie and that he can make it right between them, like it was before, and if not like it was then better at least than it is now. He hears the sobs from behind the door of her flat and the sadness rises up like a wave from the very depths of his being and overwhelms him, a crashing wave under which he feels them both drowning. He hears the sound of Audrey crying and he wishes he could do something to take her pain away, take both their pain away. He wishes he could make it easier for them both, absolve them both of all guilt and wrongdoing, all the bitterness, remove the memory of the last few months and make it like it used to be when Peter was around, when it was the three of them, when they loved each other, cared for each other. He wishes he could take her in his arms and hold her and that feeling her there against him would be enough.

He knocks on the door. He waits and listens and hears the sobs on the other side and the pain and the hurt in them feel suddenly desperate. He knocks on the door again, harder and louder, and listens against it for a break in the sound of her crying. He listens for signs that she's heard him. He waits for the sound of crying to be replaced with sounds of movement towards the door, and he waits and he listens and when he hears nothing, not even the sound of her struggling for breath amid the tears, he bangs on the door again, hammering with the underside of his fist until he hears the click of the lock and feels the opening of the door.

Chapter Twenty-Eight

The air smells of summer.

His mouth tastes of tequila.

He can feel both in his head. Softening his focus. Taking off the edges. Making details vague. Blending everything. The rhythm of the music. The evening sun. The shadows on the terrace. Her dancing her way across it towards him.

He can feel things blurring around her. Not mattering.

He watches her. Her hips bouncing to the music. Her arm holding her glass above her head. The cigarette in her hand.

He watches her dance.

Inching towards him.

Everything around her blurring to nothing.

Fading.

Completely.

He sees only her. He's aware only of her movements and the way they make him feel. The quiet excitement. The gentle knot where the sadness should be. The smile where the disappointment was.

He feels his head sway with her hips to the double bass. Feels himself nod to the cymbal and bounce the empty glass in his hand to the beat. He feels her getting closer. Coming for him.

Her little black dress. The little shimmy of her feet. Her pale white skin. The taste of tequila and smell of cigarettes. All blurring. All inviting more of the same. Telling him to let go. Telling him to get lost in them. In her.

He watches her down her shot. Shudder and throw her head back.

He watches her head with its sharp bob of black hair as it starts to roll on her bare shoulders. As she starts to sway again.

He watches her. Her shoulders. Her pale arms. Her hips.

He watches the music sweep her up and send her towards him again. Slowly. Happily. One blurred bar at a time.

He watches her getting lost in it.

Being freed by it.

He watches her coming closer. Dancing over to him.

Swaying. Laughing. Reaching out her empty glass to him.

He hears an excited trumpet and her shouting, 'More, more.'

He hears her laugh and shout, 'More tequila.'

He feels her hips against his chest.

He feels her thighs between his and watches her down another shot.

He feels her leaning in and the tequila telling him not to think about it.

He feels the sharp points of her black bob brushing his face and the sound of his own voice telling him that thinking hasn't done him much good so far. Try not thinking for once.

He smells the tequila on her breath, on her lips as he kisses them.

He feels her lips smile and pull away as the beat picks up again.

He wakes up but not alone.

He knows before he opens his eyes that she's there, next to him, still fast asleep. Before he hears the shallow breaths and murmurs that tell him for certain, he can feel the presence of her in the room. He can feel the lack of emptiness, he can feel the warmth that she brings to it.

Before he rolls over to look at her, he feels a sudden calm, as he does every morning, a foretaste of the contentment that he knows seeing her there, asleep, unaware, unconsciously happy, will fill him with. This is how he wakes up. Relieved. Happy. Rested. The first thing he does every morning is smile. His first thought isn't of where he is, at her flat or his, but that she's there and he's happy, and then he rolls over.

He rolls over to look at her, to feel the contentment that he knows seeing her there will bring, and because he likes watching her sleep. He finds her restfulness reassuring, telling him as it does that she doesn't have a care in the world and neither should he. She isn't going anywhere. He doesn't have to hold on quite so tightly. He can let go and allow it all to come to him. To them.

Sometimes he tries to remember what it was like to wake up without her. To know that he was alone. To feel the coldness in the room before he felt the coldness of the bed next to him. Sometimes he tries to feel the sadness that realisation brought with it every morning. The sadness that would quickly threaten to drown him before he'd fully opened his eyes to the morning. Sometimes he tries to feel it to remember what it was like. Sometimes he tries to remember what it was like so he can compare it to his current waking state, as if testing a once weak limb to be sure it's fully healed. Occasionally he can bring it to mind, a vague impression of what it used to be, the sadness he would once wake with in the morning before the contentment took its place.

But not this morning. He doesn't have time this morning. As he rolls over to look at her, to watch her sleeping, happy, unaware, she starts to stir. Only slightly. So slightly that if it wasn't for the morning light streaming in through the bedroom windows, she might well drift back to the deep and happy sleep that her smile says she was enjoying minutes ago.

He feels the tug of the sheets as she starts to surface, as she moves and squirms reluctantly into the light of the bedroom. He feels the movement in the mattress as she rolls to go back to sleep and then again as she rolls back to face him when sleep eludes her. He watches her. The mess of her black bob half over her face, her ghostly skin flushed pink at the cheeks and eyes, her delicate features scrunched tight as she tries to pry one eye open to take in him and the morning.

He watches her one eye squinting in the morning light, her other eye being kept tightly shut against it. He watches her squinting eye, feeling it taking him in, recognising his face, seeing what it was expecting to see, and what the accompanying smile tells him it is pleased to see. He watches her smile widen, forcing her other eye open.

Still squinting, she watches him watching her and smiles and says: 'Hey. Good morning.'

Acknowledgements

First and foremost I have to thank Scott Pack for inadvertently giving me the idea for the story in the first place - Scott, I hope you like it and if not, then maybe you should be more careful what you say in future. I am also incredibly grateful to John Bond and Tim Inman at Whitefox, and Eleanor Rees, Nathan Burton and Sally Sargeant, for helping to turn that story into the darkly beautiful book it is, and to Suw Charman-Anderson, Emmanuel Cole and Mari Yamazaki for helping to get me and the book out there. In more general, but no less important ways I'm also grateful to Clare Christian, Dave Woolf, Ali Gunn, Ivan Mulcahy, Jenny Heller and all the other editors, agents and PRs who've kept me employed and encouraged my writing over the years. And finally to Kyrstie for always knowing the right thing to do, and to Tanja, Ryan, Alex, Damon, Lisa, Kevin, Katinka, Anselm and anyone else who's ever worked behind the bar of Two Floors and kept me company and supplied with tea while I was writing.